DON'T LOSE HER

THE MAX FREEMAN MYSTERIES

DON'T LOSE HER

A Max Freeman Mystery

JONATHON KING

OPEN ROAD

INTEGRATED MEDIA

NEW YORK

Cover design by Gabriela Sahagun

978-1-5040-0165-6

Published in 2015 by Open Road Integrated Media, Inc.
345 Hudson Street
New York, NY 10014
www.openroadmedia.com

For Arlene and Richard,
Who have always been there

DON'T LOSE HER

CHAPTER 1

Diane Manchester, forty-three, pregnant and, in her words, "big as a house," shifts in her chair, uncomfortable again. It's the same courtroom chair she's had for more than a year. Recently, she had them take off the arms to accommodate her, but at eight months she feels restrained once again. She reaches down and pulls at her judicial robes and straightens a fold, while carefully controlling all emotion in her face. Is it a physical irritation making her twitch, or the images before her? Either way, she can't let it show to the others in the room.

On the bench spread out before her is the prosecution's exhibit Number Two, a sheaf of photographs showing a mass grave heating in the Colombian sun. The victims include women and children, some infants, their bodies lying awkward and twisted in the mud, mothers and babies still touching, even in death.

"Your Honor, again we object to the admittance of these horrific photographs. There is no proof my client knew anything about this atrocity in his homeland, and I emphasize that this is in his homeland, not on U.S. soil—never mind that he had no connection to those responsible for such a heinous crime."

"I agree with your assessments regarding the atrocities, Mr. Aguilar, but I will reserve judgment on your client's culpability," says the judge, sliding the photographs aside and reaching down to cradle her swollen belly beneath the bench. "You may sit, Mr. Aguilar."

3

Diane is looking out on an atypical scene in her courtroom. As usual, there is a team of federal prosecutors to her left, two of whom she's had before her in the past. But at the defense table are a bevy of lawyers, all appearing to be Hispanic, all finely dressed in expensive suits, all stern-faced and showing a palpable deference to their client, who sits next to the lead attorney. His chair is pushed back, his hands clasped at the middle of his thin torso, his legs crossed as if at a boring business meeting. Juan Manuel Escalante is a known drug cartel leader who was lured to Florida through a DEA scheme and subsequently arrested by the feds. He is charged with multiple counts of conspiracy to distribute illegal narcotics, conspiracy to import drugs, murder, and assault and coercion of witnesses as the titular head of his Colombian cartel.

Throughout the courtroom gallery, normally sparsely populated for the admittedly boring federal procedures usually held before her, Diane notes the presence of several members of the press along with a phalanx of lawyers whom she recognizes as international law wonks. Deep in one corner is a fellow judge, a senior who's hearing a big money, Indian nation versus casino technology-supplier case on another floor. He's probably jealous that Escalante is stealing some of his spotlight. There is no jury in the room. Any decision on the case before her is hers alone.

The extradition hearing of a celebrated drug cartel kingpin brings out a different crowd and certainly different stresses. Diane feels another crimp in her belly, looks at her watch, and addresses the attorneys: "Gentlemen, as it is approaching noon and we've had a long morning, may I suggest a lunch break unless there are any objections."

She looks at the prosecution table.

"No objection, Your Honor," says the head of the team.

She looks to the defense as the lead attorney begins to rise, but a voice comes from beside him.

"It has indeed been a long morning, Your Honor," says Escalante from his sitting position. His fingers are now peaked before his chin, as if in prayer. "And in Your Honor's condition, we can certainly understand your need to gather your energies."

It is the first time the defendant has spoken in two days, and it is unusual and against protocol for him to do so now. His eyes, as always, are hooded and lazy as if the proceedings are of little concern to him. The overall look is reptilian, as if a forked tongue could suddenly lash out from between his lips at any time. Though his voice is thick with accent, his English is meticulous. The head defense attorney looks down at his client in a mild attempt to silence him, but Escalante continues.

"We would want nothing but the best of health for Your Honor and her child."

Diane looks down and meets Escalante's eyes: Was that arrogance on display, or a threat? *Can I hold him in contempt or should I warn his team about any further directed comment? Do I rise above it?*

She slides her chair back and begins to stand.

"Thank you for your concern, Mr. Escalante," she says, gathering the photos of the mass grave and straightening them, making sure that the images are pointing outward for all in the courtroom to see. "Fortunately, *my child* and I will be just fine."

Following the judge's lead, the court bailiff calls out, "All rise." The judge steps down and leaves the room through the door to her private chambers. Her longtime judicial assistant, Martin Andrews, is just inside.

"What the hell was that?" he says as he helps her out of her robe. He had been listening to the proceedings.

"Don't know, don't care."

"Really, Judge—was that a threat?"

"I don't know, Marty. But I'm sure the U.S. Marshals Service will know about it before Escalante gets to lockup downstairs, and there'll probably be a YouTube video posted before that."

Diane tries to downplay the line about her and her baby's health as simple grandstanding. Sure, she'd gotten threats from defendants before, a few more direct and visceral than Escalante's. Every judge got them. If you let it get to you, you'd better leave the job.

"But for my health, and that of my baby," she says, gathering up her purse and phone from her desk, "I'm going to lunch."

"Want company?" Andrews asked.

Diane looks askance at her friend, whom she'd brought with her from her position as a prosecutor to the federal bench.

"Do I ever?"

"No, ma'am. See you in an hour."

Out on the street in the warm sun and fresh air of a Florida spring day, Diane stops at the pedestrian crosswalk, thinking about hot fudge sundaes and the Constitution. When the white stick figure on the pole lights up, she crosses, thinking about where to go for lunch, and the jurisdictional boundaries of extradition.

Halfway down Clematis Street from the courthouse, she cups her palm and wrist under her bulging belly and thinks of the eight-month-old baby growing inside her, and then of the photos of the mass grave: the women and children.

Stop it, Diane! Lunch is for stress release. It is not a time to think about the case, or the twists of the law, or the admissibility of evidence, or dead children. Leave it alone for an hour. Relax!

The obstetrician said the only way he was going to let her continue working was if she avoided undue stress. She needed to relax, forget the case, and do what was right for herself and her child.

She actually stops in front of the windows at the Oh My Chocolates store and sighs, but with the thought of white walnut raisin bark and alpine dark truffles in the back of her head, she moves on.

Across the street, she picks up a familiar figure, a woman dressed in a business suit but wearing running shoes. She is pushing a baby carriage quickly, in a hurry, as she always is when Diane sees her at lunchtime. Childcare down the block? Pediatrician appointment? Diane imagines what lies ahead, juggling career and motherhood.

Can she keep her judgeship? Could she stand to do without it? She and her husband, Billy, have had this discussion. He argues that he works mostly out of his home office, so he'll step up. But she knows his singular passion when he's focused on a case or a financial deal.

"You'll get up in the middle of a teleconference with Uruguay's economic minister to change a diaper?"

"Sure," Billy said. "Depending on the strength of the odor."

Diane smiles at the thought, shakes off the image of Billy and diapers, and keeps moving, her destination now settled. When she reaches the short block of Narcissus Avenue, she crosses and has just stepped up on the curb, heading for the awning that reads NATURE'S WAY CAFÉ, when the screech of tires on pavement causes her to snap her head around.

A white van jolts to a stop next to her. When a side panel door slides open, a figure leaps out, and Diane's arms are gripped by fingers that drive into her biceps, splitting the muscle there. As she's pulled into the van, she speaks aloud for the first time since telling Marty, "For my health, and that of my baby, I'm going to lunch."

"What the hell . . . ! Hey! My God, what the hell! Ow, ow, my baby! Help! Help!"

CHAPTER 2

There is something about dead high tide that always makes me uncomfortable, especially on a day like today, when there's barely a breeze off the ocean: a day when masses of full gray clouds hang fat out on the horizon, too far away to be threatening, but gorged with moisture and barely moving, like big slumbering dogs you know to let lay.

At a time like this, the water is hard to know. Its direction is caught at a high point, not moving east or west, just sitting like a pot close to boiling, but not quite yet. Even the waves seem to have stopped while that eternal switch from rise to ebb is caught in neutral.

I'm with Sherry on the sand in Deerfield Beach. We're sunning, although what we do on the beach couldn't really be called sunning because neither of us does, nor needs, such a thing. You'd be better off calling what we do at the beach a practice of ritual silence. Sherry reads, for about sixty minutes at a time, which is as long as she can stand to be inert, and then makes her way to the water, slips into the sea, and swims.

With skin brown as old leather without a single day in the sun, I read for hours at a time, only occasionally peering up over the top of today's book to watch the ocean or to track Sherry's progress in it.

At this moment, she is returning from her third trip into the water today, and I look up to see her in the shallows, both hands in the water, her full leg bent at the knee, her head down like a sprinter waiting for the gun to begin her race. Her shoulders are broad and muscled, her hips narrow. Her left leg is unnaturally large at the thigh, ripped with taut quads that chisel to the knee and then flow down into a cablelike calf. You could mistake her for a professional speed skater but for the odd displacement of weight, and the fact that when she rises full from the water you can see that her lower right leg is gone. Her thigh on that side seems to wobble a bit in midair without the ballast that was amputated just above the knee.

In one way, I am used to the sight because I have lived with her, loved her, and watched her recover from the loss of that leg since it happened. Yet, in a more disturbing way, I am not used to the sight, because I blame myself for the circumstances that led to it.

I watch as she hops up into ankle-deep water and then stands, catching her balance like some yoga guru doing the flying swan position or whatever the hell they call it. And then she hops, one-legged, to her beach chair. Those who notice stare, first at her and then at me as I sit on my ass.

Why the hell doesn't he help her, I imagine them thinking. But Sherry is the kind of woman who would refuse help if you offered. And that was a lesson about her I'd learned long before she ever had surgery.

"You've got to go in, Max, the water is absolutely perfect," she says, reaching the chair, her breathing not one scintilla heavier than if she'd just dropped in from a leisurely stroll. "I'm guessing seventy-eight or seventy-nine—really warm."

I only nod because it's the same thing she said last time, an hour ago, and the time before. Oh, I can swim, make no mistake, but mostly I prefer to do it when the only alternative is to go down with the ship. I may go in later, just to please her and prove that I am not a total lazy dog. But right now, there is a passage in this Cormac McCarthy book about lightning flashing in distant thunderclouds that has me staring out at our own horizon.

"Huh?" I say. But the need to respond is made moot by the trill of a cell phone that floats up from Sherry's beach bag. I don't react. I never bring my phone to the beach and almost consider it blasphemous to do so. But Sherry is back on duty as a detective with the Broward Sheriff's Office after months of rehabilitation and desk duty. She has proven herself physically able in myriad exercises, obstacle courses, and training scenarios.

They couldn't keep her inside anymore. Disability was not a word she would tolerate even in the paperwork they stuff into her personnel file. But active status brings responsibility, which means she is on call at all times. After the fourth ring of the cell, she reaches into the bag and answers by simply stating her last name.

"Richards."

She listens for a beat.

Then in a perplexed and uncharacteristic tone of concern, I hear her say: "Billy?"

"Yes, of course. He's right here," she says, and hands the cell phone to me, knitting together her sun-blonde eyebrows and shrugging her shoulders in a silent indication that something is amiss. Billy Manchester is my employer and my friend. He is a businessman-lawyer, eternally cool under pressure—someone who does not call me at odd times of the day when he knows I am not working on an investigative case for him.

"Billy?" I say into the cell with a touch of the concern in Sherry's reaction.

"Max, I need you. Diane is gone. Someone has taken her. She's gone, Max. She's been abducted. I need you."

CHAPTER 3

Mouth wrapped. Breathe, Diane! Kick! Come on, girl, breathe. Kick! Kick something! Anything. Oh, breathe. Breathe for your baby.

Her arms have now been pulled behind her and bound with something that cuts into her wrists. They've pulled some kind of cloth bag over her head that blacks out everything: light, images. There is nothing but darkness.

God, I can't breathe. You've got to breathe, Diane. Breathe for your baby. You have to protect her. My God, who is doing this? And why?

The van pitches from side to side, moving, accelerating, braking, turning. She tries to calm herself, breathe. She hates darkness, always has. It's one of the things she and Billy share, a dislike of darkness. They keep a night-light on in the bedroom at all times. She knows Billy's aversion comes from a childhood living on the edge in a drug-infested North Philadelphia neighborhood where safety at night often depended on being able to scramble to a hiding spot when angry words and gunfire broke out.

She believes hers came from waiting deep into the night in her upper-class suburban home, waiting with a light on for her father to come home from interminable days in his courtroom office. They have both talked about how to avoid passing this fear on to their daughter after she is born.

OK. You can't see. But think, Diane. Come on, focus and think!

She can feel someone's knee pushing down on her back, pinning her to the floor of the van. The hard metal under her vibrates each time the vehicle accelerates. It hums against her body. There are no voices. No one has said a word since they pulled her in.

Come on, pay attention, Diane. Billy would pay attention. Billy would be calculating the speed and the direction and the feel of going over railroad tracks or bridges. Do that, Diane. Come on, you're a federal judge, you're smart, you don't panic, you think. Come on, girl.

She feels the van sway again, making a wide turn—left? How many turns is that now? Two rights and a left? Shit. She doesn't know. How long has it been? Five minutes? Thirty seconds? She tries to roll, to fold her knees up to her stomach, trying to protect her unborn child.

"What are you doing?" she sputters, spitting the cloth out away from her mouth as she yells. "Do you know who I am? I'm not just some woman on the street. Do you know what you've done? You will bring a lot of shit down on your heads if you don't . . ."

A hand clamps down on her mouth over the fabric, not just covering, but clamping, the palm and fingers gripping her lips, chin, and nose and squeezing them painfully together. She gasps for breath and gets only a partial draw of air. She struggles to wrench her head away, but the grip is strong.

He's cutting off her oxygen. Again, she tries kicking, but he holds on, squeezing and crunching the flesh of her face together. She's suffocating. *Oh God, my baby,* she thinks. She begins to gag at the loss of air and then stops struggling. Only then does the hand relax, letting her breathe again.

No one says a word. The message is clear: struggle or attempt to speak or yell, and I will kill you and your child.

CHAPTER 4

I am on I-95 heading north into Palm Beach County, driving at an unsafe speed, running in the far left lane and racing up on the back bumper of anyone in my way, flashing my lights. These are acts that I would despise from anyone else, but now I am driven by the unmistakable sound of panic in Billy's voice on the cell phone.

"She didn't come back to her office after lunch. The staff got worried because they knew she was resuming a hearing at one, and she is never, ever late."

His words were tight and succinct, even more so than they usually are. Billy Manchester is naturally not a man to waste words, but I could almost feel his vocal cords tightening in his speech.

"They sent an aide out to the restaurants that she goes to and talked to the managers and waitresses who know her by sight. Nothing. No one had seen her during the lunch rush."

I knew Diane was a creature of habit. She ran her life like clockwork. As she'd risen in the ranks from West Palm Beach lawyer to statewide prosecutor and then on to the federal bench, she prided herself on efficiency, keeping ahead of the docket, taking on the toughest cases with the clear-eyed view of justice that her father, a lifelong judge himself from a prominent, third-generation Florida family, had instilled in her practically from the womb.

The only time she'd blinked in her life was when she fell in love with Billy, an equally prominent attorney in his own right. But Billy was a black lawyer from Philadelphia who, though brilliant, rarely tried cases and preferred to work behind the scenes, juggling law and investment work for a bevy of clients. Their mixed-race marriage had ruffled the feathers of Palm Beach society, but they had weathered the initial storm. The more they acted as if it didn't matter, the more their friends adopted the same attitude. When Diane announced her pregnancy, the family finally softened. A grandchild will do that.

"One of her aides came across an officer on the sidewalk in front of Nature's Way, where Diane goes for salad. The patrolman was taking a report from a bystander," Billy had said.

"The woman said she'd seen someone pulled against their will into a white van and she'd called 911 on her cell."

"It was Diane, Max. Same clothes, same description, same timeline. Someone abducted her. I need you at the scene. I'm at her office. The FBI is already setting up a tap on all the phones here in case a ransom demand is made. But I need your eyes on the street."

I was still recalling the words and involuntarily scanning the southbound lanes for a glimpse of a white van when I ran up on the tail of an SUV doing the speed limit in the left lane. I hit the brakes and the horn. No movement. I flashed my headlights. No movement.

I turned on the side spotlight mounted on the left side of the door of my 1989 Plymouth Gran Fury and aimed the beam into the SUV's driver's side rearview. He finally slid over and I punched up the four-barrel police pursuit engine and leaped up to ninety miles an hour.

The car, a classic, was a present from Billy after the resolution of a case we'd worked on a year earlier. I'd nearly destroyed my F-150 pickup truck during a chase, and Billy's often subtle humor prompted the gift. Replete with old blackwall tires and small hubcaps, the car is anything but inconspicuous. I can't use it on surveillances, but it's often invaluable when getting from place to place on South Florida's interstates and the turnpike. Back in the day, it was a standard high-way patrol car across the nation. It weighs a ton and is very, very fast.

A quarter mile from the Okeechobee exit, I flipped on my right turn signal and started working my way across four lanes of 70-mph traffic. I cut people off. I came dangerously close to back bumpers. I did the kinds of things I detest in other drivers and I apologized under my breath and kept going.

When I got to Federal Highway, I cruised through a yellow left-turn light and headed north again. When Billy had given me the address of Diane's abduction, I knew exactly where I was going. The spot was right next to Centennial Park at the east end of Clematis. At lunchtime, the downtown streets would have been thick with pedestrian traffic, folks walking to lunch, window-shopping, living life on a warm South Florida afternoon.

I knew the area because the World of Beer is just around the corner. Before I could make the turn onto Datura, I saw the spinning red-and-blue police lights that sealed off the crime scene on the next block. I spent ten bucks to park in a local lot and walked the rest of the way. I was already scanning the walls of retail stores for video cameras set up by the various businesses and spotted two on the south side—none on the north. But I was encouraged by the presence of multiple cameras on the PNC banking center and one mounted on top of the traffic signal above the intersection up on North Dixie Highway. There was hope.

"Max Freeman," I said to the uniform who stopped me at the orange-and-white striped barricade blocking all pedestrians and vehicles from entering the eastside block.

I flipped open my ID case with my private investigator license displayed. "FBI Agent Howard is expecting me."

The West Palm Beach cop couldn't have been much into his twenties. He took the license and did a full-body scan of me, prac-tically putting the photo on the ID up to my face for comparison before pulling back the barricade to let me pass. Maybe he was being careful and maybe he was doing a pre-application act for the feds. He pointed out a tall, blond-haired man in the requisite dark suit of the FBI and passed me on. I thanked him.

Agent Howard was standing, head down, speaking into a cell phone as I approached. He was a couple of inches shorter than me, a few pounds lighter in that slim way that FBI agents are. He was wearing the standard-issue sunglasses through which I knew he would have been checking my approach, sizing me up, wondering who the hell I was from behind those dark-tinted lenses.

He ended his phone conversation just before I got within hearing range.

"Agent Howard, my name is Max Freeman," I said, offering my hand. I could only see a slight movement of his eyes behind the glasses, impossible to read. He did not take my hand and remained silent, as though measuring his response.

"You're the private dick," he finally said. It was a statement rather than a question, with a slight emphasis on "dick."

It is my policy not to answer rhetorical statements. Ask me a question, I'll respond. Otherwise, I'll wait you out. I stood silently.

"Well, you've got a lot of pull, Mr., uh, Freeman," he said as if he was already forgetting my name. "Word from up the line is that I should give you some cooperation in my own investigation. That's breaking policy. You must have some connections."

I held to my own policy and waited for a question.

The agent made a show of looking around me, up at the buildings across the street, around the corner on Narcissus where the crime scene techs were focused on something against the nearby curb. Finally, he gave in.

"What can I answer for you, Freeman?"

It was a legitimate question. I can answer questions.

"I know you're only a couple of hours into this," I said, modulating my voice, purposely being deferential despite the fact that a very good friend of mine had apparently been abducted and thus was in imminent danger. But I knew where emotion fit into the profession, and knew how not to show it.

"I have no intention of getting in your way, or outguessing you, Agent Howard. The abducted judge is a close friend. I have worked for her husband for many years."

Howard did not nod or indicate in any way that he was listening. Maybe he had the same policy as I did in regard to statements.

"The husband, my friend, is the one with connections in high places. And he will be more comfortable if I'm his eyes on the street, following your investigation. I believe he will thus be more cooperative. And I believe that cooperation can only aid you in finding Judge Manchester unharmed."

Again, the agent looked up to the buildings across the street. He was going to offer an opinion, and I frankly didn't care as long as he didn't order me away. I said nothing and instead followed his sightlines to do a quick inventory.

The second floor of the facing buildings appeared to be offices or simply storage space above the commercial stores on the ground level. The blinds on most of the windows were closed. Howard would have already had agents or assisting officers canvas those rooms to talk with anyone who may have seen something relevant.

There was one PNC surveillance camera mounted on the westside wall that appeared to be focused on the sidewalk, but it could have caught something in the street. The other was on the south corner of the building, again pointed down. Howard would have already ordered the confiscation of any video from both sources. But that could take time depending on how frequently they were monitored, where their feeds went, and whether the company that controlled them would be cooperative or ask for a warrant. Nothing happens as fast as it does on a television crime episode.

The camera that was mounted on the traffic signal to the east was a better bet. It was a fairly new addition to South Florida law enforcement. The cameras were meant to capture a picture of the license plate of any vehicle that ran a red light; thus a violator could be ticketed for breaking the law even without an officer witnessing the act. The lawyers were still trying to overturn the use of such surveillance, saying it was somehow unconstitutional. If you break the law and no cop is there to see you, did you break the law? Some lawyers make money on such things.

When I looked back at Howard, our eyes met.

"We're doing the cameras," he said. He'd been watching me. "We got the description of a white Chevy van and a plate from the traffic camera already. The plate came back to an elderly couple in Delray Beach who didn't know what we were talking about until we showed them the bare plate-holder on the back of their Seville still parked in their driveway. The video techs are trying to zoom the traffic cam photos to pick up the VIN plate under the windshield glass to ID the van, but good luck with that."

Howard was not completely unlike me. He didn't totally believe in the magic of technology.

"The witness on the street said she made out three men, including a driver. She said men because they all wore black and had ski masks over their heads and faces. Two of them pulled the judge into the open slide door of the van and they left in a screech, according to her.

"Another wit, up there," Howard pointed to an open window on the second floor across the street, "looked out at the sound of the screech and noted the van blowing through the light and heading west."

He then pointed down at the huddle of technicians at the curb.

"Despite the shit you see on CSI, they're not going to find tire tread size and the composite makeup of vulcanized rubber and then match it to the manufacturer and run down the purchaser and an address of the van owner before the next E*TRADE smartass baby commercial."

This I knew, believe me. I had also surmised the rest of it, or Howard wouldn't still be standing here.

"We're still looking for the van, wherever they finally ditch the thing, but this scene is just about done, Mr. Freeman. You might as well join your friend over at the courthouse and wait with him for the ransom call."

I looked into the dark lenses of the agent's glasses, maybe finding his eyes. The feds never tell you everything. Like good poker players, they always hold something back.

"Was anything found here?" I said.

The sunlight flickered on his lenses when he tilted his head, subtly looking away.

"Diane was going to lunch, carrying her purse, and considering her court status, always kept a cell phone in that purse," I said.

Howard took his time.

Even if Diane had turned her cell off—and she never turned it off—the signal could have been traced and triangulated to determine her location, sometimes within a few yards.

"We found her purse three blocks away up past Quadrille," Howard finally said. "It appeared to have been tossed out the window. The cell and her wallet with cash and cards were still inside. There was no indication they even opened it, but we're having it printed just in case."

No chance of tracking the cell signal. No chance these were idiots who would stop at the 7-Eleven to buy beer with her charge cards. They'd gambled big, but they were not just your average thugs. They were smart and they didn't care about small change. I knew those facts would take this abduction to a whole new level, a whole new motivation.

I thanked Howard for being candid and for his time and he accepted my handshake.

"I'm sorry about your friend," he said. "We will get her back."

"Thank you, sir," I answered. "I know we will."

CHAPTER 5

Now, she noted a slow turn, the way the van crawled, the screech of worn brake pads beneath her ear, still pressed against the floorboards. Diane had calmed herself. The knee that pinned her down had eased up when she stopped struggling and she'd curled herself up. She felt another inching right turn. The wheels bumped over a small ridge and then she heard the distinctive sound of metal sliding against metal coming from outside the van, the sound echoing. Garage door? Big one. In a large empty enclosure. Warehouse?

Brains not brawn, Diane, she thought. *You're a 140-pound pregnant woman. You can't fight them. You have to outsmart them.*

No one had said a word during the entire ordeal. No shout, no orders or directions given. She had seen two—no, three—men, including the driver, before they'd pulled the cloth over her head. But in her memory there were no distinguishing features. Dark clothes, maybe dark eyes inside the mask on the face of the one she did see. But were they the eyes of a white man? A black man? Asian, Hispanic? She couldn't say for sure. It had all happened so fast; it was insane.

She felt the van stop and heard the sliding van door through which they'd dragged her being opened. Again, hands came up under her arms and dragged her out, this time with two people, one on either side, holding her up. She gained her foothold and stood, realizing for the first time that her shoes were missing. They must have come off when they pulled her into the van. They were flats she'd bought when she was at six months and her ankles had begun to swell. It was a totally bizarre thought, one that came from some involuntary synapse in her brain, but damn, she'd liked those shoes.

The surface she stood on now was cool to the bottoms of her feet, flat and hard like concrete. When the men pulled her forward roughly, she grunted in pain, her belly again feeling heavy, swinging a split-second behind each movement. It felt like it did when she rolled over in bed too quickly to answer the phone, or spun too quickly to catch an elevator door at the last moment.

In the last month, it was as if her stomach was an attachment; the weight of the baby and swollen placenta sometimes seemed independent of her own body. She'd grinned at the feeling the first time she noticed it. She was not grinning now.

They marched her across a hard flat floor, twenty-six paces. She was now counting, paying attention, determined to keep her head working instead of panicking. Then they hesitated a moment, and she could feel the hands under her armpits lift slightly, drawing her up. The top of her bare foot scraped across an immovable object. The hands continued to drag her up. She felt a flat surface, warmer like wood, and she stood on it. They were going up steps.

When she hesitated, the man on her left yanked at her. She moaned, and the gesture of pain seemed to cause the man on the right to stop and ease his grip slightly. She needed to remember the reaction from the one on the right: Was it a sign of compassion? *Keep a focus on him,* she thought. *Try to keep track of him.*

It took her a couple more steps up before she caught the rhythm and began to count: one, two, and three . . . seven. A landing, then a turn to the right, and then seven more.

At the top, they turned left. She tried to see under the hood, but there was nothing but blackness. Maybe the lights were off. Maybe the place was windowless. Maybe there was some sort of loose elastic around the hood and they'd somehow cinched it, but she could feel it around her shoulders. *It's dark, just dark. But these guys are still moving as if they know each step without seeing. Where the hell are we?*

It was fifteen paces on another wood surface at the top of the stairs and then the sound of old hinges crying, followed by an abrupt turn to the right. When she was spun and pushed backward roughly, she panicked and thought they might actually be tossing her over the side of some elevated walkway. A bubble rose in her throat. But before she could scream, the backs of her knees hit something soft, and she sat heavily on some kind of chair . . . no, sofa . . . no, mattress.

She heard the hinges again and then the clack of a door being closed. Silence. She tried to calm herself on the mattress. She felt the roughness of the fabric beneath her with her fingertips: wool, scratchy, thick wool. She breathed in the air. She could smell the heat, the odor of old wood, stale air, dried cardboard, and a slight, pungent whiff of sweat. Not hers.

She thought of her heartbeat, then of her baby's heartbeat, then admonished herself to focus and went back to her own heart rhythm. *Calm yourself and listen,* she commanded. She breathed deeply several times. Had they dumped her alone in a closed room? Finally, she took in a lungful of air, held it, and concentrated. There was another breath in the room, a most subtle sound of air moving rhythmically, in and out, and in and out. Not far away and to her right.

"Who are you, my keeper?" she suddenly said. "My captor?"

Silence.

"I know you're here," she said.

She listened again to the nearby breath, but now it was gone or was being held.

"I can see you there," she lied, and tipped her head in the direction she thought the breathing had come from.

"I can see through this stupid hood and I know exactly where we are. Do you really think you can kidnap a federal judge and not have every law enforcement agency in the United States coming after you?

"They'll find me, you know. And it will be very hard on you all. Do you know the penalty for abducting a federal judge?"

This time, she was quiet for several seconds. *You can't hold your breath forever,* she thought. After what seemed an impossibly long time, she heard it. The breath was louder, no doubt from the effort to hold it in the lungs for so long.

Then Diane heard the creak of wood and the slightest swish of fabric. She thought she actually felt something. Was it her imagination or was that air against her? Was it the actual displacement of the oxygen in the room as her captor moved? She tried to sit up, to get her feet flat on the floor, but the baby made it impossible to use her stomach muscles. And with her arms bound at the wrists behind her, it was a hopeless task. She tried to roll over on her side to aid the effort and heard the structure beneath the mattress creak.

Or was that the floorboards again? Was he moving? Was he nearer? Was he close enough to slap her, strike her with a fist, or kick her swiftly in the stomach? She stopped moving and listened again. She squeezed her eyes shut and felt the moisture in the corners.

"Please," she said softly. "Tell me what you want. Please, let's get this over with so I can take care of my baby. Please."

CHAPTER 6

I left my car near the crime scene and walked to the federal courthouse, using the route I assumed Diane had taken to go to lunch. I knew I would walk it again later, in reverse, the way she would have. And with each step, I would try to put myself in her shoes, to see what she would have seen, to absorb what she would have felt—the wind from the east, the heat rising up off the concrete sidewalks, the sun, higher than it was now, bright on the top of her head at midday.

Had there been any warning? Had she seen it coming, the threat and the menace? Had they tipped their hand, or was she completely surprised by the attack?

Attack—I didn't want to use that word about Diane in her condition, carrying her and Billy's child low in her eighth month. I'd seen her only a week ago in their penthouse apartment overlooking the Atlantic. She'd been waddling around in the kitchen, making fun of herself, bumping her belly against the marble countertop, mocking herself as she opened the refrigerator door, and backing up while simultaneously making a *beep, beep, beep* noise like a tractor-trailer in reverse.

"Heavy load here, boys!"

Billy stood aside, smiling and looking back over his shoulder at me, gesturing with his palm at his wife: "Poetry in motion."

They had not come to this moment without hours of discussion, lying in bed side-by-side in the early morning hours and late at night when questions are often laid bare in quiet air.

Billy was my best friend, and even though I had only known him for a few years, a long relationship between our respective mothers in Philadelphia tied us together. We knew each other's demons.

Billy had grown up in the faltering neighborhoods of North Philly, whose streets were lined by boarded-up and decrepit homes stained and wasted by the change from blue-collar factory jobs in the inner city to the concentration of white-collar office and consumer-oriented jobs downtown. His father left before Billy could know him, a man made angry by his own hopelessness and lack of education and the addictions he'd ultimately bowed to.

Billy's mother endured the violence his father visited on her, but never took her eye off the goal of making her only son the beneficiary of lessons learned. Billy had cocooned himself with books and chess and learning and the avoidance of the plague of the streets. He looked back on his own childhood as something endured and to rise above.

My own upbringing as the son of a third-generation South Philly policeman had its own bitter taste. My father, too, was often a raging drunk, a wife beater who succumbed to his anger and need to glorify himself by lording over those he could, most often his family—those closest to him.

Billy's and my own mother had eventually, or maybe inevitably, found each other at a Center City church and borrowed each other's strength to rid themselves of their tormentors. But both Billy and I carried an inevitable question into adulthood: Would I ever bring a child into this kind of world?

Now, in his early forties, with the strength and connection and love of his wife, Billy had come to answer yes to the question.

As I entered the federal courthouse and headed for Diane Manchester's chambers, I cynically wondered if he'd made the wrong decision.

A man dressed in a dark off-the-rack suit and wearing an audio plug in his ear stopped me outside the judge's hallway door. I gave him my name as he eyeballed me. *Federal security,* I thought. He spoke into the wrist-cuff of his suit and then opened the door to let me enter.

I'd been in Diane's chambers a few times and knew the layout. This was the outer office, typically paneled in cheap government-issued wood and adorned only with the standard displays of the judge's law degrees and official certificates on the walls. There was an equally plain, catalogue-purchased desk where her secretary usually sat taking myriad phone calls from lawyers, bailiffs, bureaucrats, prosecutors, and fellow judges.

But today, her secretary was not in his usual chair. Martin Andrews was instead sitting in one of the waiting area chairs, staring at an empty wall as if transfixed by some minute flaw or stain or perhaps an image of the unthinkable. A man who could have been the outside guard's twin was in the desk chair, working at Andrews's computer, tapping and studying, tapping and studying.

"Marty," I said to Andrews, who had yet to look away from his wall despite my entrance. The look of recognition came late to his face.

"Oh, Mr. Freeman," he said finally, and started to rise.

I stepped to him instead and, closing the gap, forced him to stay seated.

"You OK?" I said, extending my hand. He shook it without vigor.

"I'm afraid I'm quite useless," he said, looking from my face to his own desk.

I shared the glance over my shoulder. "They can do that to you," I said with a touch of conspiracy in my voice. "Don't take it personally, Marty. They'll need you before long."

I started to turn, but Andrews reached out to touch my sleeve with his fingertips to stop me.

"She'll be all right, won't she, Mr. Freeman?"

Even the sharp ones will plead for reassurance when they know it's too early and too impossible to know yet.

"Yes, Marty. She'll be all right," I said, being equally cavalier with the unknown.

When Andrews turned back to the wall, I asked the man at his desk to let Mr. Manchester know I was there. Then I turned to the unmarked and unadorned door to Diane's inner chambers and waited. The man did not take his eyes from the computer display before him as he also spoke into his sleeve. The door opened and another suit motioned me inside.

The judge's chamber was essentially one huge room with three of the walls lined with floor-to-ceiling bookcases. There were three doors and no windows. One door led to Diane's courtroom, one to her private bath, and I'd just walked through the third. The dominant feature in the office was a ten-foot-long oak conference table surrounded by chairs and positioned in the middle of the room.

This would be where the meetings with case lawyers and prosecutors and trial participants were usually held. I'd seen the table often strewn with opened law books and documents and case files and half-filled coffee cups and the wrappings and residue of late-night dinners.

Today, there were four men huddled at one end, focused on two laptop computer screens. Newly strung wires ran across the polished surface leading from the computers to the multi-button telephone hub at the center. The device, the size of a small mixing bowl, looked like a kid's computer game handset, with a digital readout display at its center, several color-coded buttons on one side, and a perforated speaker section, all sitting on a raised, three-legged base. It was the hub of all incoming and outgoing office calls, be they private or conference. The FBI agents had obviously tapped into it and were ready to record and feed all information into their own computer database instantly. No one had to say they were waiting for a ransom call.

At the far end of the room, Billy sat at Diane's own broad but far from ornate desk. He looked up when I entered, closed his laptop, and stood. I'd never seen him look so stiff, unemotional, and blank. He was staring at my face as if in assessment. His coffee-colored skin seemed to have lost all lines and texture.

Always dressed in the finest suits, he'd somehow grabbed a plain, dark jacket and slacks that were eerily appropriate for a funeral. He stepped around the desk stiffly, devoid of the easy and athletic movement with which he usually carried himself. I was forced to judge that he was holding it together by pulling inside and showing nothing, neither personal pain nor anger nor panic.

The agents at the table glanced up as I stepped past them. One started to greet me, but hesitated as I headed directly for my friend.

I reached for Billy's unoffered hand and squeezed it in spite of him and pulled him close to me, touching his shoulder with mine. I didn't even try to speak. It would have been an insult to a man of his intellect and experience to toss out a comforting statement like the one I'd given Andrews outside.

"Thanks for coming, Max," he said, the tone so flat it made me wince.

If there had been even the slightest hint of panic in his first phone call to me, it was now forever gone.

"Mr. Freeman," a voice behind me said.

I turned to see one of the table men, who had waited an appropriate time for Billy and me to greet each other, and had now stepped forward.

"Agent Duncan," he said, offering his hand.

I took it.

"Mr. Manchester has requested your presence, sir. And it is, we believe, in our interest to have you here."

I looked into the freshly shaved face of a senior agent whose words did not match the look in his eyes. I guessed him at near sixty. He'd been red-haired once. Now, the gray was filtering back from his temples, and deep crow's-feet stamped the corners of his eyes. A familial balding pattern had left his scalp exposed and a veined and red-splotched nose exposed his dependence on too much liquor to salve the grinding visions of ugly human deeds he'd seen over a career.

"I understand that you have some law enforcement experience," he said. "And will thus be familiar with the jurisdictional parameters under which we work."

He was telling me that he was the boss. The FBI was in charge. Don't get in the fucking way, and don't even think about doing anything either active or overt.

But I am nothing if not active and overt when the safety of my friends is at risk. I had been a cop in Philadelphia for several years, had been in the detective bureau for a short time before the stink of bureaucracy sent me back to working the streets. Then one night while responding to a Center City holdup, someone's bullet pierced my neck and my return fire blew the heart out of a thirteen-year-old child.

I'd come to Florida to get away. But some things never leave you. I had a head full of such things. And one of them was the inability to sit still when someone needed me.

"I fully understand," I said to Duncan, meeting his eyes, giving him my best "sir, yes, sir," attitude.

He motioned me to the table.

"We have tapped into all the communications and computer lines here in the judge's office in anticipation that whoever is responsible for Judge Manchester's disappearance will make telephonic or digital contact," Duncan said.

"We are also coordinating with all local law enforcement on a BOLO for the white van observed leaving the scene. And there is another team tracing all possible routes from that scene to access any additional video from both government and private security cameras."

Duncan looked up at me. "But as you might guess, that will take some time."

Perhaps the agent was trying to discern how long I'd been off the job: whether I'd been brainwashed by the movie and television depictions of the government's Big Brother access to every mounted camera on every street corner and shop entrance and satellite lens in existence.

I knew it didn't work that way, even if it was in the interest of law enforcement to have the average citizen and especially the idiot criminal element believe it. It might be a deterrent, but it wasn't true. Few of those cameras are monitored, or even maintained to ensure that they're working. And there is no overwhelming computer net that links them all together. That fantasy has been around since Patrick McGoohan starred in the television series *The Prisoner*, and it isn't any more a reality now than it was back then in 1967.

The government net is increasing, and such surveillance might be scrapped together in a matter of weeks, but it wasn't going to happen during a commercial break.

Duncan stood at ease, as if his required update was finished. He waved a hand in Billy's direction.

"If you would like to join Mr. Manchester in putting together a list of possible contacts, you are welcome to stay on as long as you wish."

I looked at Billy, who had returned to Diane's desk.

"What about the State Department?" I said to Duncan.

The man raised his eyebrows.

"You already know the judge was working on the Escalante extradition," I said. "The kidnapping of judges and journalists in South America is a well-known byproduct of the drug wars there. Would the idea that they might adopt the same techniques here not be an immediate summation of motivation?" I said, adopting the agent's galling use of technical lawyer-ese.

I watched Duncan's eyes. The man was a rock. He didn't give a single "tell." No twitch, no crinkle of facial skin, no flit of an eye—a formidable poker player.

"That, Mr. Freeman, is not my purview," he said, and turned away to his telephonic-digital-whatever-it-was that his team was focused on.

"Thus the State Department," I said. But it could have been a statement to the wall. I went back to join Billy.

He had reopened his laptop and was tapping away at keys in a way I had no chance of keeping up with.

"He threatened her, Max."

"What?"

"Marty Andrews said Escalante made a veiled threat in open court this morning by commenting on her health and the health of our baby."

I stayed silent because I could feel the warm spark of anger flaring behind my eyes.

Finally, I glanced over at the gathering of the feds.

"These guys know that?"

"Of course," Billy said, not looking up from his computer. "They've sent someone down to the lockup cell to speak with him. But I've got my own Wi-Fi set up here and I'm pulling together some contacts I have in Colombia. Businessmen, but very connected businessmen. Word gets passed very quickly among the moneyed class. This kind of thing will have ripple effects."

I noted that Billy was not using Diane's name. He was going impersonal, probably as a coping mechanism, but it was jarring to hear.

I also noted the lack of any stutter in his speech. Billy is a face-to-face stutterer and has been since childhood. Whether it was from the physical abuses by his father or Billy's own penchant to avoid people and find comfort in books and computers, he'd developed a stutter that occurred only when he talked face-to-face with others.

Over a phone line or even out of sight on the other side of a wall, his speech was flawless. But when talking directly to another person's face, command of his voice and tongue eluded him, and his stutter was pronounced.

Though the odd handicap kept him from ever being a court-room lawyer, it in no way stole from his brilliance in knowing the law and the inside workings of government and business. His dual degrees in law and business, from Temple University and Wharton, only honed an already exceptional mind. His connections were worldwide. His client list was long and distinguished, and he was as adept at legal counseling as he was at steering those clients toward wealth-building investments and opportunities.

Billy knew where the money was, both here and overseas. And he knew those who had it. Thus the list of friends and people who owed him was enormous, and powerful.

But I also knew what money could do. And the beauty of being a private investigator instead of a cop was the advantage of using it.

"Can you pull together every major federal cocaine bust made in the tri-county area over the last couple of years on that thing?" I asked.

Billy didn't look up, but cocked his ear, thinking, trying to guess my angle.

"Yes."

"Get me the addresses of those busts and names. If Escalante is involved with this, then the sellers he's been feeding product to might be the ones with ears."

"I'll get you a printout," Billy said, agreeing with my strategy without saying so. "And I'll get you some bribe money."

"Twenty-dollar bills," I said. "Thieves and dealers don't trust hundreds anymore."

"Just tell me how many," Billy said. "She's out there, Max, and I need her back."

CHAPTER 7

*O*K, *shit-hits-the-fan time," Rae whispered when they finally got there. She knew it was coming, knew it when Danny gave her the instructions and then when that asshole Geronimo looked her in the face and just pointed his finger. Danny had told her the woman was coming and all she had to do was watch her, keep an eye on her, don't let her do anything stupid or try to get away or scream or pound on the door or anything. Just watch her and don't say a word.*

Say nothing—that's the one thing Danny really hit hard on. And that's what Alvin the Indian from fucking Keewaydin who everyone called Geronimo meant when he pointed his finger at her. Not a word. No voices. No words. No accents. No skin touching skin. Absolute silence until it was over.

Yeah, right, no skin touching skin, unless you meant Geronimo's braves shoving the woman through the door of this crappy little room onto the crappy little cot. So now she's here. Your job? Just watch her in silence.

Rae could tell in an instant that it was some rich bitch, even with a bag over her head. She could tell by the Ann Taylor suit and the hint of expensive perfume still seeping off her. Yeah, even a trailer-trash girl like her had been to the mall in Traverse City and had tended bar at the Grand Traverse Resort and Spa, where the big money wives dressed up and flaunted it, sitting at the bar and crossing their legs with that shush of expensive nylons and dress fabric that never gets worn from excessive use or the touch of an iron.

And just as quickly, Rae could tell the woman was pregnant from the way she swung with her bloated belly and protected it as she kinda bounced on the mattress when the braves shoved her, shielding her stomach above all and not giving a shit if her head hit the wall.

Goddamn Danny! I knew it. I just knew it.

My man Danny, gotta sure thing going again and what happens? Goes right into the crapper.

"This'll be a sweet gig, Rae. We take a free trip down to Florida, get outta this ass-freezing weather for a few weeks. We go down there and do this job for a few days and, hey, you're part of it, baby. You aren't just sitting around and waiting for me, you know, like you always complain about."

Yeah, she did bitch about those times when he was jacking cars for other guys who didn't have the skills that Danny had or the moxie to get out in the daylight hours and slide a cod-buster under the door jamb and record the owner's key signature and then come back the next night and hotwire the thing. Sure, Danny was good, but all that meant was that she was standing around in the boring bar watching the Land Rover owner sip his martinis and making sure she gave Danny a call if the guy happened to get up to leave.

Waiting on you to have the fun, you with the skills and the contacts and the balls—yeah, she did get tired of that.

So he says this time is different.

"I got you in on the deal," he says. "You're part of it, babe. They need someone like you and I told them you were perfect for it and they're paying us both, like, a shitload of money and then we just party awhile afterward, sit in the sun, go down to Margaritaville, you know?"

You never learn, Rae, you just don't learn, and now here you are, sitting in a fucking hot wooden room like a fucking jail cell with a woman with a bag over her head who has probably been kidnapped for some kinda ransom by a bunch of lunatics downstairs along with your man, Danny.

And the bitch is pregnant. The one goddamn thing you yourself have avoided like the plague all your life and held up like a badge of honor every time another one of your friends went and popped out another kid that put them further on the dole and deeper in the welfare ditch and you smiling and nodding at all their little, "Isn't she cute and such a little doll," and telling them, "Congratulations," when you really meant: "Dumbass. Whyn't you just jab another stick in your eye?"

Rae knew the usual outcome all too well because she was one of those babies. Apparently sired by a man she knew only as her mother's ex.

More babies—Jesus!

So now here you are with another pregnant woman. Another one in trouble but it's feeling more and more like you're in cahoots with what's putting her in trouble and fuck that. Fucking Danny. Gonna be so easy. Now the woman says she can see you through the hood and knows where you are. Bullshit. You can tell because when she says it her head isn't even turned in the right direction. She's trying to trick you like everybody else who thinks they're smarter than you.

How many dozen of them have you seen at the resort or over at the Indian casino: tourists walking in and lording it over the locals, the hicks, and the help. She's lying and you know she's lying. And then the bitch says she's a federal judge and holy hell is coming down and you really fucked up this time and goddamnit, Danny, maybe the woman ain't lying about that!

CHAPTER 8

The room stayed quiet, but there was noise outside the door: metal grinding on metal and the sound of hissing, like air pressure releasing but at a lower octave. Diane would hear a pop; then the low hissing would go on and on until she heard the clanging sound of something falling on a hard floor.

She could smell the odor of something burning. At first, she started to panic: Were they setting fire to the building? Would they burn the place down so that they didn't leave evidence? Would they simply burn her alive after such a bold kidnapping on a street corner? Burned alive: the thought made her quiver.

In her mind, she revisited one of her first cases as a prosecutor, a fire on an old sugar plantation out near Clewiston in which the manor house burned to the ground. There'd been only one victim, the wife of the prominent elderly owner, dead of smoke inhalation in her own bedroom.

Diane had been called to the scene because when firefighters arrived they'd found the bedroom door locked from the outside. When they'd battered their way in, they knocked back the flames but discovered the burned body of the woman on the floor just inside. The battalion chief had noted fingernail scratches on the inside enamel of the doorframe.

In subsequent interviews, Diane found that the woman had been suffering from Alzheimer's and that her husband, who had been in the company of a local brothel owner that very night, admitted that he locked his wife in for her own safety when he went on his regular sexual forays. His was a storied name in the history of the county, but Diane had gone after him with a negligent homicide charge and made it stick despite the politics. The sitting judge had sent him to Starke, where he'd died before his sentence was fully served.

Her father, by then an appellate court judge, had admonished her not for being strident in the face of political pressure, but for showing up at the scene. Leave it to the detectives, he'd told her. But Diane had always felt that many in law enforcement and the courts saw her as the pampered, rich-kid judge's daughter. She'd always been determined to stick her nose into it and check out the scene firsthand if she could. That one may have been a step too far.

Now, the recollection of the medical examiner carrying out the woman's charred remains made Diane shiver. Would the relatives of a dead plantation owner hold a grudge and try to burn her to death for her actions nearly ten years earlier?

Again, Diane calmed herself. *You don't kidnap a federal judge just to kill him or her—at least not right away,* she thought. *You've got to get something for your trouble, for your risk.* She was rationalizing, but she couldn't completely stifle the fear that knotted in her throat. She could still smell the odor of something hot, but it wasn't smoke, and it did not increase.

Something was happening on the first floor from where they'd taken her up the stairs, but still there were no voices. Not a distinguishable word was said. Not outside, nor in this room where she knew, just knew, someone was still sitting or standing nearby watching silently. It had been hours now, she was sure of it, even though she told herself over and over that her anxiety only made the time go slower.

It was hot, but somehow not humid. In a Florida summer, it would be intolerable in a place like this where the hot air and humidity would rise and make it a sauna. But it was March, supposedly the peak month for beautiful Florida weather. She had figured out how to puff out the fabric of the hood on her face to create a bit of a gap, a pocket in front of her nose and mouth so that she could breathe easier. But it was still a cloying, almost gasping affair when she let herself start to panic. She had to control it for herself and for her child.

"May I have some water?" she finally said, knowing her captor was there. "I'm very thirsty. The baby needs the hydration. You must know that, sir."

Nothing but silence. She quieted again, straining to hear the breathing sounds she'd heard before. How big was this room? Had he moved far enough away to keep her from hearing him breathe?

"Please," she said. Her throat was parched and tight from anxiety, and her plea came out as a grainy whisper: "Please."

She heard the floorboards creak, once, twice, a third time—and then it stopped. She tilted her head up as if she could see the figure approaching even though the hood was opaque.

When she felt something against the bottom of her chin, her first reaction was to pull away, to buck at the touch. But no violence followed—only the damned silence. She took four breaths and then leaned forward again. After a beat, she felt pressure under her chin, followed by the feeling of something poking and then sliding up under the hood: not a finger but a straw. The sharp edge of a plastic straw rubbed at the bottom of her chin until she managed to maneuver it into her mouth and suck on it, bringing the liquid into her mouth. Coca-Cola, strong and syrupy, flowed.

She hadn't been a Coke drinker since her youth, but the coolness of it and the slight carbonation were like rushes of fresh air. She took in more of it, knowing that in the long run the sugar and caffeine would help keep her alert and partially energized. She leaned into it and tilted her head down, thinking she might use the lift of the straw against the fabric of the hood so that she could peek a glance at the floor or bed. But suddenly, she felt a push against her forehead as she was forced back. The straw was pulled harshly out and straight down. Again, Diane heard the floorboards; he'd stepped back.

She let the silence go on for three beats and then said: "Thank you. You are very kind."

CHAPTER 9

Waiting for something to happen is the most difficult part of organized law enforcement, and it was one reason I was glad to be out of it. The feds in Diane's office were ordering in more coffee. Billy was working his sources on the computer. Everyone in the room was waiting for one thing: the bleating of the phone and the call that would make some form of ransom demand for Diane's life.

With the exception of a few nutcases out there, criminality is a simple, logical outgrowth of human need: greed, retribution, sexual gratification, power.

The odds were stacked against the possibility that three maniacs would mistakenly sweep a sitting judge off the streets in the middle of the day. The fact that they were smart enough to ditch her phone and credit cards and cash meant they weren't run-of-the-mill idiots. They had another motivation, and the FBI glommed onto the answer that Diane's involvement in the Escalante case was that motive. I shared their supposition, but I couldn't just sit and wait for the next step to be dictated by the other side.

With Billy's approval, I left the courthouse and went to the main branch of American in downtown West Palm Beach.

Inside the lobby, I asked for Mr. Armistead as Billy had instructed and was quickly met by a man in his late fifties with the kind of combed-back gray hair that was gelled into minute, perfect rows leading from a high forehead to the perfectly clipped back of his neck. He had a weak chin, which he tried to hide with one of those macho mustache-and-beard combinations they call door-knockers.

Still, he was wearing an expensive suit and had a ring on his right hand that probably indicated the graduating class of some Ivy League university. But after adjusting my handshake to avoid the ring's bulk, I didn't give it another thought.

"Mr. Freeman," Armistead said, and with a come-this-way gesture he led me to a corner office, which I quickly surmised was not his private one but an open affair any bank officer could use on the fly.

The art on the wall was a Florida watercolor of swaying palms and white-capped ocean and taupe beaches. There were no personal photos on the immaculate desktop, and Armistead did not even give the computer screen a look when he sat down.

"Mr. Manchester has given us his instructions. And if you will only sign for this, Mr. Freeman, and please show me some form of ID, we can take care of this as quickly as he has urged."

A photo ID: the guy was giving me a hundred thousand dollars in cash on an ID and a signature. I always admired Billy's contacts. I didn't want to be him, but I did admire his connections.

I showed my Florida driver's license and signed. Mr. Armistead glanced at the ID. I was sure that he had already sized up the courier sitting before him: a tall, lean man whose specific age would be difficult to guess because of his athletic carriage and tanned and healthy complexion from extended periods of outdoor living. He might have been put off by my oxford shirt minus the tie, and my un-ironed khakis. And he may have noticed my scuffed leather boat shoes but probably hadn't yet detected that I wasn't wearing any socks.

It's a look I've cultivated because it makes people think: Cop? Boat captain? Salesman? Tourist? It's bland enough to cover a lot of bases and keeps me from sticking out. In my business, you don't want to stick out.

Giving a hundred grand in cash to a guy who looked like an

upscale deckhand or an aging Applebee's waiter might not have been among Mr. Armistead's usual banking duties, but again, Billy's name smoothed all doubts. The man pulled a stuffed, softbound attaché case from under the desk and pushed it toward me as if it might be unlucky to hold on to it too long.

I didn't bother opening the case, and the banker's stone-faced look indicated that he certainly would not encourage it, even in the quasi-privacy of the office.

"Thank you, sir," I said, and he only nodded.

I walked out of the bank with the attaché and went back to my car, which I'd parked deep in the corner of the lot in a Floridian's favorite spot—under the shade of an old banyan tree. Shade, even in March, is coveted by those of us who know better than to put anything in the corrosive direct rays of a subtropical sun. You could bake bread on the front seat of a sedan parked on asphalt without shade in a couple of hours.

After working an eight-hour shift in summer, it's every office worker's wonder that the polymer plastic making up radio knobs and door handles and gearshifts isn't melting and dripping onto the floor mats when they get to their cars.

I had also backed the Gran Fury into the spot up next to a ficus hedge to give me some cover when I popped the trunk and lay the attaché inside. I opened the case. I don't care who you are or how rich you've become, seeing that much cash in twenty-dollar bills will make you blink your eyes and catch your breath. I took out six thousand three-packs in purple bindings and closed the case. Then I took my keys and reached far into the back of the trunk.

After Billy had given me the Fury, I had a friend weld a steel drawer up above the space where a spare tire should go. You couldn't see it if you just opened the trunk and looked in; you needed to know it by feel. I unlocked the drawer, retrieved a bundle wrapped in oilcloth, replaced it with the case full of money, and relocked it.

I closed the trunk, surveyed the landscape for interested or furtive eyes, and then got into the driver's side. Once settled behind the wheel, I unwrapped the oilcloth to expose the SIG SAUER P226 Navy handgun I'd been given by Rob Maine, a Florida gun expert who'd become another new friend. He'd been aghast that I was still harboring my old 9-mm police-issue handgun. He knew I was living out on the edge of the Everglades, and said the moisture was going to turn the old 9 mm into a hunk of rust despite my regular care of the weapon.

"Use the SIG," he said. "The SEALs do and it isn't completely waterproof, but it's phosphate-coated, and a hell of a lot better than that old thing you've got."

I dropped in the fifteen-round magazine and checked the ammunition, thumbing the first two out, looking for rust. Maine had also "gifted" me a box of 9-mm rounds that he'd sealed around the primer area with a diluted mix of clear nail polish.

"Wouldn't want you to snap a wet load when some gator's got you by the balls out there."

I worked the slide. Everything was clear.

I do not like guns. I don't like the trouble they can lead to, or the aftereffects they can leave behind. But I was going somewhere with a wad of cash in my pocket to meet a guy who knew some guys who knew everything there was to know about drug dealing in this area of South Florida, and that combination demanded backup I wasn't going to get. I slipped the gun under my seat and started the Fury.

Clarence Quarles—they called him CQ. And even though a cat can sometimes change some of his stripes, more often than not you're still going to find him near the same litter box he grew up in.

Clarence was a tall, skinny, chocolate-skinned athlete who had the gift of some combination of bone density and fast-twitch muscle that could catapult his six-foot-seven-inch frame to heights you could only gawk at. His splayed fingers seemed to do magical things on a leather-covered ball, making it move and spin and float in the air, giving it a radarlike attraction to an orange hoop just twice its circumference. He could run, inexhaustible, like a gazelle, and had a shooting range that made NBA scouts drool and defensive players cry.

I had met him through a friend, a teacher in fact, who had a seemingly mystical effect over Clarence that had led the kid from a despicable neighborhood on Tamarind Avenue in West Palm Beach to a prep high school in New England to a scholarship at Boston University. There was something in CQ that had kept him from signing a pro contract as an undergrad, had kept him in school studying economics, and had kept him coming back to this place on spring break to see his family and shoot hoops like he'd never left.

If you ever asked him why, he'd stretch out those impossibly long arms, turn his pale white palms to the sky, and quote Popeye the Sailor Man: "What? I yam what I yam."

It made people shake their heads. It made people wonder. It made me smile. Billy knew and loved the kid and would be appalled that I would bring him into this mess. But I knew CQ had connections. And I was going to use any and all means to find Diane.

I parked the Fury in the street fronting the Dunbar Village housing project within eyeball distance of the basketball court. I knew CQ hung there—a mama's boy come back to the roost. His mother's home was thirty feet away from the rusted gate entrance to the court. From her porch, she had watched her boy from the time he learned to walk. And CQ knew she was watching: that fact may have saved him.

When I closed the door of the Fury, the noise caused a dozen sets of eyes from the court to look over, while another untold number that I couldn't see surely peeked out from gauzed curtains and dusty venetian blinds. A tall white man in an old-school police car didn't just pull up to this neighborhood without being noticed.

Knowing this, I headed directly to Mrs. Quarles's front porch instead of the court where I had already spotted Clarence sitting idle on a bench, surrounded by four or five other players. Before I reached his mama's front yard, her son got up, picked up a basketball with one hand as if he were snatching an errant cantaloupe from the ground, and started shooting free throws at the far basket.

As usual, Clarence's mother was sitting on her porch, a lap full of sewing in the folds of her day dress, her tapered and weathered fingers busy with close work.

"Good day, Mrs. Quarles."

"Yessir, Mr. Freeman," she answered, looking up at the sky. "I believe the Lord has done us right today."

"How have you been, ma'am?"

She moved her gaze from the azure sky over to the courts where the players had gone back to more important things than assessing the stranger who'd put a wrinkle in their day.

"I got my boy home. And I rose for yet another day on this earth, Mr. Freeman," she said and turned a smile on me. "So I'm on the plus side, sir."

"Indeed you are, Mrs. Quarles," I responded, taking my time, knowing the ritual. Since her son's tremendous athletic skills had turned him into a commodity in high school, no coach, no recruiter, no so-called adult fan, was allowed to address or approach him without the permission of his mother. If you broke that rule, you automatically lost access. That's how it was and it was upheld by CQ and thus by everyone else.

"That's some kind o' old-time vehicle you got there, Mr. Freeman," the elderly woman said, again without looking at the subject of her sentence. "Reminds me of bad times."

Her tone was conversational, carrying no other meaning than a simple statement. But the message was there.

"Yes, ma'am. She's an old classic. Billy gave it to me as a present."

"Is that right? And how is Mr. Manchester? We don't see him as much as we would like to." The mention of Billy improved her demeanor. A hint of a smile came to her face. "He still livin' on top of that big ol' palace down on the beach?"

"Yes, ma'am, he is. And although he is in good health, Mrs. Quarles, he is working very hard. In fact, I came by today to see if Clarence might be able to help Mr. Manchester with something."

The elderly woman looked at me, studied my face in the way I was sure she had studied the eyes of every recruiter or coach or vice principal of a private school or any other man who came to her porch bearing propositions for her son.

"If it's for Mr. Manchester, I'm sure Clarence will want to help," she said, now looking past me toward the court, indicating I was allowed to speak to her son. I took my foot off the first step and my elbow off her banister.

" 'Cause I know Mr. Manchester would never put my boy in a bad situation," she said. The inflection was a mix of question and command.

"No, ma'am," I said before turning away. "He wouldn't."

I slipped inside the fence of the basketball court and walked toward the far end. The players, all African Americans ranging from elementary school children to prematurely gray, yellow-eyed men, lowered their chins but raised their eyes, cutting looks at yet another white dude in search of CQ.

"Yo, Coach," someone yelled from the deep corner of the court. "I gotta sweet jumper, too, like to light up yo' field house like a star."

The comment elicited a number of guffaws from the other players.

"Hey, man. I take CQ a dozen times one-on-one. He ain't that good," the young caller said.

More sneers from the others and then from a group on the bench: "Shut up, nigger. You can't take CQ's mama with that raggedy-ass game a' yours."

"Why don't you come out here, nigger, an' I sho' you what's raggedy-ass?"

I kept walking, though I felt a grin pulling at the side of my mouth. If a white man had used such a racial epithet on the playground, or anywhere else for that matter, words or fists would be flying. Here it was ritual. I did note that when the braggart commented that he'd beaten CQ in one-on-one games in the past, CQ himself had never turned from his concentration on his own basket. I saw him simply shake his head and shoot another free throw.

As I approached, I watched him bounce the ball twice, then position it delicately in the web of his elongated fingers. With a fluid motion like the slow whip of a willow tree limb in the wind, he shot the ball in a parabola that I knew was too high for a standard free throw. Yet the orb rose with an exaggerated backspin, pierced the hoop without touching any part of the rim, and because of the spin, struck the macadam and bounced back perfectly to CQ, who had not moved from his spot at the free-throw line.

I was three steps behind him, and he had not turned his head.

"That the way Pistol Pete Maravich did it, Mr. Freeman?" he said, still not turning, but again positioning the ball on the tips of his fingers and letting go another shot, exactly the same, with the same rotation and result.

"So I've heard, CQ," I said. "He didn't have anyone to rebound for him when he was a kid, so he developed that backspin so he wouldn't have to chase the ball."

CQ shook his head.

"Ol' school, man. But you do what you have to do, right, Mr. Freeman?"

This time, he turned, cradled the ball in one hand, and reached out the other, offering it. The young man's palm swallowed my entire hand like I'd slipped it into a manila envelope. And I do not have small hands. "Maravich was a legend," I said, looking into CQ's strikingly black eyes, the corneas so dark it was impossible to detect the color there. They made you stare into them a bit longer than was naturally polite.

"True," CQ said. "But can you imagine a guy playing in the NBA today with the nickname 'Pistol'? Man, the press would crucify that dude."

I was still looking into the kid's eyes, but felt myself smiling at his grasp of the world around him. "Probably true," was all I said.

Clarence bounced the ball a couple of times and let an awkward silence sit for three beats. "Y'all didn't come to play, did you, Mr. Freeman?" he said with a smile of his own.

"No. I came to ask a favor, CQ, for me and for Mr. Manchester."

The statement caused the young man's lips to seal and his eyes to avert for the first time.

"OK," he said, stepping toward the empty benches at courtside. "Let's talk."

So what did I need from him? CQ asked. I just had to name it. Mr. Manchester was his friend. He'd been supportive from a distance, not like the others who wanted to be close just for the sake of prestige or spin-off money or any residual self-gain they could get from "knowing" CQ.

"He's cool. And I met his lady once and she was cool, too. What do you think I can do to help?"

I gave CQ the facts in low tones on the courtside bench. The other players had left us alone. I explained the kidnapping of Billy's wife and the instant speculation that her case dealing with the extradition of a Colombian drug supplier had in all probability been the motivation.

"We think they'll keep her close, hiding her until they think they can use her in some sort of trade to keep their man from going to court here in the States."

CQ had followed the logic. He was a college-educated twenty-one-year-old. In fact, he was smarter than a typical college kid because he knew both sides of the street: the campus and classrooms where he was learning macroeconomics, and the local corner where a more visceral form of business theory held sway.

"So you're looking for Mrs. Manchester and because you think there are drugs involved, you figure I might have access to relevant information, being that I have such wide connections within the drug underworld?"

Crafting his synopsis, CQ had discarded all hints of ghetto cant in his voice and diction. The metamorphosis was impressive, but I wasn't sure if he was employing it because he was pissed at me for making assumptions, or to show that he understood exactly what I was asking him to do.

"Y'all need a CI. Right?" he said, instantly switching up the lingua franca. "Somebody who know everybody in the 'hood and got an ear for the street scut."

"Right," I said—no use hiding my intentions.

He stared out over the empty half-court for a minute, spinning the ball in his huge hands, letting it slide over his skin. With each revolution, there was a hissing sound.

"Are you providing incentive, Mr. Freeman?" he finally said, cutting his eyes at me.

"I am. I've got two grand in my pocket and more if the information pans out. Unmarked cash. You pass out the first taste, and then I'll personally deliver the follow-up if your source has more."

Again, CQ spun the ball.

"That ain't the way the cops do it."

"I'm not the cops."

The ball stopped. CQ looked me directly in the eye, the way he'd been taught by his mother, the way that meant he understood what was being asked of him and that he was promising to do what he said he would.

"For Mr. Manchester and his wife, yes," he said.

He reached out a hand. I reached into my pocket first and then gave him a handshake containing a disposable cell phone and a packet of a hundred twenties.

"You make the call to me and then ditch the phone, CQ. No blowback on you. We're not putting you in jeopardy."

He looked past me, staring first at the ground and then raising his eyes past me in the direction of the porch where his mother still sat.

"Yeah, you are, Mr. Freeman. But it's cool. I know the game, and I'm better at playing it than you are."

I thanked the young man, knowing he was correct, but justifying my actions as I walked off the court.

"Yo, Coach. Yo, check it out, Coach," yelled another player who fired a twenty-five-foot air ball that again elicited hoots from the others.

As I moved past CQ's front porch, I cut my eyes to Mrs. Quarles, who was still in her chair, watching me with a relaxed but suspicious look on her aged and mottled face. She returned my nod, but not with full approval.

The Gran Fury was untouched under her protective eye, and I climbed in and keyed the ignition, rumbling the 420 V-8 to life, the noise helping me keep at bay the ethical argument that I knew was going to haunt my thoughts. But I had other stops to make, including one to a lawyer Billy would be loath to contact on his own, even though it was an obvious connection to the Escalante empire.

When I'd pulled away from CQ's neighborhood under the baleful look of his mother, I knew I was running without rules. And in the world of both the good and the bad guys, someone running without rules can be dangerous.

CHAPTER 10

I need something to drink. My baby needs something to drink."
Whine, whine, whine, Rae thought, looking over at the hooded
woman on the bed. Christ—these rich bitches, always whining. She
just stared at the figure, arms still bound behind her, propped up at
an angle against the wall now, letting her bloated stomach take the
softness of the mattress.

"The baby needs hydration. You must know that, sir. You must
know that a child needs water. Please."

Rae remembered the time one of her mother's boyfriends put up a
sign in their trailer home above the kitchen sink in a place you could see
from just about any spot in the front half of the trailer, which in reality
wasn't but one room with a stupid bar counter separating the kitchen
area from the so-called living room.

The placard was shaped like a traffic sign with a red circle and a
red stripe lashed across the words NO WHINING—like it was the law
or something in their home. And he hadn't been staying there more
than two weeks, James or Jimmy or some damn out-of-work long-haul
trucker dude. He was another of her mother's beaus, as she called them.
Putting up a damn NO WHINING sign in their home! Asshole would just
point at the sign when he thought Rae or her mother was complaining
too much.

He wouldn't even turn his head away from the big-screen television set he'd lugged in, obtained no doubt from some electronics theft ring that was actually in cahoots with the drivers of tractor-trailers who hauled the stuff from Detroit or Grand Rapids up north. He'd just point his finger at the goddamn NO WHINING sign, and Rae would walk out the front door, flipping the bird at the back of the guy's head as she left.

"Please. Please," the woman had whispered. Rae looked down at the Big Gulp that had been under the chair since Danny brought her lunch, a Coke and a taco from the 7-Eleven. The drink was warm by now, but she picked it up and stepped to the bed. The woman turned her head, and Rae poked the straw from the Big Gulp up under the hood, poking until the woman finally got it into her mouth and started sucking, a little at first and then as if her damn life depended on it. Not so haughty now, right, Ms. Rich Bitch? Us hicks ain't so much shit on the heel of your shoe when you need us, huh?

Finally, the woman started pulling at the straw, and Rae could see that the opening at the bottom of the hood was starting to gape. She was afraid the woman was trying to sneak a look at the floor, the room, even get a look at her, so she yanked the Big Gulp away.

Now you're taking advantage? Now you're trying to get over on me? She wanted to yell at the woman, but she held her tongue. Silence, Danny and the asshole Geronimo had said.

Instead, Rae retreated back to her chair and sat and stared at the hooded head across the room. Rich bitch trying to get over, like they all did. Always conniving, trying to figure out how to get their way, make their businesses more profitable, and put more in their pockets, and all the time sounding like they were doing you a favor. Yeah, she heard the big shots, talking at the bar about their big deals and methods of financing. Talking about their hidden interest rates and sweetening the pot with government subsidies they'd never be on the hook to pay back—pulling a profit they couldn't dream of without those tax subsidies.

Oh yeah, they'd chat and whisper the internal dealings without the least concern over doing it in front of some backwoods bartender girl *who'd be too stupid to understand the ways and methods of the big-business boys.*

So was Danny any different? Hell, sometimes it was the car and truck and heavy equipment owners themselves who'd get him to steal the damn vehicles just so they could write it off on their insurance. Isn't that fraud? Isn't that a crime? Oh no. That's the game, baby. You need to know how to cheat without getting caught. It ain't a crime unless you get caught. The old "If a tree falls in the woods and there's no one there to hear it, does it make a noise?"

Hell, Rae had been working the Grand Traverse Resort and Spa bar on a Sunday afternoon with a basketball game on the big screen and heard the NBA commentator say that a player "would never make the big time if he wasn't willing to push the envelope, do what needs to be done. It's not a foul unless you get caught by the ref. That's his job. Not yours."

The business boys drinking their lunch had looked at one another and nodded, and tapped their fists together. You tell it, brother. That's the way it's done, right there on national television. Cheat if you can get away with it.

Rae sat watching the hooded woman and slipped the Big Gulp back under her chair.

"Thank you," the woman said. "You are very kind."

CHAPTER 11

I didn't have an appointment, but I knew that Johnny Milsap, Esq., attorney at law, would greet me with an extended hand when he found out I was walking around with cash money. Just like on the street: I'd be different than some detective or prosecutor calling in a favor with the promise of a break or a reduced sentence. Johnny did his business under the rubric made famous by an old-time Philadelphia counselor and politico who was caught on tape braying: "Money talks and bullshit walks."

I'd be talking his talk.

Not that I was making moral judgments. I'd already made two other stops, one to see a bail bondsman whose reputation was spread among the users and losers in the drug trade as the man to go to when you were in jail on a possession-with-intent-to-distribute charge, and the other to see a retired DEA investigator who owed me and still kept his finger on the workings of the cocaine importation trade on the Miami River in Miami-Dade County.

Neither of them seemed to mind taking Billy's money as a "consultant's fee" for any information, rumors or otherwise, they might come up with about who might be involved with Diane's abduction.

For a man I considered a low-life lawyer, Johnny's offices were decidedly conservative. He was on the sixth floor of a building on Las Olas Boulevard in downtown Fort Lauderdale. There was a community college across the street. The main offices of the biggest newspaper in Broward County were catty-corner. Just across the Intracoastal Bridge on Sixth Street was the county courthouse and jail complex where Johnny did his work. The reception area for Suite 609 was done in beige and lavender, with a thick carpet and artwork on the walls that was a couple of grades above Motel 6, but prints nonetheless. There were eight chairs in the room, all of them empty.

Milsap did most of his work defending drug charges against his various clients and being kept on retainer for bail service and for questioning the proper procedures of collection of evidence and the strength of warrants. His wealthier clients did not come to his office; they had their people do it.

But his more street-level clients were sometimes unpredictable and always carried the possibility of danger if their cases didn't turn out the way they'd hoped. The receptionist at Milsap's office was behind a sliding, pebbled-glass window, so you felt like you were visiting the urologist or the local psychotherapist. I could tell by the thickness that it wasn't bulletproof glass, and knowing Johnny, I wondered why not. I ignored the stupid-looking bell on the shelf and rattled the window with a knuckle instead.

The glass slid open halfway, and a receptionist with streaked blonde hair and the doe-eyed look and complexion of a seventeen-year-old met my gaze with emerald green eyes that hadn't a clue behind them.

"May I help you?"

I wondered if she knew she'd be the first one to take a bullet if one of Johnny's pissed-off clients came in with a grudge against her boss.

"Please tell Mr. Milsap that Max Freeman is here to see him," I said with as little inflection as possible.

"Is Mr. Milsap expecting you?" the tiny rehearsed voice said.

I gave her a deadpan look that I imagined was worn by every detective or numbers enforcer or racetrack operator who ever actually came in to see Johnny.

"Not until you tell him I'm here," I said.

The girl did not alter her Alice-in-Wonderland look as she said, "One moment please," and then slid the window shut.

I did not sit and instead took two steps closer to the door leading to the attorney's inner office. It wasn't a long wait. In less than a minute, the handle clicked, the door opened inward, and Johnny Milsap greeted me with the practiced smile of a back-lot carnival barker or adjustable-rate mortgage broker—take your pick.

"Well, Max Freeman, friend and confidant of the illustrious Billy Manchester himself. To what do I owe this unexpected pleasure?"

He offered his hand. I stepped past it and walked directly into his private office.

Milsap's desk was second-rate, faux oak, and devoid of any files, a computer, or even pretend photos of family or friends. He probably had a law degree from some innocuous university, but it was nowhere in sight. There was a wall of bookcases behind him, but they looked so regimented and obviously untouched that I was reminded of a book dealer I knew who could order books by the yard in whatever color matched your wallpaper just to supply ambience. The framed art on the other walls were repeats of those in reception, and I actually had to give Johnny credit for not having black velvet paintings of Elvis up there.

I sat down in front of his desk and Johnny took up his post behind it.

"Please have a seat, Mr. Freeman," he said with only the slightest hint of sarcasm in his voice. "What can I do for you?"

Elbows on the armrests of my chair, I folded my hands in front of me, looked unblinking into the attorney's face, and stifled my urge to strangle the man. He must have read my eyes.

"First," he said, clearing his throat, "I would like to offer my condolences to your employer over this terrible atrocity involving Judge Manchester. It's horrific, unconscionable."

News of the kidnapping of a federal judge would already have been flashed on CNN and rippled through the legal community.

Milsap knew that as Billy's investigator I would be focused on nothing else. But being coy at such a time was not below him. Again, I held my tongue and my homicidal urges in check and instead reached into my sports coat pockets and stacked ten thousand dollars in cash on Milsap's desk.

"I'm paying for information, Johnny," I said. "You have more connections to drug distributors than any lawyer in South Florida, and it is a possibility that Mrs. Manchester's kidnapping may be the work of minions from the Colombian cocaine pipeline. I'm asking you to ask around, to listen carefully to the scuttlebutt among your clients. If you hear something useful and pass it along, there will be more of this coming."

Now, it was Milsap's turn to be silent. He looked from my eyes to the money. It talks. Especially when it's sitting stacked up in front of a man like him.

Milsap and I had crossed paths a couple of times in the past, once when he was representing a Delaware investment group that was buying up the life insurance policies of elderly black women. Milsap acted as a go-between who would pass those names on to a white-collar degenerate who then paid a mentally challenged drug addict to smother the women if they began to outlive the actuarial profit of those policies.

Through Billy, I was put onto the case. When the shitstorm came down, Milsap claimed he never knew where the names were going, and never recognized them when they started showing up on the obit pages.

"It was a fiduciary responsibility on my part," he told detectives who started sorting out the story after the killer of the women died at Sherry's hand. "I had no idea."

Now, I was actively putting myself in bed with him. The sour taste in my mouth was starting to build with each second he delayed a reaction.

"You understand," he finally said, nodding at the cash. "This retainer would be considered the formation of an attorney-client relationship, Mr. Freeman. Thus any conversation between you and me would be considered privileged. Any information that I might access and discuss with you would, I hope, be considered as such."

"Be as slick as you need to be, Johnny. You get me something that gets us closer to the scum who took Diane Manchester, I pay you. I don't need names. I don't need affidavits. I need to be pointed in the right direction."

Again, Milsap looked at me and then at the pile of bills.

"I know Judge Manchester was working on the extradition case for Juan Manuel Escalante, Mr. Freeman. And I know you and Mr. Manchester are smart enough to be aware of that particular businessman's connections and outreach. If in any way my assistance . . ."

"Your name doesn't come up, Johnny. I'm not DEA. This is freelance and it's mine alone," I said, knowing there was an edge to my voice.

"OK, OK," Milsap said quickly, raising his palms. "I'm just saying."

"Yeah, I know what you're saying, Johnny." I reached into my pocket to pull out another disposable cell phone and dropped it on top of the cash.

"I know you've used one of these before, Counselor. Untraceable, with a single number loaded into it. I've got its mate, also untraceable. You get anything, you call me. No way to connect it back to you."

The attorney's hands were now moving across the desk to enfold the phone and the pile of cash.

"And if something good should come of my information," he said, pulling in the money as though he'd just won a huge poker pot. "Perhaps one good turn from a fellow member of the Florida Bar might someday be returned by Mr. Manchester himself?"

I stood and gave the lawyer another eye-to-eye look.

"Don't push it, Johnny."

CHAPTER 12

Diane didn't know how long she'd been asleep or how long she'd been dreaming. She'd tried to stay awake; had felt her eyelids fluttering, and resisted. She jumped several times when her head bobbed forward. But in the end, she failed.

She'd tried to be brave. *I'll fight these bastards. I'll kick someone in the balls and escape. I'll scratch someone's eyes out.* Instead, she lay down on the mattress. She'd tried to cry, conjured a face for her baby, pulled a vision of Billy and his smile, and then squeezed her eyes tight to force the glands to produce moisture so she could feel the tears run down her cheek. That failed, too.

Instead, in exhaustion brought on by anxiety, she slept and dreamed. She'd gone back to the time when she was a child, to the first time she'd felt vulnerable and alone, unloved and scared. She might have been six, maybe seven. She'd had a fight with her parents, both of them at the same time, which was rare.

While on a vacation in southwest Florida, she'd been left in a rustic cottage with a babysitter while her father the judge and her mother had gone to some exotic Florida dinner at the nearby Rod and Gun Club and denied her even the possibility of being left alone. She'd argued she was old enough to be left on her own. She'd thrown a tantrum, replete with tears, and declared loudly that she was no baby.

She'd stalked to a room and closed herself in, refusing to even meet the sitter. Then she'd snuck out through a window and onto the grounds of the old Everglades City hotel. She'd bumbled about near the docks and boats and marshland that surrounded the near-century-old place in the half-dark, and had become frightened by the unfamiliar calls of night birds and insects and the moonlit splashes of feeding fish and the underbrush rustle of nocturnal hunters. She'd found misguided refuge in a worn, wooden boathouse and cowered there until she was found by a collective staff of anxious searchers and her frantic parents.

The dream seemed so real—the sensation of wet tears on her face, the fear of being abandoned, the exhaustion from searching the darkness for a way back, hunger from a missed meal, the smells of damp canvas and caustic oils, and the shouts of unfamiliar men's voices calling out her name. Why had her parents abandoned her? Why had they not protected her? Why was she all alone?

When Diane jolted out of the dream, she blinked open her eyes and was met only by the darkness and the cloying feel of the hood still over her face. She could feel the moisture of tears against her cheeks and realized she'd been crying. Choking against the close air, she began grabbing at the cloth, wrenching at it to pull it from her face. In frustration, she cinched it tighter around her throat instead. Strong hands suddenly clamped onto her wrists, and Diane began screaming for help.

She may have let loose two, maybe three cries before the sound of a door bursting open was followed by three heavy steps and a clap of thunder in her right ear. The blow spun her. Her body reeled, the creaking bed frame screeched, and the heaviness of her belly swung a fraction of a second behind the rest of her body, sloshing behind the force that sent her hard against the wall.

Silence, or maybe deafness, followed. The flashes of light she saw were from the slap to her face, not the removal of the hood. She squeezed her eyes shut against the pain, saw more swirls of light and color behind her eyelids. Then through her undamaged ear, she heard the first words since being in her court chambers—guttural, threatening, deep, but controlled words:

"If you cannot control her, we will find someone who can."

She heard the door slam. Then the stunning quiet took over again. *You're still conscious,* Diane thought. The pain at the side of her face was humming, and there was a ringing in her ear, like a high-pitch tinnitus. She curled her back and bowed her head. *Does trauma to the mother cause damage to the fetus?* she wondered. *If you go unconscious, maybe it does, and if you stop breathing, definitely. End of heartbeat? Stay alive, Diane, no matter what.* She again listened to the silence.

Then she concentrated, tuned her good ear: Was the captor still there? The one who had obviously been upbraided for letting her scream? She stilled her own heart rate and breathing, and settled herself, then listened intently to the air—to the vibration of it, the movement. Maybe the electric air of the disturbance itself made it hard for her to get back to the acute listening she'd been trying to cultivate. Was she alone, or not? Was her guard still here? Was he pissed because she'd gotten him into trouble? Was it possible to hear anger?

She made a tactical choice.

"I'm sorry," she said.

No reaction.

"I'm sorry I screamed and got you into trouble. I panicked. I won't do it again."

Nothing—no response. No "shut up, bitch," or "It's just a job for me." No scraping of chair legs. No sliding open of a shut window, just to change the air and take a breath.

Diane listened closer for the breathing she'd detected before. Certainly, any human being would be feeling something after the threat from that guttural voice that had just berated her overseer. Anger like that raises the blood pressure and increases the respiration. No one could not be affected.

Then she heard it: a ticking, a wispy *click, click, click*-ing. She knew the sound of texting. She made it herself when she used her phone while court was in session. She thought of it as a quiet, incognito way to communicate even when you weren't supposed to be doing it.

My guard is texting someone, reaching out, outside of this room at least, she thought. A connection to the outside was something, she told herself—a possibility.

"You can understand that I'm afraid, can't you?" she said aloud. "I'm a pregnant woman grabbed off the street and stuck in this room with a bag over my head. You can understand that I'm scared, for myself and for my baby.

"You were a baby once," she said, taking the chance, making the calculated move, working the only possibility for compassion that she could think of.

"You have a mother, too. Wouldn't your mother be afraid for you?"

CHAPTER 13

When she was sure the woman was asleep, Rae carefully, so carefully, slipped out of the room to pee, to see Danny, and to bitch. On the landing outside, she looked out over the open expanse of high empty ceilings, crisscrossing rafters, and caged industrial light bulbs hanging just above her level and casting an orange glow over the space below. On the ground floor, she looked first to her right, at the pile of metal and destroyed upholstery and stacked tires that had once been the white van Danny and the others pulled up in when they'd arrived with the woman. Danny was sitting there alone on an intact removable backseat. The cutting torches and gas cylinders and safety mask were beside him, standing as if his only friends.

He seemed to sense her presence. When he looked up, she could see the flash of alarm in his widening eyes and his palms came up to warn her back. She thought, Fuck it, Danny, I got to pee, and crossed her legs and frowned in a pantomime of need.

Then she followed his eyes across the room and saw the other three men sitting at a square card table, corralling a pile of bills in the middle, each holding a fan of cards in their hands. Geronimo the asshole looked up from his cards when Danny stood, and read that something in the air had changed. He turned his face up to where Rae stood, then followed her sightline back down to Danny.

Danny shrugged his shoulders once, grabbing at his crotch and then gesturing up to the landing. The Indian dipped his chin and with an almost imperceptible nod, gave his permission.

While Danny moved to the staircase, Rae moved down so that they could meet at the bottom step. She sneered at the "What the fuck you doin'" look on Danny's face and pushed past him to the only bathroom in the place, in the corner next to a half-glassed-in office. Danny followed, and when she stepped in through the bathroom door, he came in, too. She didn't try to stop him.

Rae let him close the door and then spun in front of the old-style porcelain commode, pulled down her shorts and panties in one motion, and squatted, all without once looking him in the eye. Elbows on knees, she sat there—waiting, knowing him. He couldn't stand the silent treatment. Danny hated when she wouldn't talk to him, refused to argue out a disagreement, flat-out stoned the idea of discussion. He'd get frustrated, angry, then come back pleading.

She knew this was her power over him. It wasn't long before she felt him come over and stand in front of her. She was looking at his jeans, the old cowboy belt buckle, the plain gray T-shirt he always wore, eschewing anything with a print or logo or insignia, and then she felt his curled index finger under her chin and she let him lift her face to his.

"I'm sorry, baby. But it's not going to be long," he whispered, knowing he was breaking Geronimo's rule against talking.

"There's been some kinda glitch. One day, babe, maybe two. Then we're done, we get the money, we're outta here," he said, kneeling down.

Fucking Danny, she thought. She looked straight into his cornflower blue eyes, the ones that few girls in Leelanau County could ever resist. She was no exception. But she also knew that he never said he was sorry to anyone else in this world.

"Goddamnit, Danny, is that woman a federal judge?" she hissed. "Is that a kidnapped federal judge up there you got me watching?"

She kept her eyes on his, using her advantage, turning the blade of guilt. Danny put his finger to her lips, even though she was barely *whispering and knew the unbreakable rule, and he inched forward and crouched down, pressing in between her knees, opening her thighs with his chest and forcing her elbows off. Then his face came forward, and she lost contact with his eyes and felt his lips on her forehead.*

"She's bullshitting you, Rae. She ain't no judge. It's gonna work, Radar. You know it's gonna work. You just gotta hang in, do your part, and we're golden."

She let his lips lay there, their cool touch actually tingling with the perspiration of her forehead. He was using her nickname, Radar, what friends had called her from childhood, spinning off her given name, but also recognizing her uncanny ability to know when something was going to happen before it happened.

Early on it was simple things, like her announcing the arrival of an ice cream truck long before anyone else could hear its music. Later, it was her correct predictions about her girlfriends' romances, and her uncanny ability to intuit classroom pop quizzes. The crowning event was her impromptu warning while joy riding in the blackness of night on abandoned railroad tracks in Dave Knowlton's old-school Dodge convertible.

It had been a teenage joy ride thing for years. Knowlton had figured out how to ease his daddy's junker car onto the abandoned tracks using the crossing at Kimberly Road. The wheelbase of the car was the exact same width as the track, and he would pull up parallel on the crossing and drive his wheels carefully onto the rails. He'd let a little air out of the tires so the weight of the car would make them sit securely over the iron. Everyone would then pile in the back and onto the hood of the Dodge.

All Knowlton had to do was slowly accelerate down the track. You didn't even have to steer. The rubber wheels hugged and followed the rails and hummed in the darkness of the woods. It was like flying. The effect was even scarier when Knowlton turned the headlights off. Thirty miles an hour felt like ninety.

One night, they were "rail sliding," as they called it, when Rae sensed something even she could never explain. The hair on the back of her neck started tingling. An anxiety rose into her throat.

Finally, she couldn't stand it anymore and screamed, "Turn on the lights, Dave! Goddammit, turn on the lights!"

Knowlton spun his head around. "Come on, Rae, you scaredy-cat . . ."

But her next "Goddammit, Dave!" caused him to give in and flip on the headlights. And there it was: a dormant, hundred-ton flat car squatting thirty yards in front of them that would have surely sheared the heads of everyone in the car. Knowlton yanked the wheel, and they jolted off the rails and came to a bouncing stop on the railway ties.

"Radar," they called her. The name and reputation was set. You better listen to that girl 'cause she knows what's going to happen.

Yeah, Rae used that, too. She learned how to count cards at the blackjack tables at the Indian casino at Peshawbestown and because she used that new talent in front of her friends, it bolstered the image that she could somehow look into the future. Who was she to dissuade them?

But now Danny was using it to mollify her.

"You know it's gonna work out, Radar, 'cause you always know."

With his left hand over her shoulder, he inched closer, forcing her thighs farther apart and pulling her into him, her chest into his, her butt sliding on the seat, her exposed genitals opening. She knew what he was doing and let him.

"The damn woman's pregnant, Danny—you can't bullshit that," she whined, using her little girl voice. "I'm alone up there watching her and they got her arms tied behind her and she's hungry and thirsty and I'm hungry and thirsty and what the hell? Did you know it was gonna be like this? 'Cause if you did, I'm gonna kick your ass."

By then, Danny had moved his lips off her forehead and brushed them over the curve of her ear. She felt his warm breath tickling her there and she knew that he knew the effect it always had. Then consciously she slid her butt even farther forward on the toilet seat until her moistness touched his cowboy belt buckle; the shock of cold metal against her broke the spell.

"Goddamnit, Danny," she hissed as she pushed him away. "What the hell is going on with the freakin' cutting torch and the van all in parts!"

Danny backed off and just shrugged his shoulders.

"Geronimo said get rid of it," he said. "The tools were already here, and I was bored. It ain't the way I'd get rid of a stolen car, but what the hell? I don't know a damn thing about Florida, and the places I'd dump it probably don't even exist down here. It's not like I got anything better to do while we're hiding out in this sweatbox anyway."

"Chop it into little pieces and get rid of it? Was that Geronimo's idea?" Rae said with a tone in her voice that sounded both knowing and ominous at the same time. It made Danny turn.

They locked eyes for a moment, and Rae knew Danny had picked up on her meaning and that they were thinking the same damn thing.

The kids back home may have made fun of Geronimo behind his back, but the rumors about the big Indian kept those jokes to a whisper. Everyone knew Alvin worked for the casinos. Danny said he was just a leg-breaker for the bosses when some dumbass bettor got in over his head and needed to be convinced to pay up. But when a group of kids sitting around at a fire pit on a September evening started telling ghost stories, the rumor always came up that Geronimo had done away with more than one missing casino problem by cutting up the bodies with a big old frontier bowie knife and hiding the pieces in the woods around Kalkaska County.

"You know that's bullshit about him dicing up bodies, Rae," Danny said. Rae turned away as if she hadn't even heard and changed the subject.

"You gotta get us some food and something to drink besides fucking Coke, Danny. Because that woman's gonna get sick and she's right about that baby, it needs some damn nutrition."

She was lighting into him and ignoring the rise in her voice when a knuckle suddenly cracked sharp on the door and brought instant silence.

Danny looked up into her eyes and blinked once. Then he nodded. Rae mouthed the words, "Make this right." He nodded again and stood and left.

CHAPTER 14

A sunset smeared with soft reds and shades of purple was coloring the western sky when I left Attorney Milsap's office. I thought briefly about the view from my river shack out on the edge of the Everglades: someplace quiet and serene. Someplace where pregnant women weren't kidnapped and drug dealers didn't feast on addicts and capitalism didn't turn the world greasy and greedy.

But who are you kidding, Max? Out there in your one-room hideout, you listen to the night-hunting owls and herons and gators and fish gulping smaller fish every black evening. Is that the nature of all things? Does the world feed on itself until Darwin's biggest, smartest, and most adaptable become so fat yet so insatiable that they bring on their own demise?

"You are one cynical bastard, Max," I said out loud.

I needed to see Sherry. I put my three phones on the passenger seat beside me—one for CQ, one for Milsap, and my regular cell, which Billy would call if anything changed—and headed for Victoria Park.

Sherry's house was in an old Fort Lauderdale neighborhood that had ridden the ups and downs of South Florida real estate with only minimal damage. In the late 1940s and early 1950s, a post-WWII boom created a population surge in Florida headed by young soldiers and pilots and Navy men who'd come to train here and had fond memories of a place in the sun with fresh ocean breezes where cheap homes could be built or purchased for them and their young families. In places like the aptly named Victoria Park, single-story houses with barrel-tiled roofs and hardwood floors popped up on open acreage and even on created land, where entrepreneurial developers dredged out tons of swampy marl both to build up a solid foundation for home-building as well as to create canals to the sea. As the people moved in and then spread out to create lakefront suburbs in the same manner, "old" neighborhoods like Sherry's became quaint and "historic," tucked under the shade of old live oaks, gumbo limbo, and silver palms.

After one of the inevitable real estate dips in the 1990s, Sherry bought a small bungalow on a cop's salary and it became her respite from the world around her. Since the loss of her leg, I'd spent as much time here as I had out in the Glades shack.

"Moving in, Max?" she'd tease, but with a certain edge. It was a part of our relationship we still hadn't quite sorted out.

When I turned the corner onto her street, I could see her little MG, newly outfitted with hand controls for the brakes and accelerator on the steering wheel, parked in the driveway next to my F-150 pickup truck. I pulled the Fury onto the swale in front of the house and called Billy on my regular cell.

It was a quick and morose conversation that ended with an agreement that I would meet him at the federal courthouse in the morning. My friend didn't sound like he would be sleeping soon, and I wasn't sure I would be, either. We'd both done what we could do for now. Bad people had the upper hand, and it was not where either of us liked to be.

I got out, locked the Fury, and walked between the cars to Sherry's gate, which opens to a walkway leading to the back of her house. Before I reached the patio deck, I could hear the familiar liquid plunking of one foot kicking and the soft, rhythmic splash of swimming strokes. Sherry had outfitted her backyard pool with a jet pump system that created a steady current against which she could swim. She had done this before the accident as a supplement to her distance-running workouts, and now it had become a sort of savior for her head and body.

The aqua glow from the submerged pool lights reflected up into the leaves of the oak whose boughs spread above her backyard and formed a canopy. The mixture of green leaves and shimmering blue gave the natural roof a calm but surreal feel. I stepped up onto the wooden deck and for a minute just watched her swim, the lithe body, skin whitened by underwater lights, moving with an effortless rhythm that belied the strength behind each stroke.

It took a second, more focused look to pick up on the unnatural movement of her hips. She had learned somehow to curve her single right leg in and perform a one-beat kick that resulted in an odd *kerplunk*, but still afforded her a straight and true course. The body adapts. Human beings adapt. It's what we do.

I sat down in a lounge chair, put the three cell phones down on the table next to me, and closed my eyes.

I felt droplets, first on my arms, then on my chest, and then on my face. In my half-consciousness, my mind went to blood. With an internal vision of red, an actual taste of metal gathered on my tongue.

"Max? Are you awake? Max—wake up, babe."

Sherry's face was above me, her wet blonde hair tucked behind her ears. But the ends still dripped water on my cheeks.

"Jesus!" I said, startled.

"No, just me," she said. Then she bent closer, putting her still-cool lips on mine. The taste of chlorine replaced the metallic hint of the blood that had somehow seemed so real a moment before. She pulled over another lounge chair and sat, using a towel to cover the stub of her missing leg.

"You OK?" she asked as she looked into my face. Her cold fingertips were now on my arm.

"Yeah, yeah, OK," I said, shaking my head. "Wow, must have dozed off. What time is it?"

She looked back at the large-faced clock by the kitchen window that she used sometimes to time her workouts.

"Almost nine."

"Shit."

"Why? Got somewhere else to be?"

"Uh, no. No. I just . . ." I ran my hands over my face.

Sherry stared at me a few seconds longer. I must have passed her evaluation.

"You want a beer?"

"Yeah, sure," I said.

She wrapped her towel around her waist and then hopped, one-legged, across the patio to the back kitchen door.

I hadn't gauged how draining my anger and anxiety over Diane's abduction had been. Sometimes you spend hours on surveillance or a stakeout, keeping your senses honed until your eyes burn, and your mind begins to play you. Sometimes you run hard and fight furiously until you think you can't take another step, and then you take that step.

But an emotional hurt, a constant internal push to do something that's just out of reach, a feeling of frustration and helplessness, will strain both body and soul. Soldiers know this state; so do prisoners of war. To fight against it takes even more energy. Only a few can do it. Others break.

"How's Billy?" Sherry asked, returning with an ice bucket filled with four bottles of beer and setting it on the small wicker patio table next to my three phones.

"Scared. Frustrated—and working every source he's got to find information," I said. "I just talked to him. He's touched State Department contacts here and in Colombia. He's pulling favors from people in financial circles from Miami to Caracas, anyone anywhere with even the slightest connection with Escalante."

"They're going with the drug lord angle," Sherry said, less a question than a statement of fact. She'd been in law enforcement for a long time and was the daughter of a Florida highway patrolman. She knew that you go with the obvious first. Hit hard with what you have, especially when innocent lives are at stake; if you jumped the gun, tough.

"But no ransom demands?"

"Not a word," I said. "They've got taps on Diane's office, the federal prosecutor's, Billy's penthouse, and the courthouse cellblock where Escalante is being held."

"They didn't move him?"

"No. He was there for the hearing when Diane was grabbed so they took him to the internal lockup downstairs. For security's sake, he's being kept there under armed guard. Billy said he isn't going anywhere."

"Is Billy going anywhere?"

"I'm going to pick him up in about, uh, eight hours," I said. "He says he's done as much as possible from the courthouse and needs to get back to his own computers at home."

"He says the media hawks are outside the federal building, but he figures that early in the morning I can drive him out of the basement garage and get him to the penthouse without anyone seeing him."

I took a long pull of the cold beer and wasn't sure I even tasted it.

"They'll be at the penthouse, too," Sherry said.

"Yeah, well, you know Billy. He's already arranged for a limo to pull up in front of the building while we go around back in my pickup. You know the media cattle. They'll all go for the limo to get the shot of the devastated millionaire husband of a kidnapped judge, and we'll slip out the freight entrance."

I leaned my head back again and stared up into the blue-green glow spackling the overhead leaves. Diane rolled out of her chair and hopped behind me and put her hands on my shoulders and started kneading the tightened muscles there. It was something I usually did for her, massaging her swimmer's shoulders and the calf of her good leg after the insane workouts she put herself through. The gesture almost made me feel guilty—almost. I let her continue.

"The circles are spreading out," she said, working with both hands. "The TSA and U.S. Marshals are all over the airports in West Palm, Lauderdale, and Miami. Coast Guard's doing their thing, doubling up on the suspect boats they've already tagged as possible drug mules."

"But Escalante's people aren't stupid enough to try and move an unwilling kidnap victim through obvious channels," I said. "They've got hundreds of private and commercial docks they could use to float her out of here. Never mind the private airfields and corporate jets they might commandeer."

As Sherry dug her strong fingers into my neck, trying to work the muscle fiber loose, we did the familiar dance we often did when she was on a sheriff's case or I was deep into some investigation for Billy. We were riffing off each other, stating the obvious but also posing the possibilities.

"They do these abductions all the damn time down in South America and over in the Middle East: multinational businessmen, judges, journalists, family members of the rich. It's usually about money, isn't it?" Sherry said.

"I remember the case in Colombia where they held that woman politician for eighteen months," I bantered back. "They kept moving her, town to town, building to building, until they got the president to give the drug lord a cushy, non-extraditable term in a local prison. A country club deal."

I let out a low groan when Sherry's fingers found a particularly hard knot and pried in between the strands of muscle, working them loose. The woman had a talent for finding a way in.

"The difference down there is that whole communities are dependent on the drug lords or scared shitless of them," I said. "You're not going to find that kind of intimidation here. Somebody hears something, sees something, and thinks they can profit off the information, they're going to spill it."

"The sheriff has already put out the word," Sherry said. "Everywhere from drug task forces right down to patrol. My friend over at the state attorney's office was told the same: if you've got someone in a cell with info, squeeze him with a deal."

I let my head drop, chin down near my chest, stretching the neck fibers, letting Sherry go deep.

"That takes time. Promises work too slowly. It's a recession: money talks and bullshit walks," I said, thinking of Johnny Milsap.

"You're quoting soiled politicians, Max."

"We've got to get Diane back."

CHAPTER 15

She woke to the feeling of something touching her face. Her first reaction was to fight. But Diane was a fast learner. Coming out of her exhausted sleep, she recalled that the last time she'd cried out she'd been rewarded with a blow to the head. This time, she held back and let full consciousness come first. The grip she felt was pinching her lower jaw, shaking her awake, but in a less-than-forceful way.

The shroud was still over her head; the blackness that met her open eyes was becoming . . . not normal or acceptable, but expected. From under the drawstring, she felt something probing up from her neck, something small and sharp-edged; but again she stifled her panic. *Not a knife blade*, she thought, *or a razor*. Whoever was holding her jaw was also trying to work the object up to her mouth without creating an opening where light, or any view of the world, would be exposed.

When Diane moved her head and rolled to one side on the bed, her captor allowed it. Then she moved her mouth to accommodate the probe. Another straw, she discovered, letting her skin feel the object, the rounded edge now at the bottom of her lip, working its way into her mouth. Water? God, she was thirsty. And she'd been given the soda before, though clumsily. She hesitated, but gave in. If they wanted to poison her, they would have already done so. She took the end of the straw in deeper and drew on it.

What came onto her tongue was cool, the consistency of thick milk, but flavored with some kind of faux-fruit taste. She drew in more of the fluid, and the pincers at her jaw, obviously someone's fingers, loosened. She swallowed. She let her taste buds work and her mind take over. This wasn't some half-melted milk shake—not that sweet. But it was definitely something more than, say, strawberry-flavored milk. She stopped drawing and took a breath, but kept the straw in her mouth. Could it be some kind of nutrition drink? Food in a bottle—Ensure or Boost or some other concoction? She sucked more into her mouth and swallowed. She didn't resist, because she knew instinctively that it was sustenance, something for her and for her baby.

The last time she'd met with her obstetrician, the doctor had said the baby would be gaining almost half a pound a week now. Was she starving her own child? It was hard to calculate how many hours she'd gone since last eating, but the anxiety and fear had drained her. She needed something to give her the energy to think, to assess, and to survive.

Her baby was everything now. It hadn't always been so. Only two years ago, she'd been already in her forties and single: career-oriented, too busy with her legal aspirations and following the family tradition. The lawyers and the society men of Palm Beach were just part of the game they all played. She'd never been serious about any of the men who'd dared to court her. She knew her family name was intimidating to them—all but Billy.

He was refreshingly different. Yeah, she'd heard of him—the *GQ* good looks and the quiet, unassuming demeanor of the black lawyer who never took on cases that would put him in open court. The gossips couldn't quite figure out his pleasant but curt style because they were ignorant of his severe stutter. She'd heard the stories of women who'd approached him and been mildly rebuffed with courteous but blunt thank-yous and curt nods before he'd suddenly turn away.

But then she'd met him at a fund-raiser for Women in Distress. She was there as a judge and symbol of the so-called vigilante justice system. Billy was there as the biggest benefactor to the program for the past eight years. They were introduced and, belying his reputation, he talked with her.

Yes, there was the stutter, but his eyes held hers, and he didn't look away. Her father had instilled the same attribute in her at an early age: look everyone in the eye, prove that you're listening, really listening to what they say, and that you value them and the time they are spending to talk with you. And when Billy told her she had the "most g-gorgeous gr-green eyes he'd ever s-seen," she knew it wasn't a line a stuttering man would ever just use.

After that first meeting, they'd dated: quiet, personal dinners where she learned of his background in North Philadelphia, the barely present father who'd inflicted so much physical and emotional pain on Billy's mother. In those most intimate moments, he'd told her the manner in which his mother had ended that abuse: the poisoning, her premeditated killing of his father, her torturer.

The stories moved Diane, but it wasn't sympathy or compassion that convinced her that this was a man she could finally commit to. She simply fell for him, despite the social upheaval that would result from her marrying a black man. She just loved him. And this baby, their baby, was the result of that love. *Damn it, Billy, where are you?*

Diane kept sucking at the straw until it came up dry at the bottom of the empty bottle or container. At the bubbling sound, the straw was abruptly pulled from her mouth and out through the bottom of the hood, which was again cinched tight. Diane heard, yes, she swore she actually heard, the air move as her captor must have withdrawn from the bedside.

"Thank you," she said. "Thank you very much for caring. And my baby thanks you, also."

Work that angle, Diane, she thought. Everyone has a mother. It's limbic. No one can avoid that reality or that recollection. You've got to be inhuman, or a psychotic monster, to look at a baby and not feel something. But had she been taken by monsters? She rolled back onto the mattress, her eyes open against the black cloth. For some reason, she felt she could think better if her eyes were open, even though her view was of nothing. She lay there for a few minutes, formulating.

"Let me ask you something," she finally said, keeping her voice as conversational as she could: not antagonistic but not condescending, either. It was her courtroom voice, the neutral one she used when addressing witnesses.

"It seems you are a compassionate person. Can you at least tell me your name? Or even something I can call you? We're here alone together in all of this. You can at least talk to me. You don't have to tell why you've done this, or what your plans are. Just talk to me. You've let me know you're here by giving me something to feed my baby. Can't you just say something?"

Silence.

Again, Diane heard the creak of wood. Is he sitting in a chair? A straight-backed wooden chair against the wall? Sitting there with a gun in his hand just waiting for the order to kill her? Or is he just staring at her? Or was that muted clicking sound she'd heard really a cell phone he's using to text someone? She tried to form a picture in her mind. Were the walls concrete? Was the door metal, like a cell? Were there windows? Were they glass, and thus breakable?

The silence was causing her imagination to run rampant. She'd never been good at silence. In her work, she was surrounded by people: attorneys asking questions, aides making requests, bailiffs giving reports, other judges discussing changes in rules. Outside of court, she was a sociable woman, attending conferences and fundraisers and society dinners.

Billy was the quiet one, always listening, always taking in the conversations and sights and smells, and rarely speaking. Though his stutter put him in that situation, Diane knew there was an upside to it. He liked the fact that she could take over in a social situation. He was glad to be able to ignore a social function he considered a chore. Billy might be able to stand this silence and wait it out.

She didn't think she could. She needed to know. She needed to do something. She was blind, pregnant, and at the mercy of physically bigger and stronger captors. If she tried to get up, she'd be shoved back down. If she called out, she'd be slapped quiet. If the only way she could act was by talking quietly, she'd do it.

"Do you speak English?" she asked. If indeed her kidnappers were somehow aligned with Escalante, maybe they were South American. Or would they be locals who worked in his drug distribution enterprise?

She'd read the files on Escalante, knew of the ruthlessness of his multiheaded businesses in Colombia and the internecine battles with both the government there and other drug distributors vying for trafficking routes and supplies. The photos of village citizens, children, caught up in the crossfire of the drug wars had made her blanch. Even if Escalante hadn't done the deeds by his own hand, it was by his order that certain outcomes were achieved. If these were men of the same cloth, a dead American judge would mean nothing to them.

Stop, Diane, she told herself. *No negatives now—don't go there. Your father always taught you optimism.*

Her father had been a judge for forty years. As a child, she'd learned from watching him come home from court with the wear in his eyes and the tired, slumped shoulders of a man who had carried a burden all day and had not been able to leave it behind in the courthouse. When she was older, he would quietly discuss the day's deliberations and rulings and the inevitable moral and ethical dilemmas that could not be discussed on the bench or with attorneys.

Those burdens belonged to the judge. He'd told Diane the truth when she first donned a robe: "You stay optimistic, Diane, because you will see and hear so much of the evil in this world that if you don't, it is too easy to lose faith in all mankind."

It had been her parents who guided her, through school, through college, and into law as she followed the family tradition. But she'd thought that she'd given up that inevitable link during her adulthood and had become her own person—which she'd achieved on her own. But now she questioned that independence. She wanted their help. She wanted Billy. She wanted someone to sweep in and rescue her, and the weakness was pissing her off. She had to gain back her strength and do something.

The silence continued from the other side of the room. Her captor was there; she could feel the air from his breath. *Use what you have,* she thought.

"Can I have some more?" she said. "I'm still very hungry."

She heard the creak of wood and felt the shift in the density of the space around her. She sniffed, trying to discern from the odor of cologne or sweat or breath something that would help her gain an image, an internal picture, an advantage. But all she gained was the feeling of fingers tipping her chin up and the straw beginning to probe again up under the hood.

CHAPTER 16

If I slept again, I wasn't aware of it. After picking apart the case by her poolside, Sherry and I had lapsed into a silence that under other circumstances both of us would have enjoyed. Instead, she gave up on the neck massage, sat, and shared a second beer with me, and then excused herself to go to bed. I stared into the blue-green light and found myself waiting for one of the three cell phones next to me to ring, to call me to arms, to give me a direction or an enemy or a hope.

At some point in the night, I caught myself massaging a dime-size disc of scar tissue at my neck, letting my fingertips glide over the unnaturally smooth skin, probing it, measuring it, remembering it and the day that bullet had ripped through skin and muscle and barely, just barely, missed my carotid artery.

Being an officer of the law had seemed like a destiny for me, an odd sort of birthright, though emulating my father would never be a motivation. My career had been checkered. I was not smart. I was not ambitious. I was relatively big and athletic, not afraid of long shifts, and could always defeat boredom by studying people—their movements, routines, facial expressions, body language, and interactions with one another—which made me a good street cop, but not an internal climber.

When I'd given up my short stint as a detective, I'd gone back to the streets, on a third shift walking a beat in Center City. When the shooting that ended my career occurred, I never even felt the first shooter's round pierce my neck. They told me later that I continued to the storefront and on one knee actually turned over the body of the boy, pressing my hand to the hole in his skinny chest created by my exiting bullet.

Later, in the hospital, commanders offered me a disability payout to leave the force, and after killing a child in the street, I agreed. I took the money, invested, and then moved to South Florida. I left the place and the profession that had formed me with the hopes that I could leave the past behind. But like every human with a modicum of self-actualization, I learned no one can bury the past deep enough. It is always there, scar tissue stirring the present.

Before sunrise, the birds began to flit in the canopy above Sherry's pool: wrens with their tea-kettle calls, mockingbirds with their loud *clack*, and the annoying green parrots, a colony of which had somehow taken up residence in the neighborhood and was known to go screeching through the trees like a bunch of squeeze toys.

I got up, gathered my three phones, and went inside to take a shower. I grabbed something to eat out of the refrigerator and, as was my habit, I leaned across the bed where Sherry lay sleeping and silently kissed her good-bye on the side of the forehead. I was once told it was a cop's kiss, knowing every time you went out on a shift, there was a chance you might not be back. Whether it gave your loved one any peace was debatable; maybe it only made *you* feel better. Maybe it was selfish. But if such an act is a display of selfishness, then maybe selfishness is overly maligned.

I took the F-150 instead of the Fury. I was thinking about the incognito nature of my morning trip. Billy's plan was for me to arrive at 6:30 a.m. at the federal courthouse's underground parking lot, where I'd be cleared to enter by security. Then I'd meet Billy at Diane's office, where he had been living for the past two days. From there, he had arranged for a limousine to leave the garage ahead of us. We'd soon follow in my pickup, staying in cell phone contact with the limo driver. When he got to Billy's condo, we would slip in behind the building, where Billy would have on-site security personnel allow us up on the basement freight elevator. Maybe the whole plan was unnecessarily elaborate, but both of us had seen the media at its worst, and if the limo distracted the hounds, then Billy—the anxious and aggrieved husband of the kidnapped federal judge—wouldn't have his ducking head and profile flashed on CNN all day.

When I arrived at the courthouse, I took Tamarind Avenue around to the back and stopped in front of the lowered parking garage gate to give the uniformed officer my name, my private investigator's and driver's licenses, and the business card of the FBI agent in charge whom I'd met in Diane's office the last time I'd been here.

It still took ten minutes for the guard to clear me. Inside, I parked as close to the elevator as possible and noted how sparsely populated the garage and the hallways inside the building were. It was an eight-to-five kind of place; the day-to-day workers—clerks, bailiffs, secretaries, lawyers—wouldn't start flowing in for another hour or so.

Yet when I locked my truck and looked down past the pillars to the east end of the garage where a corridor leading to the holding cells was fenced off, a man clad in the black paramilitary uniform of a SWAT officer was standing with an MP5 automatic rifle slung over his chest. When I took the elevator to the first floor, I met a uniformed Palm Beach County officer on duty at the security and screening checkpoint.

While I emptied my pockets of keys and change and three cell phones, I looked out through the glass-front doors and could see two news vans already parked, or perhaps still parked, out in the public lot. No one was doing any early stand-up reports for *The Today Show* or the many local morning newscasts, but I knew it was only a matter of time before they would.

Even though I hadn't tripped any signals when passing through the metal detectors, the officer on the other side still wanded me. Once cleared, I headed upstairs to Diane's chambers. Outside her doors, I was met again by men I assumed were federal agents, who radioed my presence inside and then passed me through after obtaining clearance. Things were tight. They're always tight after the fact, after the hijacking, the bombing, the homicide, the riot, or the abduction.

Law enforcement is a reactive entity—often closing the gate after the horse is out. It is that way out of necessity. A free society can't function any other way. But tell that to a father who signed a petition against those stoplight cameras and whose daughter was later run down by someone blowing the light in his neighborhood. Tell it to the guy who derides the TSA for slowing his business travel and then finds out his family was on the plane blown out of the sky by a terrorist wearing a shoe bomb. Tell it to the folks who lobbied for less regulation and then found four feet of toxic sludge in their backyards when the nearby coal plant's retention wall collapsed.

People never want government telling them what to do until something hits them between the eyes. Then their reaction is to blame someone for not keeping them safe. You don't want rules and regulations? Welcome to chaos.

The reception area of Diane's office was empty, her assistant nowhere in sight. If schedules and attorney inquiries and requisite daily handlings of bureaucratic housekeeping were being done, they weren't being done here. When I walked through the door to her chambers, the silence was telling. There was one agent sitting close by the electronics that had been set up to monitor and record all incoming calls. There were empty coffee cups and several editions of the local newspapers stacked around him. The lone agent nodded at me, stood to shake my hand with one perfunctory pump, and then looked into my eyes awaiting any question or utterance I might offer. I said nothing.

Billy was still behind Diane's desk, staring into the computer monitor there, his fingers dancing on the keyboard. He did not look up as I stepped to his side. With nothing to report himself, he waited on me in vain. He looked as bad as someone whose loved one was missing and had spent days without sleep, banging out emails and making phone calls to anyone who might be helpful or could be bribed or cajoled with favors or pressured with economic ruin to hand over any information that might lead to the whereabouts of his wife.

I put my hands in my pockets and after a full minute I finally said: "You ready to go?"

Billy looked up at me with eyes I didn't recognize: the flesh around them was pouched and swollen, the whites striated with red veins, the pupils focused and burning with a deep anger and volition that would have caused me to reach for my handgun had I seen them in the head of some street criminal in my patrol days.

To my question, he only nodded and then stood with a wobble in one knee and a hand that had to go out on the nearby bookcase to steady himself. I instantly wondered how long it'd been since he'd been out of Diane's chair, but I knew better than to reach out. I let Billy gain his own balance, but I hooked his forgotten suit coat off the back of the chair as he led us out of the office.

"I've g-got to g-get home, M-max," Billy said as we headed down the corridor towards the elevators. "I've got m-more c-computer p-power in m-my own office than they d-do here and m-my c-contacts aren't always g-going to b-be f-forthcoming unless w-we're on a s-secure l-line."

If he was pulling in his national and international players, the big economic guns that he'd cultivated and with whom he'd shared his financial expertise, I could see why they would be reluctant to talk openly to him while he was sitting in a federal courthouse. Billy wasn't a scammer. As far as I knew, and admittedly I knew little about big-time finance, he played it legally and above-board. With his background at the Wharton School and the myriad friends he'd met there and throughout the law community, his clientele was varied and far-reaching.

He'd made them money over the years, and I knew he'd tapped them for some of his philanthropic endeavors. He knew they would help in any way they could, but they weren't comfortable flaunting it. The real players don't put their business out on the street. They keep it confidential. Just like in the underworld, if you're a player you don't talk about it out in the barrooms or at open lunches or on unsecured phone lines. Wannabes brag; the real ones just quietly and effectively go about their business.

As we walked to the elevators, a few early birds began to appear. A black janitor with his wheeled refuse can and a broom slid his way into our path, and Billy stopped and took the elderly man's hand, which was offered in a muted gesture of consolation and hope. Further down, a middle-aged woman stopped to wish Billy well and "knew, just knew" Diane would soon be home. Before we reached the elevator, a knot of suited men turned their faces to us. All nodded their heads in greeting and uttered sentences of support. Among them was a silver-haired man of medium height whose eyes were focused on Billy, but not intently.

"Mr. Manchester. I was just on my way to your wife's office, sir," said one, who stepped forward as though the spokesman for all.

I determined that the man was in his late sixties or early seventies. The suit was pinstriped with an American flag pin in the lapel. His facial skin was flaccid and devoid of anything resembling a tan, unusual for Floridians. His rheumy gray eyes worked an expression of sincere empathy onto his face.

"Judge Krome," Billy said. They both extended their hands and shook.

"I can't imagine what you must be going through," the judge said. "It's terrible—just terrible."

Billy stood mutely, nodding, looking the man in the eyes but then skewing his sight away. It was so uncharacteristic of him not to always look a person in their eyes when he was speaking to them or when he was being spoken to that I felt a tick of embarrassment. All of us swallowed the silence.

Then instead of simply understanding the situation and moving on, the judge continued. "Have they, the authorities, I mean, have they heard anything at all?"

"No. No word," Billy said.

Again, I had to feel for my friend. If you are not within Billy's inner circle, he is not comfortable talking in extended sentences. He wouldn't admit that his stutter bothers him, but he knows it bothers others who only know him from his reputation and are sometimes stunned or wonder if they are the butt of a joke when he is caught having to use his jagged speech. With strangers or simple acquaintances, he has always found it best to hold himself to the use of single-syllable words and tight sentences.

Perceptive people pick up on the vibe. This guy didn't, and it was starting to piss me off.

"Well, I assume that the Marshal's Service and the FBI are here and working? I haven't been updated at all. Have there been any developments?"

Now I couldn't help myself from stepping forward, using my body language to tell the guy to back off and let us pass. In turn, the judge seemed to have discovered me there for the first time and took a step back. He looked me up and down. I wasn't in a suit, was in fact dressed casually in a pair of faded jeans and a short-sleeved, poplin field shirt. My hair wasn't at official length. I had no badge or firearm.

In his courtroom, no doubt I would have gained his ire as improperly attired for the business of judicial comportment. But at six foot three, I towered over the judge, and when I started to move my broad shoulders into his line of vision, at last he got the point. Billy did not move to introduce me or to make any excuse for my presence.

Finally, the judge said: "Well, if there is anything I can do, Mr. Manchester . . ."

"Yes, Judge," Billy said. "Uh, I m-mean n-no, s-sir. The authorities, as y-you know, are d-doing wh-what th-they c-can."

We continued down the hallway, the heels of Billy's dress shoes clicking on the marble tile. He may have whispered the word *asshole*, under his breath. Or maybe I did.

"All of the m-men in that group d-deal m-mostly in economic crimes," Billy did say. "Krome's been here for twenty-five years b-but has n-never m-moved into the sp-spotlight or the role of administrative judge as his v-vitae w-would w-warrant."

We arrived at the elevator door, and I pushed the DOWN button.

"I m-met him once at a f-fund-raiser. He was d-doing little m-magic tr-tricks f-for the other attendees. P-pick a c-card, any c-card t-type of st-stuff. M-making c-coins d-disappear and f-finding th-them in s-someone's n-nose. . . . Th-there's s-something about a jurist d-doing sleight-of-hand tr-tricks th-that s-seems, w-well, inappropriate."

Inside the elevator, I pressed the button for the garage floor.

"He's in th-the m-middle of a b-big m-money tr-trial and w-was pr-probably g-getting m-more m-media attention th-than anyone else in th-the b-building."

I did not finish Billy's sentence: "Before this all happened." But I did look over at him, and he must have felt my eyes on the side of his face.

"Wh-what, M-max?"

I shrugged—wondering why he was going on about the judge's current case.

"I t-tapped into the c-courthouse c-computers from D-diane's desk. R-researched every c-case, including th-those immediately p-past and awaiting: wh-what judges are s-sitting, wh-what c-cases th-they're w-working, wh-why th-those c-cases w-were br-brought here, who the s-suspects are, who's d-defending, who's pr-prosecuting. Th-three of the m-men st-standing th-there are d-doing b-big-m-money c-cases."

The elevator stopped and the doors slid open. We stepped out and started for my truck.

"I have to keep asking, 'Wh-why D-diane?'" Billy said, again musing aloud.

"Wh-what d-did th-they t-teach you about criminality, M-max? Always l-look f-for m-motivation, r-right?" he said, looking at me again.

I just nodded. It was unusual for Billy to ask questions to which he already knew the answer.

"And follow the money," I said.

Billy hesitated for a fleeting second, then spun and headed for my truck. "N-no p-possibility unconsidered."

Billy called his limousine decoy when we were two blocks from his apartment building and sent the empty car to the half-circle front drive. We watched from a safe distance. Despite the early hour, there were still three camera guys lying in wait. Often in these times of diminishing news budgets, local newspapers and television affiliates will send only a photographer to a criminal perp walk or to tag a person of interest. All they want is the photo or the video clip.

They're smart enough to know that the shouted questions of reporters rarely get answered, anyway. And who says a cameraperson isn't smart enough to yell the same old: "Why'd you do it? Are you scared? What does it feel like?" But pity the poor assignment editor who sends no one and then the competition gets some guy tearfully falling apart on camera and blathering into an open microphone. So they cover their asses.

Billy and I watched as the news guys reacted to the limo, rushing to follow it to the front entrance. Then we drove around back to the sublevel garage, used Billy's resident key card to get in, and took the service elevator to the penthouse floor.

Upstairs the elevator opened onto a short, nondescript hallway and yet another door that led to Billy's private entrance. His vestibule was tiled in gleaming marble, his front door a solid slab of polished oak. He keyed it open, and we entered his domain of subtle luxury.

Despite the fact that no one had been home for days, the air was fresh and lightly scented with some kind of automatic aerosol. Billy skirted the sunken living room, dropped his keys on the pass-through kitchen counter, and went directly to the wall of sliding glass doors that opened onto his deck twenty-one stories in the air. He opened them wide, and I could feel the ocean air billow into the apartment, bringing its own brand of salt-tinged freshness.

Billy stood out on the patio with his hands on the rail looking out over the Atlantic, staring out at the ruffled surface of the sea. I gave him a few minutes to breathe, to close his eyes and let the breeze take him where his head needed to go—a respite, if only for a short time.

I looked out over the thousand square feet of living space: the tongue-and-groove oak floors, the glass-topped dining table, the leather couches, the ebony statuary and art objects that were mostly museum-grade and would eventually be loaned or simply given away to charities and collections as Billy and Diane experimented with different styles.

There were, of course, some never-changing favorites, including the copy of Eduard Charlemont's painting *The Moorish Chief,* which dominated the southern wall. As I looked in the eyes of the guard whose duty it was to protect the women of the palace, it was not lost on me that I had seen them in the truck on the way over. They had the same stoic burning that now inhabited Billy's gaze; not angry, but defiant and intent. The lives of his wife and his unborn child were in jeopardy.

As a man who used the strength of his intellect and knowledge as his sword, Billy's battle was known to me, but not his tactics. On the other hand, I was ready to kick ass and do whatever it took to whoever was responsible.

I walked out to the patio entrance but did not clear the threshold.

"You want a wine or something?"

"No, thank you, Max. I don't need it."

I stayed quiet. It would come.

"I planted a listening device in Diane's chambers," he finally said. His speech was clear and uninterrupted. It was something we'd developed without planning: him standing outside at the rail and me just inside the apartment, or the other way around. Without being face-to-face, his stutter disappeared. "I also hacked a line into the computer system there so that I can monitor it. Whatever they know or find out, we'll know at the same time."

Again, I let the sound of ocean breeze carry us. In the time I'd known and worked for Billy, I had never known my friend to do anything illegal. Now, he'd stepped over a line, and I wasn't sure what that might mean in the future.

"You don't trust them?"

"To give us everything they have? No."

Billy's voice held a tinge of cynicism that I recognized as my own, but that I rarely heard him use.

"They'll follow kidnap protocol," I said. "They're trained in this, Billy. They've done it a lot."

I don't always go in for the FBI-bashing that many cops do. The feds are professionals and, like any other, they have their good and bad. But even raw logic tells you that a surgeon who does two dozen heart transplants a year is going to have better odds than the one who works at the local hospital and does one.

But I also know that every scenario is unique, involving different personalities, motivations, and levels of acceptable risk. One size does not fit all. But government agencies, by the nature of the huge numbers they deal in, are in love with one-size answers and procedures. If you're the family, though, you don't want to hear stats and probabilities and one size: you want your loved one back.

Billy was covering all the angles, even if he had to step out of the lines to do it. As I watched from behind, my friend took a deep breath of ocean air, his lungs filling and his back seemingly expanding as he straightened. Then he squared his shoulders and turned to look at me.

"I've g-got other p-possibilities f-for you, M-max," Billy said with a nod toward his office.

I followed. The room consisted of two walls of floor-to-ceiling books and one wall of shelved CDs. The fourth was dominated by a huge video screen. Billy was at his desk, fingers on a keyboard with his back to me. The screen was tiled into six different blocks, most with data undecipherable to me: maybe stock evaluations, or lists of contact names, or schedules of who knows whom. In one block I recognized a satellite photo of downtown West Palm Beach that showed streets and the tops of buildings, a Google photo I knew could be widened to reveal the whole city or pinpointed to a specific intersection.

And in the top right block on the screen was a photo of Billy and Diane, posing on the beach on their wedding day, a turquoise sea behind them, a light in their smiles and eyes that I had seen from the day they met and had never seen diminished.

"It m-may s-seem t-to you th-that I am grasping," Billy said as he turned in his seat, took a printout from the copier, and handed it to me. "B-but anything l-less f-feels l-like g-giving up, M-max. And w-we d-don't d-do th-that, d-do w-we?"

I looked from the list of names and addresses on the paper to Billy's eyes to confirm the thought, but he was already focused on something else. He was looking up at the block in the upper right-hand corner of the computer screen.

CHAPTER 17

All I had was an address somewhere in Pompano Beach, somewhere on A1A, somewhere where the man who had scared Diane Manchester more than any person she'd sent to prison supposedly lived.

Whether or not the feds were willing to expand their theories beyond the drug cartel leader they had locked up in the basement of the courthouse, Billy wasn't taking their seeming inability to look beyond the obvious as his own. Diane had put a lot of people behind bars in her years as a prosecutor and judge, and Billy had come up with a list. These weren't the ones who did the most time or lost the most money or were necessarily the ones who were the most ruthless or sociopathic or had outwardly threatened or condemned her. They were the ones she remembered late at night, the ones she whispered about to Billy—the ones who really rattled her.

This one went by the name of Giovanni Maltese. He'd been out for a year, plenty of time to reconnect and set up a retribution kidnapping. Maltese was a gangster of the East Coast Italian variety who had been anything but typical. At one time, he ran most of his overlord's cocaine distribution system from South Florida to environs in New York State. Maltese was not a hands-on made man. He procured, which meant he made the deals, set up the delivery lines from importers in Florida to outlets in the north, negotiated the price, and kept anybody who thought they might move in on his organization's franchise from actually doing so by making the cost too high in terms of both business and bodies. And although Maltese never pulled the jobs or the triggers, he hired all those who did.

For a prosecutor like Diane, he was the big fish that could not be allowed to get away. And according to Billy, she'd worked him like a talented flats fisherman works a bonefish with a fly rod. She was relentless and cunning and resourceful and above all patient, intentionally feeding him delicious possibilities, working his greed and ego until she hooked him in the mouth with enough interstate trafficking charges that even his own people were ready to give up on him and let him be sacrificed. Then when the case finally came to trial, she refused to deal.

What made Maltese atypical was that the word got out that he was willing to deal, break the code of silence, and be the rat. And Diane let him swing; no federal witness protection deal. No negotiating the sentence with the standard, "You give me this, I'll give you that."

"Th-the m-man scared th-the sh-shit out of her, b-but sh-she refused to b-budge," Billy recalled. "Sh-she s-said, 'He p-poisoned ch-children, f-fed addicts, got rich off p-people's w-weaknesses. W-we'll get th-the rest of his organization on our own.'"

Whether she knew that Maltese's willingness to deal would get out to the kingpins he worked for or not, Billy said, she went for the fifteen-year prison term she had in the bag and sent the man away.

"W-was sh-she uncompromising? Yes," Billy asked and answered his own question. "St-stubborn? Yes, especially wh-when sh-she s-sets her p-path. B-but th-that's m-my hope, M-max. Th-that's wh-who sh-she is and t-that's wh-why w-we'll get her b-back."

In the Fury, I headed toward Pompano Beach, got off the I-95 exit at Atlantic Boulevard, and drove to the beach.

This was yet another part of Florida, an oceanfront wall of

high-rise condominiums that the cynical described as concrete ant hills: thousands of people living stacked on top of one another and each, depending on how high their floor was and how their condo was positioned to the east, with a view of the Atlantic Ocean. A few would have Billy's kind of view, many others just a glimpse of watery horizon. But the address I had for Maltese was on the west side of A1A. Buildings here were one or two stories, with a few motels in the 1960s mode: stucco framing jalousie windows, hand-railed stairways, numbered parking spaces. The signs ran the gamut from THE OCEAN VENETIAN to THE LUCKY GUY MOTEL.

When I finally found the address I was looking for, there was no sign. The place was one story, took up two full lots including a corner, and held no adornments offering free HBO or Wi-Fi. I pulled into a half-empty parking lot and tucked the business card I'd taken from the desk of the probation officer I'd met earlier into a black vinyl folder, determined to look official.

It wasn't the big, open reception area that tipped me off. Nor was it the open-door hallways that led off in three directions or the smiling, middle-aged woman at the front desk. It was the odor, the slightly pungent smell of too much disinfectant trying to cover the olfactory hint of open medications or stale wardrobes or urinary miscues.

"Welcome to Atlantic Shores. How may I help you, sir?"

ATLANTIC SHORES ASSISTED LIVING INC. read the top of the sign-in page the woman pushed across the countertop toward me.

"Hi, I'm looking for Mr. Giovanni Maltese," I said honestly.

"And you are?"

I opened my folder, took out the probation officer's card, placed it on the counter, and ignored the sign-in sheet. When the woman read the card, her smiled disappeared.

"Mr. Maltese is over at the beach. With Peter," she said, putting extra emphasis on the second sentence. "Where's Mr. Mobley?"

"Uh, Mr. Mobley's on vacation," I said, guessing she was asking about Maltese's regular probation officer and apparently guessing right.

She looked again at the card I'd given her.

"Well, they're out there staring at the ocean like they always do this time of day," she said, nodding her head back toward the front door.

"Thank you," I said, and reached out my hand to retrieve the card. She gave it back. I still hadn't lied about my identity, at least not with my mouth. Someday I'd have to ask Billy if that would hold up in court, but not today.

I stepped back outside and took a deep lungful of clean air. A year out after a fifteen-year stretch in the federal lockup at Coleman, and Maltese was in assisted living? From the sheet Billy had given me, the man was fifty-four. His wife had divorced him while he was in lockup, and there were no children. Usually, these guys squirrel enough away before they go inside so that they aren't destitute when they get out. Maybe the nest egg was paying the bills here. I'd have to ask.

I scanned the monster-size buildings across on the beach side of A1A: the Coastal Sun, the Royal Beach Club, the Avalon—concrete honeycombs with as much style as shoeboxes standing on their ends and packed as close as building codes would allow. I followed a sidewalk to the edge of the street and spotted a crosswalk and a sign that read BEACH ACCESS. I had to wait for four cars to pass despite the bright yellow markings for pedestrian right-of-way. You do not step out in front of moving vehicles in Florida the way you might in Philly or New York. They will flatten you, your bicycle, your walker, and your baby stroller, and then curse you for getting in their way.

The beach access was a crumbling asphalt path most likely grudgingly carved between two towers. It allowed the regular public to visit the public beach. It was like walking a back alley in midtown, but at the other end I could see a slash of blue horizon and could smell salt on the breeze. As I came out of the funnel, I spotted two figures: someone in a wheelchair accompanied by a man dressed in what hospital people call scrubs. I stepped to the side of the standing man.

"Peter?" I said. The face that turned to me was in his mid-twenties, cleanly shaved, and from the dusky skin tone and eyes so dark you'd say black before brown, Hispanic.

"Yes," he said, his tone slightly surprised and his eyes darting over my shoulder in the direction of the assisted living building. "Does someone need me?"

"No, no. My name is Max Freeman," I said ditching the probation officer ruse and offering my hand. Peter took it, his expression changing from concern to perplexity.

"I'm a private investigator from up in Palm Beach County, and I'm here to talk with Mr. Maltese."

I gestured past the young man to the person in the wheelchair. The figure there had not turned his head or indicated in any way that he was aware of my presence. He was dressed in tan slacks and a pale windbreaker with the collar turned up despite the warm temperature. A baseball cap with the bill turned in the correct way to shield his face from the sun was pulled down.

"Well, Mr. Freeman, I am afraid you will have a difficult time doing that," Peter said, and I could hear the slight Spanish accent in his wording. "Mr. Maltese does not talk these days."

I nodded but gestured to the sitting figure. "May I try anyway?"

The man named Peter hesitated, but then politely stepped back and indicated with an open palm—give it a shot.

I knelt next to the wheelchair and made the same introduction to Maltese I had to his aide, but he continued to face out to sea. From up close, I could see wide wraparound sunglasses under the cap. His hands were clasped in his lap, mottled loose skin barely covering the thin bones that made me think of bird skeletons I would find occasionally in the Everglades during drought times. His thin legs protruded from the wheelchair seat, draped in the fabric of his trousers like cloth hanging on a towel rack. He may have been fifty-four, but looked ninety. Prison takes its toll, but in this case it had taken more. I let the silence sit for several beats and then stood.

"Does he hear?"

"Yes, but I think only when he wants to," the aide said, perhaps a glimmer of a smile at the corner of his mouth.

"Talk?"

"You would not describe it as talk, no, sir."

When I gave him a quizzical look, Peter continued, moving in past me to bend at Maltese's side.

"When Mr. Maltese was in prison, they told me he was injured by the other inmates," Peter said while zipping down the front of Maltese's windbreaker and then unwrapping a soft cotton scarf from the man's neck. Exposed was ochre-colored, crumpled flesh like cooked chicken skin that had been heated from the inside out. It ran from under Maltese's boney chin down past where an Adam's apple should have been and into the collar of his white T-shirt.

"They told me the others pinned him down and poured Drano, you know, the pipe cleaner, down his throat. The acid, I guess, did what they wanted it to do.

"He coughs. He growls sometimes when he is not happy. He moans when he is deeply saddened. But talk? No, he does not talk."

"How does he communicate, then?" I asked, fighting against empathy. I knew the man's background, what he had visited on others through his ruthless enterprise. "How do you know what he wants?"

"Since I started taking care of him last April, we have discovered a language together," Peter said, tucking the scarf back into place and re-zipping the jacket collar. "I know when he is hungry and when he needs the bathroom. When I wash him, I know that he likes it. Sometimes, when we have a soccer game on the television, I can tell he is smiling inside."

"So he can see?"

The aide looked out at the Atlantic, where the afternoon sun sparkled off the wind-rippled surface as if a thousand diamonds had been cast into the sea.

"The doctors say yes. But I think he sees only what he wants to see. He likes the ocean, even when it is stormy or wet. If he sees it or hears it, I am not sure. I just know he likes it."

I kept pressing.

"Can you take the glasses off?"

Again, the aide hesitated and looked into my face. He was being protective. I realized it was his job to do so; still, there was more there than simple guardianship. The kid cared.

After making some assessment of my intentions, he made a decision.

"Sure," Peter said, moving again to Maltese and carefully slipping the dark sunglasses off.

Again, I knelt before the man, whose eyes were open, aimed out at sea, the irises a gray color that showed no recognition nor cunning, no depth nor guile.

"Mr. Maltese, do you remember a woman named Diane McIntyre?" I asked, using Diane's maiden name, from when she prosecuted his case. There was no reaction, not even a blink of eyelids. "Do you know Judge Manchester?"

Again, no flinch or change in the coloration of his skin or rhythm of his breathing. I was talking to a wall. I stood again.

"Does he write? Does he get mail? Does he get visitors?" I asked the aide.

"No one has ever come, and I have never seen him put pen to

paper. They never told me where his family is, or if he has any. I think I am all he has."

The man called Peter looked down at his charge and put his hand on Maltese's thin shoulder. A sound like a muffled sigh came from the man's scarred throat. Peter looked up into my eyes and smiled.

"See?"

"Yeah, I see," I said, reaching out to shake the young man's hand. "I'm sorry to have bothered you."

I returned to the Fury and sat in the driver's seat looking back to the entrance of the beach access. Did I think I would see the two men jogging back across the street high-fiving each other over putting one past the idiot private dick? No. Could Maltese have hired some of his former underlings to kidnap the prosecutor who sent him away and in effect sealed his fate? Maybe; but why now, fifteen years after the fact? I wasn't optimistic.

I knew that if Billy decided to, he could make Maltese and Diane's fear of him into a federal case and get the FBI to pull every telephone record and mailed correspondence ever attached to the one-time mobster. But I was convinced that the crumpled human being I'd just seen was beyond retribution or vengeance. We couldn't wait on search warrants and records checks. We needed to find Diane.

CHAPTER 18

He kicked her awake.

"Pooh," Diane moaned, only slightly, and shifted on the mattress. She felt the baby move again. It seemed as if he'd been kicking for hours. He wanted out. He wanted freedom.

When had she started thinking of her unborn child as "he"? She wasn't quite sure. Together she and Billy had decided not to be told the sex of the child, a secret the obstetrician had kept even when showing them the sonogram photos. But her mind had taken over. You can't call him it! Billy had already picked out a name, Adam, the firstborn. She'd gone with a girl's name, Victoria, though she wasn't sure about the inevitable shortening to Vicky.

But now she was thinking "he." She wondered if the physical abduction, the threatening and punishing, was such a macho, warlike, mannish thing that she'd let it drift into her own belly.

Again, she felt a poke from within—maybe a foot or an elbow. It was only speculation, a game she'd played back when she was lying in bed with Billy visualizing the fetus inside her, trying to imagine the soft skull and fifteen inches of height and a suckling response already causing him, perhaps, to suck his forming thumb. Those comforting yet anxious previews were now obscured in the heat and dark and boggling fear surrounding her.

The cloth of the hood was still on her face, the humid odor of her breath forming on the fabric. How many hours had it been? How many days? Each time she came out of a foggy half-sleep, part of her expected to be back in her apartment, wrapped in the cool muslin sheets with Billy lying next to her. It had to be a dream, a horrible nightmare, and a trick on the mind.

But when she opened her eyes, the blackness was still there, the smell and the taste of the cloth and the realization that this was no dream. "Ooh," she moaned again, and rolled her hips to press her stomach against the bed, trying to ease the ache in her shoulders that had been so unnaturally strained with her hands tied behind her. And then she heard the creak of floorboards, and yes, she believed she could actually feel her captor now whenever he moved to her side. The belief was strengthened when she felt the straw again poking at the bottom of the hood. She let it work its way up to her lips and drew it into her mouth.

The concoction they were now feeding her came warm and smooth into her throat, and she took it greedily this time. If they were poisoning her, so be it. If they'd spiked the supplement with drugs, what were her options? Her obstetrician had warned her against dehydration. She'd even taken to keeping a bottle of water on her courtroom dais while she listened to the presentation of evidence and testimony.

"Can you help me to the toilet again?" she asked when she was done drinking. "I'm sorry. The baby, you know—he pushes on my bladder and I have to go."

The first time she'd asked to pee, she thought she might be led to a bathroom, behind closed doors where she could remove the damn hood—not to be. Instead, her captor had grabbed up a fistful of fabric from the arm of her dress and half-dragged her to somewhere in the room, maybe a corner, and then forced her to sit down by clipping at the back of her knees and pressing on her shoulders until she felt the roundness of a seat meet her buttocks.

Was it some kind of portable toilet? It felt similar to a "head" she'd used on a sailing yacht she'd taken with her family to Bimini years back. By blind feeling with her cuffed hands, she was able to rise slightly and pull down her own underwear and position herself. It was humiliating, knowing that within reaching distance her captor was watching her. She'd tried as best she could to keep her dress down around her knees, but could not cover the sound of her water hitting something that she assumed was a bowl below her.

You do what you have to do, Diane thought. Was this part of the captivity? The raw humiliation of the prisoner? She'd read about such things, reports from prisoners of war and details from the diaries of abductees. Some simply wallowed in their own voids. At least there was a modicum of civility here. Was that a good sign? A sign at all?

But if it was a forced humiliation she wasn't going to let it happen.

"It doesn't bother me, you know? I've got brothers. With brothers, you learn to pee in front of men," she said. No response. Just silence.

Though she knew she was being watched, Diane had seen enough investigative reports as a prosecutor and judge to be thinking ahead. *Not if*, when *the Marshal's Service and FBI find me, they're going to need evidence on the case of my kidnapping. I will*, she swore to herself and her child, *survive to tell my story*. But she knew plenty about forensic evidence.

Taking her time on the makeshift toilet, she used her hands, bound behind her, to feel the surface of what she was sitting on. She needed to find smooth spots where she could roll her fingertips like they do in booking to leave her prints behind. Would it help? Would her captors know to wipe everything clean? Obviously, she couldn't know, but just the act, the clandestine act of doing something, anything, lit a spark of defiance in her brain. *Think, Diane. Outsmart them if you can. It's all you've got.*

When she was finished, she tried to stand on her own. There was no cleanup. She reached down and pulled up her underwear. She felt slightly dizzy. Was there spotting on her underwear? Was the anxiety and the fear and this wretched nightmare having an effect on her child? She wobbled on her feet. This time, her captor actually took her by the arm, clamping it and guiding her instead of pulling her by the sleeve. The tips of the guard's fingers seemed small to Diane. She tried to analyze the touch, to gauge the angle, maybe judge the height of her captor. This trip to the toilet had also surprised her with a new sensation of tingling in her feet and legs upon standing.

Her doctor had warned about the swelling that might occur in her legs and feet during the pregnancy, but she'd stayed active, had even gone down to the beachfront pool in her and Billy's building to swim in the evenings after work. But in this captive state, lying on a mattress for hours on end, her circulation was next to nil. This time, she resisted, just slightly, from being led back to the bed.

"Can I just stand for a minute?" she asked, showing deference with her tone of voice. "I just need to stand and move my legs, you know? I'm getting so stiff and the blood needs to move to get down to my feet and organs and the placenta for my baby."

She was working the angles, making herself more human to him: not just a thing being bargained for a price. If her captor had even a sliver of compassion for children or motherhood or humanity, she wanted, needed, to touch it.

She took a shuffle to her right, put pressure on her foot, and then took a full step back to her left. She bent her knees. She took a full step to the left and again flexed her knees, waiting to be grabbed or pulled.

"Do you remember when your wife was pregnant?" she said, taking a chance. Silence.

She took another step to the right, and then back again. She arched her back and let out a groan at the effort, feeling muscles that were cramped, maybe even bruised, from the rough handling she'd received as they shoved her in the van and sat on her.

"Maybe your mother? With a brother or sister?" Silence.

"You know I'm already in my eighth month and I can feel the baby kicking?" she tried again. "If you put your hand right there on my belly, you can actually feel him."

Silence.

"Do you think you could at least free my hands so I could feel my stomach? You certainly can't think that I could overpower you or escape. I'm a fat, pregnant woman. I just want to use my hands to rub my stomach, feel my child, and calm him."

More silence.

Then she felt the hand grab her arm above the elbow, not the comfortable, leading hand but a fingers-digging-into-muscle, pissed-off hand. She knew she'd gambled with the attempt at personalization. He dragged her across space, the seven steps she'd counted to the toilet, this time stumbling steps, and then spun her and backed her up again until her knees were clipped by the edge of the mattress. She sat down hard on the bed, her back stiffening this time so as not to bang her head on the wall.

Not a word was uttered—not even a *humph* from the effort the captor had used to issue the silent message: shut the hell up.

Diane sat, huffing into the cloth of the hood, smelling her own deteriorating breath coming back at her. *I went too far*, she said to herself. *Christ, maybe this guy was a toss-away kid and has no memory of mother or family. Hell, maybe he was abused by his parents as a kid, and all I've done is goad memories that just pissed him off more.*

She stayed silent and listened, with a newly acute sense of hearing. Hadn't she read somewhere that when one sense is removed or lost the others try to compensate? She couldn't see, but she could hear.

And there it was, that muted clicking sound: not teeth chattering in a closed mouth, or nervous foot-tapping. Not careful knuckle-cracking. This was tapping, not rhythmic, but fast. After a pause there was more tapping—definitely texting. And then nothing.

She lay back. *How long will this go on? How long?* She felt the baby move again deep in her abdomen, that surreal, tiny push from the inside out that only one living thing in all of existence can feel. Then she heard the creak of a chair or floorboards. Again, she thought she could feel the air move.

When something touched her elbow, she flinched and felt fingers take hold of her, firmly but not with malice. Then the grip pulled her and rolled her more to her side and she followed the unspoken instruction. And then she felt and heard, instantaneously, a quick pull and snick at her wrists and her hands fell free. The grip at her elbow disappeared.

CHAPTER 19

Midafternoon: I looked down at the next address on Billy's list and shook my head. I'd driven more than an hour south on the Florida Turnpike toward Homestead, and then another half hour southwest past Florida City, the last civilized place on the southern peninsula of the state before the long jaunt on the Overseas Highway to the Florida Keys.

I was now on Ingraham Highway—good luck with street signs. The eight-mile-long roadway is named after James Edmundson Ingraham, one of those "visionary" industrialists who was convinced in the late 1800s that the Florida Everglades could be drained and channeled and turned into a utopia of profitable farmland. Nature, of course, had her say, and now the road that bears Ingraham's name runs from the entrance of Everglades National Park at its western terminus to the largest state prison in South Florida, the Dade County Correctional Institution, to the east. In a historical sense, both beginning and end seem apropos.

On either side of the two-lane road were open fields of farmland as flat as a pool table and lined with knee-high tomato plants. At variable intervals, the plots would inexplicably end and butt up next to forestlike acres of mature avocado trees, lush and green and generations old. The next carefully zoned field would be lined with rows and rows of towering royal palm trees, standing like soldiers before the march. This was a part of Florida you never see on post-cards, more akin to Midwest plains than the subtropics. With few signs and no discernible addresses, I was left to slow down at each turnoff or gate entrance to search for a mailbox or mile marker or number or clue.

After a few aborted turns down tractor-rutted service roads and a stop at a corrugated steel warehouse shell, I finally came upon a walled and ornamented entryway that appeared residential—residential, considering its location, but palatial considering the six-foot-tall bronzed sculptures of rearing horses that flanked an iron gate. A family crest read ARENAS. Through the gate, I could see a long, palm-lined driveway and a terra-cotta-colored barrel-tiled roof in the distance.

I was in search of Manuel Arenas, age forty-one, convicted six-teen years ago in federal court for unlawful distribution, possession with intent to distribute, and importation of cocaine. Diane had prosecuted the case against Manuel and his older brother, Eduardo. The eldest brother was ruled not guilty for lack of direct evidence. When Manuel was convicted, Diane had asked for the maximum penalty, fifteen to life.

Billy had explained to me that the younger brother had refused to implicate his sibling and took the weight himself, testifying that he alone had used his family's agricultural business in southern Dade County as a cloak for his own illegal activities. In court on the day his sentence was announced, Manuel Arenas, then twenty-three years old, had raised his hands with fingers pointed as if forming duel handguns, aimed at Diane's face, and spit four times while jerking his wrist in mock-firing before bailiffs could wrestle him out of the room to his echoing cries of "You will die, bitch! You will die!"

Billy's depiction of Diane's own recollection of the moment, and the fact that it still resonated with her years later, included the look of total rage on the young man's face and the complete conviction that a deep wrong was being done to him—and that she was responsible. The undisputed fact that Arenas had imported tons of cocaine into the United States using a variety of means and through his own family's legitimate business ties and operations seemed to roll off his back.

In fact, he'd been recorded in phone taps bragging about how he used hollowed-out railroad ties into which he stuffed coke. He'd brought tons into the country as framing material for outside gardens. When the DEA got onto that scheme, he'd claimed that he himself had discovered how to blend the coke into a paste that could be molded into decorative flowerpots and imported into Florida, and then crushed and refiltered into high-grade cocaine. At trial, his only defense had been that it all was simply business.

Now, I stood at the electronically locked gate of the Arenas family compound, waiting to ask if he'd carried out his long-ago threat to a federal prosecutor. With no badge, no authority, and no expectations, I pushed the intercom button on the gate.

"May I help you?" a man's voice asked.

"My name is Max Freeman. I'm here to speak to Manuel Arenas."

"And what is your business with Mr. Arenas?"

"I'd like to ask him about Judge Diane Manchester."

There was a pause, but not one that seemed inordinately long.

"Please come in, Mr. Freeman," the voice said. The gate, triggered from within, began to open.

The entry drive was grand: sixty-foot palms, multicolored bougainvillea adorning either side, a covered porte-cochère under which I pulled the Fury. When I parked and stepped out onto the shaded tile drive, a man was already standing next to a set of double oak doors. They were massive and appeared to have been hand-carved.

"Mr. Freeman," the man said with a tick of Spanish accent as I approached. He extended his hand and I took it.

"Eduardo Arenas," he said in introduction, and waved his hand into the entryway of his home. "Please, sir."

I nodded and stepped through the doorway into the coolness of air-conditioning turned a bit too cold and the fragrance of fresh-cut flowers a bit too cloying. The interior was as grand as the outside: polished marble, glittering chandeliers, pale leather seating, a variety of artwork on textured walls, all awash with sunlight pouring through two-story glass windows that formed the back wall of an expansive great room. As I stepped down from the foyer into the room, a woman dressed in a maid's uniform approached with a tray.

"Coffee, Mr. Freeman?" Eduardo Arenas said. "Or something else?"

"Uh, no. No, thank you," I managed. I admit I was slightly put off by the welcoming tone and deference considering I had shown up unannounced. But I was not here to be clever or unassuming.

"I would like to speak to your brother, Mr. Arenas," I said. "Is he available?"

Eduardo was a man small in stature, maybe five-eight and 140 pounds. He had dark, perfectly coifed hair, black eyes, and some age lines in his face, but fewer than one would expect for a man nearing sixty. He was dressed in dark linen slacks and an intricately patterned white guayabera shirt.

"I have sent for Manuel, Mr. Freeman. He is out working in the groves," Eduardo Arenas said, motioning me to sit as the maid placed the coffee service on a glass-topped table before leaving. "May I ask what your visit is in reference to?" The man's English was perfect.

"I assume you recognize the name of Judge Manchester," I said. "Are you aware of the recent news of the judge?" Arenas sat and poured us both a small china cup of dark coffee.

"Her maiden name is McIntyre. She was the prosecutor in my brother's federal trial," Arenas said matter-of-factly. "Many years ago . . . and yes, I keep up with the news, Mr. Freeman. The kidnapping of a judge in the United States is very big news."

Arenas sipped his coffee and sat silent, waiting for another question.

"I work for Mr. Billy Manchester, the judge's husband. And as you might guess, we are looking at all possibilities involving her disappearance. Mr. Manchester said that his wife was very afraid of your brother, Mr. Arenas," I said, matching the man's direct tone. "Even after many years."

Arenas put down his cup, looked down between his knees, folded his hands in front of him, and sighed.

"Manuel was very young then, Mr. Freeman," he said, still looking down. "He was young and foolish and caught up with himself and the times."

I said nothing. I'd heard too many stories begin the same way. I knew Arenas would go on and I let him.

"Manny made his mistakes, no doubt. He was a young man too proud, too boisterous, and perhaps through the fault of his own family, too arrogant about the things he had and the things he thought he deserved."

Arenas finally looked up, his forehead and the corners of his dark eyes now holding the age lines that seemed absent only minutes before. His expression didn't hold sadness as much as a look of a recognized guilt.

"I was the older one, supposedly the more mature. I was the one who should have looked out for him, taught him lessons. I did not then, Mr. Freeman. I want to believe we have both learned a great deal over the years."

I held my silence.

"During my brother's incarceration, our family continued to build," he said, raising his palms to indicate the opulence surrounding him. "We now have contracts with the state and supply most of the decorative palm trees for nearly every roadside off-ramp and rest area and government facility in South Florida. We are a serious and legitimate business, Mr. Freeman. We hold no grudges, nor do we harbor ill feelings for the dues we had to pay for past transgressions.

"On our mother's grave, my brother had nothing to do with whatever has befallen Judge Manchester."

The speech came off as heartfelt. Yet I'd heard such orations before, from political speeches to confessional soliloquies to parole board pleadings. I was about to ask a question when noise from an adjoining hall drew both our attentions. Manuel Arenas entered the room pulling a broad-brimmed hat from his head and held it in his hands as his brother stood.

"Manuel, this is Mr. Freeman. Mr. Freeman, this is my brother, Manuel, the foreman of our family's work crews, planters, and harvesters. He has been in the fields since five a.m., as he always is."

The younger Arenas was wider at the shoulders, thicker in the forearms, and grayer at the temples than his older brother. He was dressed in dusty jeans, workman's boots, and a denim shirt sweat-soaked at the neck and under the arms. He wiped a strand of hair from his forehead with a sleeve and wiped his hand on his pants before taking my hand. I could feel the hardened calluses on his palms and fingers.

He looked me in the eye when he said "Sir," and then turned his gaze back to his brother.

"Mr. Freeman is a friend of Mr. Billy Manchester, the husband of Diane McIntyre."

No recognition came to Manuel Arenas's eyes. In fact, he looked quizzically at his brother, awaiting further information.

"Ms. McIntyre was the prosecutor at your court trial and is now a federal judge," Eduardo said.

"OK," the younger brother nodded but continued to look down.

"The judge has gone missing, and Mr. Freeman is here to ask if you might know anything that might help them find her."

Again, Manuel looked perplexed by the explanation, looking first at his brother and then at me.

"How?" he said in incomprehension.

"How was she kidnapped?" I asked, a little too loud and in a tone that might be taken as questioning his statement or actions.

"How may I help, sir?" he asked. "I don't know this person. I only work in the fields. I work with my men and with the other foremen of other crews and the truck drivers making deliveries. Eduardo deals with all the business people, the lawyers and such."

"You don't have any contact with the old drug runners?" I said as plainly and upfront as I could. Again, Manuel looked to his brother.

"Do you know a Colombian named Escalante?" I said with a sharpness in my voice that I was hoping might jar him. But he did not lose his composure.

"Those times are gone, Mr. Freeman—and so are those people," he said quietly, looking me straight in the eye without a hint of brashness or anger or contempt. "That was another life for me."

He shifted his weight from boot to boot, trying to find something to do with his hands.

"Eduardo," he said to his brother. "May I get back to work, please? We've got that shipment to make to the farm in Ocala. It's going to take until after dark to load."

The older brother looked to me, the question on his face.

"Anything else, Mr. Freeman?"

I shook my head. If these guys were bullshitting me, they were better actors than they'd been drug runners.

Manuel bowed his head. "I wish I could be more helpful," he said, and left the room. His brother waited until his sibling was gone before stepping toward the front door.

"Manny works very hard, Mr. Freeman. His family takes care of him. He sacrificed a lot and we owe him that."

"You mean sacrificed a lot by taking the punishment alone?" I said. "Is that some kind of confession, Mr. Arenas?"

The man looked directly into my face, unblinking.

"My confessions are only to my God, Mr. Freeman. Is there anything else, sir?"

"The authorities may be right behind me, Mr. Arenas," I said, accepting my dismissal.

"They will have my complete cooperation. If they want my phone records, my business contracts, access to my properties, they are theirs to have.

"I repeat my brother's words; I don't really know Mrs. Manchester. I wish we could be more helpful. I hope the best for her."

Forty-five minutes later, I was northbound on the Florida Turnpike. All I'd done was run down false leads, no better than the guys working the reward tips. I was fuming in my own brand of anger when the *chirp* of a phone snapped me out of my funk. I had three phones and pulled out the one that connected me to CQ the basketball star.

"Got something," was all the young man on the other end said.

"Face-to-face?" I said.

"Only way."

"I'll be there in ninety minutes."

CHAPTER 20

*T*ouch *your belly! Really? Do I want to touch your belly? Jesus Christ! What kind of prisoner asks the guard if he wants to touch her fat pregnant belly?*

Do you remember when your wife was pregnant? Shit! The woman still thinks I'm a man, which is probably a good thing because she's not supposed to know a damn thing about any of us. That was Geronimo's big scheme and the way these assholes, including Danny, all thought we were going to get away with this deal. No sound, no voices, no touching, no removing the hood, so she can't identify a single thing, who we are, what we look like, where she's been. That was the line Danny used to try to convince Rae that everything would be cool.

Rae knew it probably came directly from Geronimo, even though Danny was smart enough to come up with it himself. He was good at that kind of thing as much as she hated to admit it. He was good with the details, and that's why he'd been so successful with the carjacking and the pot- and amphetamine-selling at the resort and the ski areas back home. He was smooth and he was quiet and he was careful. He never talked about what he did with anyone but her. "Loose lips sink ships," he used to say, and before that, the only time she'd ever heard the line was from her rowdy girlfriends who used to laugh and say, "Loose lips suck dicks," when they were hanging at the old Crossroads bar in a booth, acting all smart-assed and scoping out the guys.

Danny had snorted at her version and had explained that the "sink ships" came from World War II and meant that sailors or soldiers who talked too much about missions took a chance of letting the Japs know what was up. Yeah, right—like they were sitting around in the bar shootin' the shit and watching the game with a couple of Japs and happened to mention where they were sailing the next day to bomb Tokyo. Christ! Her version was much better. But Danny knew that kind of shit, history and stuff. It was another reason she'd fallen for him. Quiet and smart. It was maybe the only reason she thought this whole fucked-up kidnapping thing might work out so that they'd both walk away with a load of money and a way out of the life up north.

You and your dreams, Rae. Don't you know how those go by now?

"Can you take me to the toilet again?" The whiner.

Jesus! Rae thought. She should have known. As soon as you start being nice to them, they just want more. She'd gotten Danny to go out and buy the Boost shit because the woman needed it. Even Rae knew that you can't keep somebody locked up in a room without food and water for days and not have something happen to them, especially a pregnant woman. So she gives her the stuff, and half an hour later she's got to pee. And no way is Rae gonna let her piss in that bed and have that smell hovering in the room for however long they were going to be here.

She got up and went over to help the woman up off the bed, wobbly, even with Rae holding a fist of her dress and keeping her from falling over. Stumbling. Can't put one damn foot in front of the other. Rae guided her. Same thing as your mom, right, Rae? Jesus, who needs that memory?

She'd been, what, seven, eight, nine years old? Staying home alone in the old single-wide they had on Skegemog Point. She'd be alone from the time the school bus dropped her off, doing homework on the couch with the TV on, eating cheese curls and drinking pop even though her mom might have left a tuna casserole in the fridge that day. She'd watch every kid's show from three in the afternoon until she fell asleep with her orange fingertips in her mouth like a little baby. Then she'd wake up to the sound of the car pulling up, sometime deep into the night. She'd keep her eyes closed when her mom unlocked the door and came in, the glow of the TV the only light in the place.

Rae would listen to see if the steps were quiet, and if the handbag was placed carefully on the counter. The fridge was being opened and closed. There was a rustle of clothing as her mom sat on the coffee table in front of the couch for a long minute, Rae knowing she was watching her sleep, looking at the side of her face, maybe even knowing Rae wasn't really asleep. Then she'd bend over Rae, kiss her on the forehead, and gather her in her arms and take her back to her own bed. Those were the good nights, the infrequent nights.

Mostly there were sounds of keys fumbling in the lock, a trip, and then a curse when her mom stumbled over a pair of Rae's sneakers on the doormat. Then the bump of a hip against the counter and the fridge being opened and left standing open, its light competing with the TV for a long minute.

That's when Rae would open her eyes and get up on her own. "Mama, are you all right?"

And this apparition, known by others as her mother, would sing-song slur: "I'm just hunky-dory, Rae-Jay," using her pet name for Rae. "An' I brought a treat for my baby 'cause I know they're your favorites."

Then she'd tap at the brown paper bag containing the half-drunk bottle of Allen's coffee-flavored brandy known locally as "fat ass in a glass," and a package of Double Stuf Oreos. And then it was Rae who would prop up her wobbling drunk mother, guide her through the narrow passageway to the back bedroom, and help her lie down without crashing into a bureau or nightstand or lampshade.

It was Rae who went in the tiny bathroom, soaked a washcloth under the sink, folded it, and placed it over her mother's forehead and eyes. It was she who would stare at her mother's profile, the face that everyone called country beautiful. Even as a child Rae could see it, even through runny mascara and smeared makeup: the prettiness, the curse, the ultra-green eyes that drew men in, the rich dark hair that made them stare, the flawless skin that made them want to touch her. Her mother's beauty was the exact opposite of Rae's own distinctive strawberry blonde, freckle-cheeked look. And even a kid hears the whispers of the "bitchy broads" at Tom's Pancake House: "Ain't her daddy's girl, is she?"

Even a kid could recognize her own coloring and its similarity to that of another man in town who was not her mother's ex and whom her mother avoided like vermin.

Still, it was on those drunken nights that Rae would kiss her mother's closed eyes. It was Rae who had mistaken the smell of whiskey for perfume until she was ten and went to the bar herself one night to find her mother and recognized the odor being wiped off the counter. It was Rae who knew what was going to happen before it happened. Even then. Even now.

Do I want to touch her belly? Christ no!

Do you remember when your wife was pregnant? Jesus!

And Rae led the woman back to the bed, spun her, and shoved her, a little harder maybe than she'd meant to.

Could I at least cut her hands loose so she could feel her own belly? Anything else, Prisoner? What, you wanna go for a jog around the yard? Do a few bench presses with the skinheads in the barbell club? Rae stood speechless in front of the bed. Says she's a fat, pregnant woman, what's she going to do? Well, true there. Rae knew that Geronimo would be pissed. She knew she was breaking the rules. Maybe even Danny would be pissed, but fuck it. Look at this pathetic woman lying there with a bag over her head.

Rae reached into the spot where she'd hidden the small razor blade, the same place she'd hidden her thin cell phone, the place where the old northern Michigan cops were too prudish or even too scared to search you when they booked you into county for some stupid-ass violation. She took the fold of cardboard off the blade and rolled the woman on her side and sliced through the flex-cuffs, freeing her hands.

Then she took a step back and watched. Go ahead and try something, she thought, not letting the act of kindness weaken her—I'll kick your ass.

CHAPTER 21

When I pulled up to the curb in the Dunbar Village housing project, Mrs. Quarles was nowhere in sight. That she was watching through the lace curtains of her tiny living room would be a solid assumption. When I got out of the Gran Fury and walked toward the basketball court where I could see her son repetitively shooting free throws, I stopped in front of her porch for a single second, a moment of respect and a soundless request for permission before moving on. The court was empty. CQ, ballplayer with eyes in the back of his head, did not turn until I was two paces behind him. "Thirty-nine," he said, as the ball left his fingertips with an exaggerated backspin, arced through the warm humid air, went cleanly through the hoop, and as he planned, bounced back as if on command into his waiting hands. "Forty," he said, repeating the exact movements and formula again. Only then did he turn to me, a look of seriousness on his handsome face. "Mr. Freeman," he said, cradling the ball in the crook of his elbow and gesturing to the paint-chipped iron bench on the sideline. "Shall we adjourn to my office?" I couldn't help myself. The juxtaposition of the venue and the young man's pantomime of corporate cant made me grin. "After you, sir," I said, extending my hand toward the bench. We sat and let silence hang for a full minute, maybe two. I didn't think he was second-guessing his decision as much as he was letting the quiet act as a cleansing that moved him from one activity to another; the two should never overlap. "Look, CQ," I started, "if you don't want to get involved . . ."

"No, no," he stopped me. "I made some calls, talked with some fellas. Got some info . . . but I'll tell you up front, Mr. Freeman, this tip isn't about drugs. If you think it might be a dead end, it's up to you. OK?"

Now it was my turn to be silent.

"I understand, Mr. Freeman," CQ said. "I read the newspapers. I know Ms. Manchester was the judge in the Escalante case and that everyone thinks that his cartel and their connections here on the street could have their fingers in it." He was looking out over the empty court now, not into my eyes.

"And it makes sense you'd want to find out if there was word on the streets. So you come to my neighborhood to find out what might be hummin' out here, you know?"

"I wasn't judging, CQ," I said. "Leads are leads, chances, opportunities."

After another few seconds of silence, he dug into his pocket and came out with the burner, the toss-away cell phone I'd given him.

"I ain't judgin' you, neither," he said. "Number on there for a dude name of Dez, jack-a-all-trades kinda guy who has some stuff to tell about a chop shop down Delray way where some odd shit been going on last couple of days."

I nodded and let CQ continue.

"Says he got a piece of a Ford van that has a vehicle ID number on it might interest you."

I could feel that interest materialize as a physical tingle up my hairline, an ember of hope that I had to contain immediately lest I give it more importance than it deserved.

"Of course, he also has a monetary interest of his own," CQ said, handing me the cell, his voice going an octave lower, putting on the Boston University vernacular again. "So you two will have to negotiate that on your own. He'll know your call is legitimate if it comes through this line."

The way the kid kept doing the linguistic two-step did not confuse the message. Street smart, business smart, cover-your-ass smart: Billy's friend the teacher had chosen his protégé well. I started to go to my own pocket to pay for his help, but CQ cut me off again.

"I gave Dez your two thousand up front," he said, raising his palms, refusing any money. "I hope what information he has will help Ms. Manchester. If I obtain any more, uh, leads, I'll purchase another untraceable phone and call you."

"Agreed," I said, and offered my hand to be swallowed by his once again. "And thank you, CQ."

The voice on the cell gave me the address of a bodega in eastern Delray Beach called La Preferiola. CQ had given me the guy's name as Dez, but no last name. "And if he gives you a last name, it won't be his real one," CQ said. "But the dude's got an ear on everything, and I mean everything. So you have to take his info on face value—but take it seriously because when it comes to the streets, this guy is plugged in."

I was taking it at face value, but when I reached Dez on the phone—young-sounding voice, no detectible accent, clipped and direct—he led me to a neighborhood of shops and garages and little groceries where the signage is overwhelmingly in Spanish. So I was putting a face on the "dude" ahead of time.

Here I was with cash money to pay for information about a particularly high-profile crime that might have involved drug dealers tied to one of the nearly mythic figures in the trade: it was hard for me not to start projecting. I'm figuring Dez must be Latin and wants to meet me in a place where he's comfortable and may have his own brand of backup among the locals.

I know this gig. I had more than a few informants when I was a beat cop in Philadelphia and during my short stint as a detective. We talked on untraceable lines. We met in places where the informant was unlikely to be recognized with a stranger who looks like a cop. We made the meetings short and sweet. The promise was given that real names never went into documents.

I would soon find out that a lot of those rules were going out the window on this one.

If Dez was as street smart as CQ made him out to be, he was going to be careful. And so was I. Already I had my handgun out of the trunk and felt it bite into the small of my back as I got out of the Fury. I'd thought twice about switching my car and driving my F-150, not to be so obvious, but now realized it would have been a useless move.

La Preferiola was a squat, one-story business in the middle of the block on Southwest 18th Avenue. The store's front windows were filled with advertisements in Spanish for COCINA LATINA, ULTAMAR SERVICIOS TELEFONICOS, and C.A.M., a money-transfer service providing a link to the Caribbean and South America and available in a thousand shops in South Florida. There was even a sign for overseas Internet availability for a price per minute.

It was one-stop shopping. You could come in and send money to your mom in Ecuador, call your cousin in Brazil, and send an email to Cuba, all while having café con leche and churros. The joint next door sported a red and yellow JOYERIA EMPEÑOS sign identifying it as a jewelry and pawn shop. On the other side was what we'd call a mom-and-pop grocery in Philly, with the sign LA PREFERIOLA running across the awning.

I sat for a minute, assessing. The only visible signs in English were STOP and SPEED LIMIT 30. I was a gringo in a foreign country.

CQ told me that I wouldn't have any trouble recognizing Dez. And he was right. When I walked into the store, the requisite tinkle of bells hanging on the doorframe announced my presence. A mixed odor of warm spice, cooking meat, and some undetermined whiff of cleaning agent greeted me. To my immediate right was a glass-covered warming counter with an array of rice dishes, stews, sliced pork, braised chicken, and mixed vegetables steaming in stainless trays. To the left was a counter stacked with paper directories, lists of dollar, peso, real, gourde, and Cordoba exchange rates, and a clerk streaming a litany of questions to a customer in Spanish so fast that I didn't have a chance to glean the conversation.

The narrow single room extended back past a booth supplied with one outdated laptop and into a four-table dining area. The floors were mopped clean, but I could tell that if you bumped one piece of furniture from its spot the grime would be thick.

At a small two-top in the far corner sat a man with his back against the wall, a hoodie pulled over his head and shadowing his eyes. I walked up within a couple of feet and stood silently.

"Mr. Freeman, I presume," a voice said from under the hood.

"Dez."

"Please. Sit."

The voice, again absent any discernible accent, was accompanied by the wave of a pale palm to the seat in front of him. I deferred and instead sat in the chair directly to his right where I had a wall to my own back. It was a chess move and we both knew it.

"My understanding is that you have something for me," I said.

"I think I do."

Again, the hand came up, this time holding a small strip of metal, probably a quarter-inch wide and three inches long, and stamped with a series of letters and numbers. Dez placed it on the tabletop and slid it toward me. I recognized it immediately as a VIN tag. It still had the rivet heads on either end from where it had been ripped from the dash of a vehicle. I spun the strip with my fingernail on one edge so I could read it. Then I took my cell phone from my pocket and dialed Billy's number. I needed his help. I'd read the preliminary police reports on the stolen van, but I've never been good at recalling numbers, and at times can still be befuddled when being asked for my own Social Security number.

While I waited for the line to ring through, Dez slid an *Especiales* menu over to me. *Chuleta de puerco, churrasco, sopa de pollo.*

"The chicken soup is great," he said.

When Billy answered, I read off the VIN without any preamble.

"It's the correct number for the stolen van," he said. "Where are you, Max?"

"I'll get back to you," I said, and thumbed the cell off.

I turned the VIN tag around with my fingernail and stayed silent for a few long seconds.

"True?" Dez said.

"Can you tell me where you got this?"

"I could."

When nothing else was offered, I reached into the right pocket of my cargo pants and brought out a brick of twenty-dollar bills in a way that only my lunch companion could see.

"Two thousand more," I said.

Dez did not reach for the payment but instead pulled back the hoodie to reveal his face. His eyes were gray and flat but gave no indication of menace as they met mine, unblinking. They showed no sign of being under the influence. His hair was short and naturally ash blond. He was clean-cut and owned an unblemished complexion that was, like his hands, light-colored, but what the Florida sun might supply as tan. He was a white Anglo kid in a bodega. I guessed his age to be early to mid-twenties.

"Four and I'll give you the address of the warehouse it came from . . . and an eyewitness."

"Four it is," I said, and reached into my pocket for another brick.

Dez nodded. He liked this way of dealing. No bullshit. No haggling. Easy money for him, and fine by me as well. I didn't like dealing with the black-market element, but there was nothing overtly illegal in our trade. He had something I needed. I had money to pay him. And time was of the essence.

He recited the address from memory: "2742 Northwest 60th Street, old area of Pompano Beach. Light industry, but used to have a lot of chop shops back in the day—mostly abandoned now. I'm thinking whoever chopped this one up is from out of town, because we don't usually handle it that way down here."

I looked up into his light-colored eyes at the word *we*, but didn't press.

"Carjackers who want to get rid of a car down here just drive it out west and run it into a canal. They've got dredging programs these days, but an entire car can sit underwater for decades."

I knew this to be true and let Dez go on. It was, after all, my money.

"Like I told CQ, these guys have something to hide rather than sell."

"You get any eyeballs on these out-of-towners?"

"Not personally." The young man's voice was all business.

I admit I couldn't hang a sign on him. Shyster? Thief? Entrepreneur?

"But there is someone who kinda lives in the area who sees everything that happens and is susceptible, so to speak, to questions," he said, with a nod to the money still in my hand.

I passed him the cash.

"Dude lives up on the roof across the street from that address," Dez elaborated. "Spooky guy. Be careful going up there. He doesn't like visitors, but if you knock with this," he said, slapping the bills lightly on the underside of the table, "he'll be cool."

I slid out of the chair and stood to leave.

"Hey," Dez said, and I turned back to him. "Good luck."

I was dialing Billy's number as I climbed into the Fury. He answered on the first ring.

"What do you have, Max?"

"An address and a possible witness," I said. There was a moment of silence. It was the first positive news since his wife had been scooped off the streets.

"Give me the address, and I'll run everything I can through the computer before I meet you there, Max. If it's an old building, I won't be able to get blueprints online, but I have a contact at the county planner's office who might be able to pull the file and give us a description."

Billy and his contacts. I read him the warehouse number.

"And the witness's name?"

"No name yet, Billy. But he apparently keeps a close eye on all the comings and goings in that neighborhood. I'd like to get a chance to talk with him before the feds show up and spook the hell out of him."

"We'll have to bring them in," Billy said, still hanging on to his legitimacy as an attorney even though he may have committed a dozen crimes stripping his wife's computer, bugging her office, and downloading the entire collection of files from the courthouse database.

"Give me an hour lead-time before you call them and I'll meet you there. It'll take them some time to get their team together anyway."

"OK, Max. Your call," Billy said, and hung up.

My friend trusted me, even with his wife's life potentially on the line. I was grateful. I knew that if the tip on the witness—described as kinda spooky—was good, then he was likely to give me some information for a bundle of cash a lot quicker than he would if there was a phalanx of federal agents swarming all over the block. And I had no doubt there would be a swarm. The Marshal's Service and the FBI had been shut out of all potential leads and would be itching for anything they could move on. They'd come in heavy, and that was never a way to get good info from a marginal guy who "lives up on the roof." I'd need to do that on my own.

I found the street in less than twenty minutes. I don't use a GPS, but have roamed South Florida's lesser-known neighborhoods for years while working cases for Billy, so I'm decent at tracking down addresses that you'll never find on the tourist brochures.

The building was in a row of warehouses of the old brick-and-mortar variety, different than the cheap aluminum-sided storage structures that entrepreneurs put up in the 1980s and 1990s. These places were built to last—though from the looks of the boarded windows, graffiti-marked walls, and trash-strewn streets and alley-ways, they'd seen better times. The overall feeling was gray, sun-bleached surfaces gone chalky from too much heat and neglect.

I rolled the Gran Fury around a two-block perimeter and noted a couple of junk cars up on blocks as well as a newer step van with the license tag removed. In one open bay door, a couple of guys dressed in greasy overalls and carrying tools gave me the once-over as I cruised by. This was not a place you came if you didn't have business. But it was also a place where you might hide, and no one would really care.

Given that numbers on the buildings were in short supply, when I parked at the corner of the street Dez had given me, I had to extrapolate. I picked out the two-story building that had to be 2742. The garage-style roll-down door was dull galvanized metal—and closed. Next to it was an unmarked doorway entrance with only a small, head-high window with crosshatched reinforcing wire in the glass, so that you couldn't see through to the inside. To the south of the garage door was a big Dumpster, the kind a trash-service truck would spear with its forks and lift overhead and dump.

The pocked macadam street wasn't going to yield much in tire tracks, and a scan of the row of buildings showed no security cameras and only a few outdoor lights that vandals hadn't turned into blossoms of jagged glass. It was nearing evening and there wasn't a person in sight. I calculated that the building across the street to the west was where Dez had told me the spooky guy's roof nest must be, and I worked my way down the alley.

I stepped around broken wooden pallets, rusted barrels, and a puddle of some kind of reddish ooze in the rear of the building. There was a back door that was heavily chained and padlocked. Halfway down the wall was a metal fire escape ladder that ran from the rooftop to about six feet from the ground. An intact pallet leaned against the brick wall—an obvious stair step. I stared up for several seconds—not exactly a safe approach. I'd be completely vulnerable. But what was the choice? To hell with it.

I secured my gun in my waistband and began climbing. The iron was rusted, and brownish-orange flakes came off the side rails onto my hands; but on each foot rung close to my face, I could see slightly worn signs of traffic. As I climbed, I tried to look into the second-story windows, but the dirt and grime and inside darkness made it impossible. When I reached the top edge where the rails looped over the precipice, I stopped, thinking of Dez's warning and how best to present myself to whomever was on the roof. The sound of a sharp squawking voice made my decision for me.

"Best stop right there, Copper, lest you lose that first hand and take a tumble!"

I kept my hand below the roofline.

"I'm not bringing trouble," I said, trying to keep my tone level and void of any kind of authority. "Dez sent me. And I'm not a cop."

There was silence from above. Dez had called the informant "spooky" but not deranged. I recalled his suggestion and reached into my cargo pocket for a two-thousand-dollar brick of twenties. Slowly, I raised it, flapping it a little.

"I'm just looking to buy some information—nothing more."

"Show the other hand," the voice commanded.

I pinched the brick of money against one rail with my left hand to secure myself and raised my right. Then slowly, very slowly, I raised my face above the roofline. A wizened figure of a man was in my sightline, armed with a long machete. But he backed away and gestured with the blade for me to come ahead.

I pulled myself over, money in hand, and surveyed my new situation. The man before me was small, five foot five at the most, bent over slightly not from deformity but in a fight-or-flight stance. His face was pinched and deeply wrinkled, like a dried apricot left too long in the sun. It was the color of a browned walnut. His age was indeterminate. His hair was a flurry of sun-bleached blond going gray, and his eyes were narrowed and attentive, going perhaps involuntarily from my face to the bundle of cash. He was dressed in a long, dark leather overcoat that fell to his ankles and was completely incongruous with the Florida heat. On his feet, he sported what appeared to be brand-new high-top sneakers, bright orange in color.

"Dez, you say?"

The voice was less threatening, but retained the same squawky quality.

"Yes. He gave me the VIN plate from a van I'm looking for and said you might know more about it."

The eyes, washed-out brown, maybe hazel, peered at me.

"Dez, huh? That Hispanic kid with the scruffy beard and big hands?"

"No," I said. "Dez the white kid with the smooth face and a nose for a deal."

"Humph. Yeah, that's him, always lookin' for car parts and whatnot. Come," the guy said, easing up on the battle stance and motioning to me with the now limply hanging machete.

I followed the diminutive man to the front corner of the roof where he had apparently set up shop next to a shoulder-high steel cubicle with a caged fan on top that may have been a venting shed or possibly a utility entrance into the building below. He'd propped up a makeshift awning using a bright blue tarp, the kind that Florida homeowners use to cover leaky roofs after hurricane damage. It was stretched low, I presumed so that it couldn't be spotted from the street. I had to bend deeply to duck under it.

With surprising agility, the little fellow leaped up onto a bed frame that was sitting on cinder blocks and tucked his legs into a lotus position, with the machete laid across his knees. He looked at me as if he was giving me an audience.

I was still bent under the plastic sheeting. There was no place to sit other than on the roof surface, so I followed his example and sat cross-legged before him. I could feel my shirt pull up against the butt of my gun in the small of my back.

The man just stared at me with squinting eyes, waiting.

"OK, look," I said, knowing that time was running out. If the feds were on the way, this meeting would end soon. "Dez said you got the VIN plate from the warehouse across the street. Did you see the white van? Did you see who was in it?"

The man closed his eyes for a full ten seconds. I surveyed his nest. On a small wooden table just to his right was one of those five-gallon plastic water containers with the spigot on the bottom. There were a couple of crumpled paper bags and a paper plate with food crumbs. From my seat on the roof, I could see under the raised mattress where stacks of paperback books and a spare blanket or two were stored.

Finally, the little man's eyes fluttered open as if he'd just awakened. He looked down at my hand, still holding the bundle of twenties. *All right*, I thought, and slipped ten bills from the strapped pack and handed them to him.

"Came in three days ago, they did," he said quietly, with the craggy little voice, as if someone might hear. "Like I tol' Dez—pulled up just past midday. White van, probably a '92 or '93, no markings. One of those Shuttle Columbia memorial license plates number RG3 44X."

The be-on-the-lookout with the plate number had been all over the media since the abduction, though it didn't look like this guy had a flatscreen on hand. Dez had been good at scamming the guy in the first place, knowing about my reward offer from CQ. The guy was squirrelly with his Yoda-like appearance, the syntax, and the saber, but he had an eye for detail.

"Big Indian got out of the passenger side and unlocked the side door of the warehouse," he continued. "Ain't seen that door unlocked for years."

"Big Indian, as in American or Eastern?" I said. "And how big?"

Yoda blinked again.

"Tonto kind of Indian, and tall, taller 'n you, but heavy—two hundred fifty or more. Had a long black ponytail with some kinda color-beaded knot holder. Reminded me of Chief."

"Chief?"

Yoda crinkled his brow and scowled, as if to indicate that I was an unschooled idiot.

"You know, Chief in *One Flew Over the Cuckoo's Nest?*"

My own brow crinkled.

"Chief as in 'jump in the air and put it in the basket, Chief!'"

"Right," I said, ignoring the irony of a mental case quoting a film about mental cases.

"The Indian unlocked the door and went inside the warehouse, opened the rolling door and the van pulled in."

"OK," I said, counting another hundred dollars from the pack and handing it to him. The skin of his small hands was dry and cracked, fingernails almost clawlike in length, and yellowing. But he took the money carefully, as if not to bend the new bills.

"Who else did you see? The driver? Passengers?"

"Not much of the driver when they came in. Only one else I seen was the kid."

"The kid?"

"Kid about twenty, maybe twenty-two. White kid, he's the gofer. Comes out in the night dumping metal into the trash bin, pieces big as he can carry. Humps it up in there and goes back inside."

"That's where you got the VIN plate? From the Dumpster?"

"Mighta been somethin' valuable," he said. "I know every can and bin in five square blocks. Go through 'em all. Waste not, want not, you know. I went into that one early the day after they got here. I knew they was cuttin' up that van 'cause I could smell the acetylene torch a-goin'. Waste of a good car, if you ask me. Hell, Dez coulda changed the VIN on that van and drove away."

Yeah, Dez had made more off the VIN number than he'd get from selling the whole thing.

"This kid, you get a good look at him?"

My oracle set his lips again. I opened them with another sheaf of bills.

"Yankee," he said. "'Bout a six-footer. Blondish hair, pale arms and face. A snowbird. Like I said, he was the gofer. Went out to Gilda's for hamburgers and such."

"Gilda's is the little stop-and-shop I saw out on the boulevard?" I said, guessing that the joint I saw driving in was the closest retail place around. He nodded.

"Gilda makes a damn fine cheeseburger. Fact I might go down there tonight," he said, feeling the bills in his hand, salivating on what the newly found riches might afford him.

"What else?" I said, raising what was left in my hand.

"What else you want?"

"Do you know the layout inside that building? Back entrances? First-floor windows?"

"Same as this one. Big floor-to-ceiling workshop in front, little corner office on the first floor. Storage rooms on the second floor in the back with a staircase going up. Ain't much use for windows."

I stood halfway and duck-walked over to the edge of the roof to peek over to the building. Diane could be there now, thirty yards away.

"You hear them talking? Anything?"

"Ain't made a sound 'cept the cuttin' and bangin' when they tore that van apart."

"Does the kid go for food at any particular time?"

The guy was smart enough to know the import of the question and looked at my hand again. I gave him the rest of the bills.

"Used to come out about six or seven at night, just gettin' dark."

"Used to?" I said, the past participle igniting a spark in my head.

"Gone they are," the little gnome said, his voice even quieter than before. I spun on him and he cowered a bit, but did not raise the machete.

"The kid went out at daybreak and came back in a big ol' Chrysler 300, silver color, and a temporary plate number ACI 886. One of them you can make yourself on the computer and print out on eighteen-inch copy paper and stick inside the holder, you know."

I was just staring at him, blood rising into my face. His explanation quickened and he dropped the *Star Wars* slang.

"He pulled into the shop and they closed the door. Then a couple of minutes later, out they come in the Chrysler. Looked like five of 'em, including the Indian in front. That's when I seen the girl."

He must have sensed the sudden tension that flexed in the tendons of my shoulders and arms because he slid farther back on the mattress and tucked the new money into the armpit of his leather jacket.

"Didn't see much—just the flash of hair through the side window."

"How do you know it was a woman?" I barked.

"Pretty hair. Strawberry blonde is what they call it—too pretty for a man."

Diane's hair was a deep brunette, impossible to mistake unless they'd somehow dyed it. But even so, the suggestion that she was still alive was something. I was still trying to digest the little man's revelation when I sensed him shudder again. But his focus had changed, looking past my face to a spot behind me, his nostrils flaring. I didn't make the mistake of turning my back on him when he was still armed with the long knife.

"What?" I barked again, taking a step back out of his lunging range.

"I smell Velcro and gun oil," he said quietly, still looking past me.

CHAPTER 22

When I turned to follow my Yoda friend's sightline, a long evening shadow appeared on the roof next door as if he had sensed it beforehand.

The dark outline was soon followed by a man dressed in black, carrying a long rifle at his side. For a federal sniper, he'd been somewhat cavalier in reporting to his post on the rooftop across from the suspect building.

When he saw me, he swung the weapon up and pointed it from hip level but did not bring it to firing position. It was not in his pre-operations briefing to be wary of dangerous persons in the surrounding buildings, only possible civilians. I moved slowly, standing and raising my palms to him. Behind me, I heard the scrambling of little Yoda as he scurried off the makeshift bed. Then I heard the clunk of a heavy handle being turned and the slam of the metallic door of the utility shed. Without looking, I knew that my informant had fled.

Back across the rooftop, the sniper motioned me with the barrel of his rifle to move back to the rear of the building, and I did, slowly. When I looked down over the edge of the ladder I'd climbed, there were two other SWAT types waiting on the ground below. I hated tossing my P226 Navy all that way down into the dirt, but it was the best thing to do. Climbing down with my scrotum completely exposed gave me a dreadful feeling because I knew that I was going to get squeezed when I made it down.

By the time my feet touched the ground, Agent Howard, minus the tie and with the addition of a flak jacket, had joined the other two.

"Mr. Freeman," he said quietly, through gritted teeth. "I'm disappointed."

"Yeah, me, too."

He stared at me without blinking, a skill I've never mastered.

"They're already gone," I said, slightly nodding in the direction of the warehouse across the street.

"We'll make that determination," he whispered. And if a whisper could be a snarl, he had it down. He nodded to one of the agents. "Take him to the command post—in cuffs."

I already had my hands extended in front of me.

I kept my chin up: a lanky figure in boat shoes and canvas trousers, handcuffed, being led on either side by uniformed SWAT cops who gripped under my arms as though I couldn't stand. I maintained a look of certitude on my face as we made our way through the warehouse section and on to the main street entrance to the neighborhood. I said nothing in my defense or in explanation to my "captors," and they stayed silent as well.

From the length of their strides and swiftness of their cadence, I figured out that they wanted to follow their orders and dump me as soon as possible and get back to the action at the takedown scene. Guys who train for years to use their weapons don't want to miss the chance to squeeze the trigger in a real live-fire situation.

I recognized Gilda's Stop & Shop Café, the place where Yoda said one of the abductors bought cheeseburgers. It was now surrounded by dark vehicles of different makes and models that all screamed "government car pool." A phalanx of equally dark-suited men stood around talking in twos and threes. Some of them were questioning the men I'd seen working in a warehouse when I'd canvassed the block. When I caught one guy's eye, he immediately turned to the agent in front of him. Whatever he said turned the agent's eyes on me—suspect again.

Beyond the makeshift command center, I could see a line of Palm Beach County Sheriff's Office patrol cars and a couple of local black-and-whites. And then even farther down the road, I could make out the raised dish antenna of the news vans in a pool where the media had been ordered to encamp until further instruction. As we approached the nearest group, three agents, all whom I recognized from the tracing unit set up in Diane's office, moved out to greet us.

The middle one stepped up first.

"Agent Duncan," I said, nodding, unable to reach out a hand.

"Yes, and you would be the former law enforcement member who understands jurisdictional boundaries," he said dryly. "Mr., uh, Freeman? Correct?"

Just guessing at my name? They would have had a complete dossier on me within an hour of my leaving Diane's chambers after our first meeting.

"Max," I said.

"Yes, well, Mr. Freeman, I understand that you are the primary reason that we are here and that you have information that could be important in the investigation of Judge Manchester's abduction."

Not a question. I kept my mouth shut.

"Please, Agents," Duncan motioned to the SWAT boys. "Uncuff Mr. Freeman. He is not a physical danger or a flight risk."

The team retrieved their handcuffs and immediately broke for the hot zone down the street.

Duncan did not miss a beat. "And instead of giving us this information forthwith, Mr. Freeman, you obviously decided to take matters into your own hands and thus jeopardize a possible rescue of the judge."

I massaged my wrists, taking my time, still waiting for a question.

"You're correct about one thing, Agent," I finally said. "I am the primary reason you're here, the first break in your case so far. Unfortunately, even I was too late."

The words caught his attention, but his focus was broken by a glance at something behind me. I turned to see Billy approaching, already within hearing range.

"T-too l-late, M-max? Wh-what d-does th-that m-mean, exactly?"

His face, drawn and rumpled from sleeplessness, was still a mask of stoicism. Despite the circumstances, Billy was not one to panic or jump to conclusions.

"I'm pretty sure she was here, Billy. But the informant I found said they left this morning. And he's damned convincing, even if he is a bit of a whack job."

Again, Billy's face did not react, absorbing the information. "Alive, M-max? D-did your informant s-see her alive?"

"Yeah," I said, speculating about the woman, but still stating the truth as I knew it. "Alive, Billy."

I felt a touch on my forearm from behind me and turned.

"I believe, Mr. Freeman, that we're going to have to debrief you before you go any further," Duncan said.

"Agent, I suggest you get into that warehouse and scour for as many clues as you can, and also put out a new all-points on a silver Chrysler 300 with a temporary Florida plate number ACI 886," I said, now moving back down the street with Billy toward the warehouse. "Your boys must have figured out by now that the place is empty. As for the debriefing, you can listen as we go."

Behind us, I heard the crackle of a radio and Duncan speaking quietly enough that I couldn't make out the words. But when the other end answered, the volume was still up.

"Building secure, sir—no one home."

The surveillance had been stepped up. The visual probes that slipped through any crack and under any door or window they could find had come up with nada. Listening devices got silence. Finally, the front warehouse door had been breached with a pair of bolt cutters and a handheld door ram. When we got there, the wood around the frame was splintered and a forensics technician was already dusting the knob and lock plates for fingerprints.

While we walked, I told Billy and Duncan about the homeless guy on the roof of the warehouse across the street. Duncan dispatched a team.

Then I gave them Yoda's descriptions of the young man, the big Indian, and his entourage, and the mention of a woman with strawberry blonde hair in the backseat of the Chrysler.

"Dye job?" Duncan said, just as I had thought. I shrugged my shoulders.

Agents and crime scene technicians swarmed the downstairs office and open warehouse floor, and Billy and I stepped in just in time to hear a call from the second story.

"Up here," an agent called down to Duncan.

When Billy and I followed the agent-in-charge up the staircase, no one stopped us.

The room was about ten feet square and windowless, with a cot against one wall and a marine porta-potty in one corner. A single cane chair and a futon leaned against another wall. There were no bedclothes or towels, dishes or utensils, food wrappings or litter of any kind. It was as bare as possible. Billy stood in the middle of the space, closed his eyes, and breathed.

"Sh-she w-was h-here, M-max," he finally said. "In th-this r-room—I smell h-her p-perfume."

"Uh, Mr. Manchester," Duncan said. "Before we make any rash . . ."

"Sh-she w-was h-here, M-mr. D-duncan," Billy said, cutting him off.

"But perfume, sir," the agent tried again.

"Is unique t-to any w-woman wh-who w-wears it, Agent. And I

have l-lived cl-close enough t-to m-my w-wife t-to know exactly how it smells on her, and th-that s-scent is st-still in th-the air."

"Yes, sir, Mr. Manchester," Duncan pulled back. "We will have forensics go over the room for trace evidence, of course."

"You might put someone on the Dumpster outside as soon as possible also," I said, rescuing the agent a bit. "The informant said the younger suspect tossed out stuff several times while they were here. It might give you some usable DNA."

"I'm sure they're already on it," Duncan said, but spoke into his radio anyway.

I waited until Billy broke his concentration and told Duncan we were leaving. Perhaps it was because I was with the husband of the kidnapped judge that the agent did not object. I'd given him everything I knew, as I had always intended to do. But as before, I knew the clearances and protocols that the feds would have to follow in order to wrap this scene tight. Then again, I needed to move at a pace that kept me going forward, even at the risk of stumbling or of stepping on the out-of-bounds lines. Right now, there was no evidence that Diane was not alive, and that alone pushed me to keep moving.

"Boundaries, Mr. Freeman," Duncan called out as Billy and I made our way to the doorway.

"You'll know where I am, Agent," I said, making eye contact.

"Indeed we will, Mr. Freeman."

"Th-they've g-got a tr-tracking d-device on your c-car," Billy matter-of-factly stated as we walked away.

"Yeah, I know."

"Th-they d-dispatched a d-dozen m-men t-to th-the Arenas tr-tree pl-plantation w-with s-search w-warrants."

"They've got to cover their asses, but we don't. They'll never find anything there but an older brother trying to make up for letting his sibling take the fall for riches neither of them deserved."

Billy's Porsche was parked at the end of a line of federal Crown Vics, armored SUVs, and local squad cars. He'd come in with them after giving them the address. We were too far from the sequestered media to hear if they were calling out questions, but we both knew they were aware that he was here. Long-lens cameras would be aimed at anything that moved at the so-called command center, especially at anyone who looked like the aggrieved husband.

"Let's talk in your car," I said. "Then I gotta move."

Billy opened the Porsche with his remote, and I got in the passenger seat.

"You s-said Indian b-back th-there," Billy began, getting straight to it.

"That came from the informant, a bit of a nutcase," I said, "but too detailed for him to be making shit up."

"American Indian?"

"Yeah, as in Chief in *One Flew Over the Cuckoo's Nest.*"

Normally, Billy's eyebrows would raise in perplexity when I delivered such information in an investigation. This time, he simply listened.

"D-didn't know American Indians w-were involved with th-the C-colombian c-cartels th-these d-days," he finally said.

"Back in the 1980s, the Seminoles' reservation in the Glades was a favorite spot for dropping bales of marijuana and cocaine," I said. "But the description of this Indian didn't sound like a Seminole."

"S-seminoles and a variety of tr-tribes are d-doing a l-lot b-better in the f-field of l-legal g-gambling th-than drug importation," Billy said. And, of course, he was right. Though it still wasn't general knowledge among the public, there wasn't a poor Indian in Florida anymore.

The use of Indian land and the tribe's unique standing as a nation within a nation meant that they could open a full-out casino on reservation land without control or permission of the U.S. government. Savvy businessmen and marketing moguls from Las Vegas had brought their knowledge to the Indians—at a price, of course—and turned the old no-tax cigarette stands, cheap road-side trinket huts, and side-show gator wrestling tourist traps into a multibillion-dollar industry. Every tribal member benefited whether he or she worked or not. Each member of a legitimate Seminole family was by contract awarded part of the casino profit, nowadays equal to about sixty thousand dollars a year per person. A family of four had 240,000 dollars in guaranteed income, no questions asked.

But the businessmen behind that largess, the ones who ran the casinos, concert halls, restaurants, and other spin-offs, were profiting well beyond that. And although that much money and opportunity brings in the bright entrepreneurs, talented entertainers, merchants, and marketers who make the whole thing spin, it also attracts every moocher, shyster, hooker, dealer, and con man within range as well.

Drugs in that environment? No doubt. Drug people with ties to a Colombian cartel dealing on the reservation? Not beyond possibility. But the "Chief" described by my informant could also just be a hireling, no more and no less.

Billy looked up into his rearview mirror, in the direction of the massed media behind us, and then handed me a folded copy of the day's *Sun-Herald* newspaper:

> *Manhunt for Abducted Judge Expands*
> *By Staff Writer Nick Sortal*

> *In what has now become the largest manhunt in Florida and perhaps U.S. history, federal, state, and local law enforcement authorities have "pulled out all the stops" in the search for abducted Federal Judge Diane Manchester, who went missing Wednesday during a break in the extradition hearing of Colombian drug kingpin Juan Manuel Escalante in West Palm Beach.*

> *"We will scorch the earth in the search for Judge Manchester*

and the pursuit of any and all persons involved in her abduction," said Florida Attorney General Thomas Mann during a briefing yesterday on the case that has shocked and outraged the justice system and the general public across the nation.

"First and foremost, we are focusing on the safe return of Judge Manchester, and secondly on bringing those responsible to justice," Mann said.

"Law enforcement has pooled its resources and the level of cooperation among agencies is unprecedented."

Though acknowledging that no ransom demands have been received from those responsible, authorities have focused their investigation on the Colombian cocaine cartel known as Los Lobos, of which Escalante has been the titular head for nearly two decades. Escalante was lured to Florida last year in a federal sting operation and arrested in a high-profile raid at a Palm Beach mansion and charged with dozens of RICO Act violations. Known as the Racketeer Influenced and Corrupt Organizations Act of 1970 and originally meant to fight Mafia-like organized crime, the RICO Act was broadly defined and has recently been used to deter the reaches of organized drug dealers and all their affiliates in the United States.

Judge Manchester, though a relative newcomer to the federal bench, had extensive experience in drug-related criminal cases as a prosecutor for the Southern District of Florida for many years. Escalante's attorneys were fighting to have him returned to Colombia while federal prosecutors were fighting that extradition and demanding that he face the RICO charges here in the United States where, if found guilty, he could face more than fifty years in prison.

The extradition case was in its first week when Judge Manchester was abducted off the street in West Palm Beach only a few blocks from the federal courthouse during a lunch break.

Eyewitnesses told police that an unmarked white van screeched to a halt on SW 14th Street about 12:15 last Wednesday and an unknown number of assailants pulled the judge into the vehicle and sped away. Despite the fact that private building and traffic cameras caught part of the abduction on video, the license plates of the van were found to be stolen and the vehicle has yet to be recovered.

Adding to the concern over Manchester's abduction is the fact that the forty-three-year-old judge is eight months pregnant with her first child, according to family members.

"My daughter is a pregnant woman who was only performing her judiciary duties as an officer of the court. This is an assault not only on her but on the foundation of the justice system in these United States," said Manchester's father, Charles McIntyre, a retired Florida Supreme Court justice who pleaded for his daughter's release.

"She cannot change the laws of the United States and was only hearing the case as an arbitrator of law," McIntyre said. "To harm her will make no difference in the outcome of the Escalante case and the charges against him. Such an outrageous act guarantees nothing but additional criminal charges to be brought against those responsible."

Judge Manchester's husband, William T. Manchester, a lawyer and investment manager known for his exclusive clientele list and also his pro bono work with underprivileged and minority clients, could not be reached for comment. The interracial couple was married two years ago in a private ceremony, which was controversial in the realms of high society in exclusive Palm Beach. In interviews, friends of the couple who asked not to be identified said the judge was in the late third trimester of her first pregnancy.

"They are a beautiful couple and were extremely happy together

and thrilled over the pregnancy despite all the racial innuendo slung around by the backbiters in the old Palm Beach set," said one woman who claims to be a close friend and associate. "This just has to be devastating for Billy."

William "Billy" Manchester is a black lawyer from Philadelphia with only professional rather than generational entrée to Palm Beach society as an investment specialist, while the McIntyre family has familial ties to the community spanning several generations.

Sources in law enforcement say that the State Department has been working back channels with the Colombian government in an effort to find out if Escalante's myriad connections in that country can be persuaded to assist in gaining the release of the judge.

Though the abduction, and sometimes killing, of judges and journalists in Latin America is not uncommon, this is the first time that an American judge has been physically threatened in connection with the powerful drug cartels.

Law enforcement officials say they have scoured all ports of entry and egress in both South Florida and Colombia in the event that Judge Manchester's abductors try to smuggle her out of the country. The investigation continues to focus on the drug cartel connection.

Yet in a statement released yesterday through his lawyers, Escalante denied any knowledge of the abduction and asked any and all who were involved to free the judge.

"If anyone from my native country is involved in this, it is without my knowledge or permission. This will not help change the fact that the U.S. government is denying me the legal right of extradition back to my homeland. My people are not so stupid."

In the meantime, law enforcement continues to follow several leads in the abduction, said Attorney General Mann, who asked

*that anyone with information on the case call the federal hotline
listed below.*

I folded up the paper and put it on the floor. "Nothing new there,"
I said. Billy remained quiet and didn't move, even to start the car.

"D-diane's f-father is c-considering a r-reward f-for information."

"Bad move. Brings out the nuts and they'll be swamped with
bullshit sightings and useless leads."

"L-leads are hard t-to c-come b-by," Billy said, nodding his head
in the direction of the command center. "L-look how quick th-they
jumped on th-this one."

"I'm a little surprised myself, considering where it came from."

Billy didn't flinch at the self-deprecation.

"I'm c-concerned about th-the f-full f-focus b-being on the
c-cartel's involvement," he said. "Wh-what d-did you f-find with
the l-list? Anything?"

"Doubtful so far," I said, sparing Billy the details on the Arenas
brothers and what was left of Giovanni Maltese, hating to admit my
failure to come up with a single solid lead.

"Any luck on tracing the owners of the warehouse back there?"
I said instead.

I knew it would be one of the first things Billy did when I'd
given him the address. He'd get the landowner records and trace
them through the state files. The feds would probably get to it later.

"Sh-shell c-corporations. B-but I haven't g-given up on f-finding
the pr-principals' n-names."

"The witness on the roof said the Indian opened the front
door with a key. So it wasn't just someplace they broke into. They
had a plan."

Billy nodded.

"Could be an old drug stash house."

Billy nodded again. Something was germinating in his head, but he'd wait until he'd run it around a bit to share what he was thinking. Billy was not an admirer of brainstorming.

"D-despite my entreaties to every c-contact I have in S-south America, I c-can't f-find a s-single t-tie or s-substantiated rumor that Escalante's p-people are in this," he said again, without emotion or inflection of frustration or dissatisfaction; he was just stating fact.

"If he's p-pulling the st-strings, th-then he's d-doing s-so with only a small group of tr-trusted affiliates. And as you and I know, M-max, s-something th-this b-big is a very d-difficult th-thing to d-do without s-someone slipping up and t-talking, f-for pr-profit or advantage."

I knew the feds were offering every drug-indicted detainee they had in custody a deal of a lifetime for information. I knew that they were squeezing any and all suspects with anything short of waterboarding—and maybe even that—to get a line on Diane's whereabouts.

The conundrum, of course, was the fact that no demands—not ransom or pardon or waiver of extradition—had yet been asked for by those responsible. What do you give kidnappers if they don't ask for anything? How do you determine motive if no desires are aired?

Who took Diane, and why?

"All p-possibilities," Billy said. "Remember: F-follow the m-money?"

His comment made no sense on the face of it. Now it was my turn to raise my eyebrows. He didn't look up.

"Judge Krome, the one you m-met in the c-courthouse hallway. He's n-never sp-spoken to m-me b-before th-this. N-now he c-calls me every d-day, asking f-for updates. I d-did s-some research. He's hearing a c-casino c-case. It appears he has b-been d-denying wh-what w-would n-normally b-be observed as r-routine extensions t-to th-the pl-plaintiffs."

The answer didn't do a thing for my eyebrows.

"T-two d-days ago, it appears he w-was f-forced to g-give th-them another d-delay or r-risk ethics c-committee scrutiny."

"And there's money involved?" I said.

"M-millions. If a ruling is m-made b-before a st-stipulated d-deadline in th-the pl-plaintiffs' c-contract w-with Indian c-casino p-people, th-they w-won't have t-to p-pay up. If it's l-later, th-the b-bill is due."

"And who's paying attention to this now?" I asked, not sure that Billy should be, but his mind works on more levels than mine.

"Only m-me. I ch-checked every b-big-m-money tr-trial going on in th-the c-courthouse."

"OK. And how does this tie in with Diane?"

"I frankly d-don't know, M-max. I'm drawing wh-whatever th-threads I can."

"We need a break," I muttered, hating to fall back on that old saw.

"Th-that's th-the r-response from the authorities, and th-their st-stated answer t-to th-the question of wh-what t-to d-do n-now. W-wait f-for a br-break in the c-case, th-they s-say."

Or for bodies, I thought, keeping that image to myself. I'd been there too often, starting investigations only after bodies had turned up.

"But I can't wait," I said, to myself as much as to Billy.

"N-neither c-can w-we. And p-perhaps w-with th-the Indian, you have g-given m-me another thread to w-work w-with. I'll g-get t-to it."

He was dismissing me and I got out of the car.

"R-remember th-the tr-tracking device, M-max."

"Don't care," I said—and I didn't. If they knew where I was and where I was going, maybe I'd have backup when I blew up somebody's shit. And that's exactly what I intended to do.

CHAPTER 23

Maybe it was the release of her hands—the fact that she could again cup her belly in her palms and massage her own skin, coo to her child while warming it with her own touch. Even if it was irrational, she wanted her baby to know she was there, watching, protecting. In a dream state, she thought back to the early months, to the elation she'd felt when she told Billy she was pregnant.

It wasn't as if it was unplanned. They'd talked about the risks involved in a pregnancy at her age, the changes in their lives, the challenges. But the thought of a baby, a child created by the two of them, had given her a glow that even people in the courthouse noticed.

"Aren't we in a good mood today, Judge?"

"You are looking absolutely vibrant, Judge Manchester. What, you're ahead of your docket again this month?"

And then, of course, there was the downside as her body changed in those first weeks. Squirrels in her belly: tiny, bouncing, rambunctious squirrels mixing it up. The dreaming was real enough to take her back to those early mornings trying to do the everyday things to get ready for work, and suddenly being stopped by the squirrelly stomach. Even though she knew that right now she was in a half-dream, half-awake state in a prison room, the taste of bile rising in her throat became too real to ignore, and seized her.

If I puke in this hood, they'll still refuse to take it off, she thought. *They*

*won't care. They'll make me wear it. And what if I choke? What if I gag on
my own vomit and choke myself to death and take my own child with me?*

She began to panic. Then her stomach began a lurch, a dry heave.
She fought it. Then despite the voice in the back of her head that
demanded her to leave the hood untouched, she lost control and
began tearing at the cloth, pulling at the drawstring around her neck.
She didn't care what they might do and kept clawing at the fabric as
her stomach spun. She knew about people aspirating on their own
vomit. She was driven by the irrational fear that she would drown.

She fought until the hood actually came free. A breath of clear
air hit her face and cooled her cheeks and forehead and throat. It
brought an instant relief to the nausea, even if she was dreaming it.

But now she was not dreaming. The hood was in Diane's right hand.
She went still, waiting for the slap to the head. But no one hit her. No
one pushed her back on the mattress. No one grunted or yelled at her.

Still, the days of darkness had intimidated her. She kept her eyes
closed, afraid to open them, despite the lack of reprisal. Had she
been brainwashed so quickly? You will not see. We will not let you
see. And so you cannot.

Using her newly tuned senses, she listened for the sound of her
captor's breathing. Was he asleep? Had he slipped out while she was
dreaming? How could he even tell if she was asleep or not? He could
not see her eyes through the cloak.

Open your eyes, Diane, she ordered herself. Still she hesitated. A
minute? Fifteen? Finally, she willed them open, forcing her lashes,
stuck by crusted, dried tears, to flutter. When she opened her eyes
wide again, there was no reaction from her guard. Without moving, she looked around in darkness. But her pupils had been in
darkness for days, and now they seemed to seek out the light, any
light. Across the room, the bottom edge of a door offered the single
source of a light that gave dimension and reality to her prison.

It was a single room, maybe ten feet wide. She turned and

scanned the walls for windows: none. The cot she sat upon was bigger than she had imagined. The portable toilet was in the far corner, seven steps away. Against the wall opposite her was one straight-backed chair. Something was on the floor next to it—a comforter, no, a long pad like a futon. Had her captor been sleeping right next to her all this time? Watching every movement?

Next to the pad was a white sack of some sort, a group of standing bottles, and a clock, the old-fashioned kind with the green glowing numbers. She tried to focus on the clock as if knowing the time were of utmost importance. She moved to the edge of the cot to get a closer look and was about to stand when the familiar sound of creaking floorboards just outside the door froze her in place.

Two thoughts: pull the hood back on and pretend it had never been off, that nothing had changed—or fight like hell.

When the doorknob's mechanical grind turned, her limbic system overruled. She stood and flexed her knees, and in that moment of expectation the first words she'd heard in what seemed like weeks came to her ears in a low, male, deep-chested voice: "Get her ready. We are going."

Going? Going? Going where? The words confused her.

The explosion of light that came in with the opening door stung her eyes in the way a flare must do to soldiers wearing night-vision goggles. Blinded, she rushed forward, launching herself as best she could into the door panel and feeling it give under her weight and momentum. It was less an attack than a stumble, but she heard a high-pitched yelp and a definite clomping of unsteady footfalls.

Just as she tried to gather herself for another lunge, a much greater opposite force hit the door from the other side and sent her sprawling across the room. She went down onto the iron frame of the cot, the edge catching her on a hip bone. Her cry of pain ripped the air. She looked up at the open door and got one glimpse of the backlit figure of an enormous man, taller and seemingly wider than the doorway itself. No face, but a scarf or maybe even a swath of long hair swung with his movement as he stepped into the room and backhanded her into blackness.

Consciousness—no, a true focus—crept back with the mixed odor of gasoline fumes and new car carpet. Diane had not gone completely out with the blow delivered by the big man. But the swirling movements, being dragged up by the armpits and then pushed and pulled in directions unknown, were all a blur. She recalled the stumbling, the jostling, and then a panicking feeling that they were throwing her over a rooftop to her death. But she never landed.

Then there were noises: a car engine, metal latches slamming together, the distant blaring of a horn, a siren—was it coming for her? An ambulance? A police car? Then came the movement, the pitching and a lurching stop before a feeling of momentum and speed.

Only now, with the odors around her and the realization that the hood had again been draped over her head and her hands retied, this time in front of her, did she make a cognizant assessment: they'd tossed a pregnant woman into the trunk of a car and now they were on the road.

There was no telling the amount of time they'd been moving or in what direction. Diane's senses had been so scrambled from the visions and the blow to the head that she was utterly lost. She moved her limbs as best she could to judge if anything was broken. She felt with her feet and hands the dimensions of the space around her and listened. Would you hear someone talking through the backseat of a car if you were in the trunk? Would you know if you were in the city or on the interstate, near the beach or inland? She didn't know. And soon she didn't care.

There was a constant high-speed hum of tires on a relatively flat roadway, and the odor of new car along with a tinge of exhaust. She encircled her stomach with her forearms and bound wrists and on the backs of her hands she felt a familiar texture. Someone had brought the blanket from the tiny cot and covered her. To keep her warm? Or keep her covered from prying eyes? She felt around more with her hands, let her fingers probe until she found a plastic bottle. She pulled at it and felt the shape.

She knew it could be anything; still she brought it to her mouth, and using her teeth, twisted the top until it was open enough to leak. Then she tasted the first few drops of bottled water with her tongue. Was her guard being kind to her? Did he feel bad after smashing her unconscious? She drank some more. What had her doctor said about hydration? Did her captors know this? Did they actually care about her health? If they were holding her for ransom, wouldn't they have to keep her alive, at least until they got their money?

Shit, Diane, they're holding you in the trunk of a car doing 100 mph down the highway. They punched you in the head and dragged you down a flight of stairs and tossed you into a trunk like a sack of trash. You're nothing to them but a means to some end, whatever the hell that might be.

"Get her ready. We are going," the voice had said. Was it the voice of the big man, the one she saw in the backlit doorway? She concentrated now on the words. She was good at accents. She'd lived in multicultural South Florida all her life. She knew the difference between a Florida backwoods cracker drawl and a southern Georgia inflection. She knew a Cuban aristocratic Spanish from a Castilian cadence and could distinguish a classic New York accent from a nasal, higher-pitched Brooklynese.

Those six words had been none of those. They had a straighter, clipped feeling of Midwest America, but with an indecipherable spin. What they absolutely were not was Latin American, Colombian.

If Escalante was behind all this, these were hirelings, not men from his own country, which made less sense to her. Such a man and his cartel minions didn't kidnap a federal judge and send anyone but their most trusted soldiers to carry it out.

So who are these people? What do they want and when are they just going to kill me and my unborn child?

CHAPTER 24

Fucking Geronimo. Fucker walks right up behind when I'm about to go back in that goddamn room and says, "Get her ready. We are going."

Rae was still trying to figure out what the hell that meant when she opened the door and, boom, all hell broke loose. All the sudden, she was on her ass on the catwalk and well that bitch got hers when old Geronimo put all 260 pounds to the door after it knocked her back. Then he stepped in and put her down with that fucking backhand of his.

"Get her ready." Yeah, right. The first thing Rae had to do was get a new pair of flex-cuffs on her. Hell, she didn't know if Geronimo even noticed that the woman wasn't cuffed. Fucking bitch! You give someone an inch and they take a fucking mile. She didn't know where she'd learned that old saying, probably from her mom, but ain't it the truth.

Rae had cut the woman's hands loose "so I can touch my baby, please," and what does she do? Knocks my ass over and tries to run. So then while Miss Priss was out like a light on the mattress, Rae got a new pair of flex-cuffs on her and got everything in the room rolled up and out of there so Danny could take it all out to the Dumpster. Man . . . when she saw his face, he couldn't even look her in the eye. Hey, a couple of days of babysitting and, wow, big money Florida vacation whoopee! My ass.

But the no-talking rule was still in effect so all she could do was give him her look, and even if he didn't turn to see it, she knew he could feel her eyes on the side of his face 'cause his skin was turning red right there on his neck and cheeks like it always did when he knew she was pissed at him. What the fuck did you get us into now, Danny?

Well, she kinda knew the answer to that one now, didn't she? Hell, she'd been texting Kelsey since like day fucking one and her girlfriend had been getting all the news back to her.

having fun in the sun yet?

no.

sup?

no gd fun. lotta shit.

huh?

d n another of his big ids

u in trouble?

not yet. but coming.

u not into illegal again.

yep. but this 1s big.

Rae had been trying to keep the messaging to a minimum, afraid fucking Geronimo or one of his braves were gonna catch her, but shit, this last couple of days things were getting out of hand. She'd slip out of the room when the pregnant princess was asleep, but the Indians had a hawk eye on Danny and her. All they could do was whisper and, of course, he was giving her the "everything's gonna be all right" line from that old-timey Loggins and Messina song that he said he loved because it had his name on it.

He's so full of shit. He played that song from his iPod the first time he'd taken her down to Crystal Lake and they were making out in some car he said he didn't steal from the country club lot but then admitted later that he did and had to get it back before Sunday checkout. Back then it was kinda romantic, "Danny's Song," and all. But every time they got into some sketchy situation he'd come up with that "everything's gonna be all right" again and it was getting real old.

how big?

big.

how illegal?

damn illegal.

Rae knew Kelsey was worried about her. They'd been friends forever and she was the only one Rae could really talk to about her mother and how pissed Rae was that she'd died and left her all the fuck alone. Kelsey even said that if Rae wanted, she'd tell her own mom and they'd like adopt her, make her one of the Preece family. But that was all fantasy and Rae had said, "No way." She could take care of herself and did.

Even when the worker from child welfare services showed up, she'd been able to shine them on and get them off her back and say she was with relatives. It was bullshit and her so-called aunt had just backed her story but let her stay in the trailer by herself—and why not? Rae was a hell of a lot smarter than any of her so-called family and got that job at the country club—like they needed another mouth to feed anyway. Kelsey was always there and she kept Rae's secrets and they kept their friendship. But Kelsey also had a sense when Rae was in trouble and knew this time she was in deeper than usual.

big illegal trouble in FL?

d's shit again.

it's not about a preggo judge got snatched down there?

says who?

all over the tv rae plz don't say it's that.

ok. no say.

Fuck! So the bitch had been telling the truth about being a federal judge. Independent corroboration, right? She'd heard that one a few times on those law-and-order shows and now her best and only true friend was giving it to her. If it had hit the news stations up in Michigan, then it was big stuff. Then this morning, she'd heard that overhead garage door open for the first time since they'd brought the woman in. Rae got up from her bedroll on the floor and carefully cracked the door to peek out.

A silver Chrysler 300 was pulling in and she watched as it stopped and Danny got out of the driver's seat. Shit. What? He'd gone out and stolen another car? Since it looked brand-new, Rae wondered if he'd taken it right off the car lot like he'd done that time in Traverse City. That time, she'd caught him staring at a Cadillac Escalade the dealership was pimping by putting it up on a ramp out by the roadside. Thing was six feet above all the other cars on the lot like a trophy, and Danny would just stare at it when they passed by on their way to the country club. She knew, just knew like radar, that he was challenged by the damn thing and was trying to figure out how to steal it.

Sure enough, maybe three weeks later, she gets off work and Danny calls her cell and says, "Meet me out back by employee parking." When she gets out there, he's sitting in the driver's seat of that big black Escalade. They spent the night smoking reefer in the thing down by the point and making love in the back with the tailgate open to the lake. The next day, he ditched it, taking only the mag wheels, which he said he could sell in a heartbeat.

So she had no doubt about the Chrysler 300 down there even though Danny didn't say a word when she slipped out of the room and went down to find out what the hell was up.

It was then that fucking Geronimo cut her away from Danny and without a word ushered her back up the stairs like some cattle dog cutting her out of the herd. He said, "Get her ready," and the shit hit the fan.

Hell, Rae couldn't even take her vacation clothes with her. But carefully, she put her cell down the front of her panties and just slightly up inside her so those morons couldn't tell and wouldn't dare search her there. Then they'd all piled into the Chrysler 300 after Geronimo had physically picked up the woman, carried her down the steps, and stuffed her into the trunk.

Now, Danny was driving with Geronimo in the front telling him where to go and Rae was in the backseat with the fucking braves. She'd made damn sure she was next to the window so she didn't have to squeeze between the two Indians like a white meat sandwich. Off they went.

They hit the interstate in twenty or thirty minutes, Danny driving the speed limit and using his turn signals to merge and the whole nine yards. Then they were on this wide, multiple-lane road for what seemed like hours. Rae stared out the window and couldn't even tell which direction they were going. Then there was a long, clean stretch of nothing—and she meant nothing.

They were on an interstate called I-75 and on either side was nothing but open land that looked like wheat fields stretching out to the horizon. She let herself relax but kept thinking about the text to Kelsey and her phone and whether she'd remembered to put it on vibrate. Then she giggled, considering where it was tucked. When Rae looked over from the window, she could see Danny staring at her through the rearview mirror.

"Something funny, Little Squaw?" Geronimo said the first words out of his mouth to her since he'd told her they were leaving.

"There's not a goddamn thing funny about this whole shitstorm, asshole," she'd let loose, surprising even herself, and adding, "now that the no-talking rule is obsolete."

"Obsolete? I like that," Geronimo said to Danny more than her. "That's one smart-mouth woman you got there, bro."

Danny said nothing but readjusted the mirror so he didn't have to look at Rae.

"Yeah, well, bro," Rae said to Geronimo, in for a dime now, in for a dollar. "You're the one who broke the no-talking rule."

"Don't matter now," the Indian said.

Rae felt the man next to her move, almost involuntarily, just a flinch of nervousness.

"And why not?" she asked.

Geronimo only shrugged his thick shoulders. Rae felt something flicker in the back of her head and actually felt the prickling sensation on her neck and she knew that feeling, rare as it was. She'd felt it that day in the car on the railroad tracks. She'd felt it a couple of times when one of her mother's boyfriends came stumbling into the trailer, searching for something, probably sex, when Rae was there alone and had to skinny herself under her bed and practically stop breathing until the fucker gave up and left. And now she was feeling it again and recognized it as fear.

She and Danny were way the fuck out of their league this time. It wasn't some one-day quick-hit deal and everything's gonna be all right this time, because now they were involved in the kidnapping of a federal judge. And when it finally was all over, was Geronimo really going to *just let them walk? Give them the money and let them go on their happy Florida vacation, knowing they could identify him and his little band of Chippewa brothers?*

Shit, she thought as she stared out the window at a thousand acres of Everglades swampland. No different than going out to the Sand Lakes Quiet Area down by Kalkaska, she thought—pure untouched nature. You get a few hundred feet off the trail in that oak and pine forest and nobody's ever going to find your body. Same here, she thought, looking out at honey-colored saw grass that ran all the way to the horizon.

She squirmed a little in her seat and felt the cell phone tucked up half inside her and thought of her friend Kelsey. At least she'd know where to dig for their bones.

CHAPTER 25

I was already in a back booth at Lester's Diner, working on one of their famous fourteen-ounce ceramic cups of coffee, when Sherry walked in. She was wearing her business suit, slacks that covered her prosthesis, and a jacket that covered the 9-mm Glock she carried in a belt holster on her side. Despite everything going on, my first thought was, *Damn, she's pretty,* and I told her so when she slipped into the bench across from me.

"Am I?" she said. She has a habit of answering every compliment with that question.

"You're very beautiful today."

"Am I?"

"You handled that perfectly."

"Did I?"

"You're the smartest woman I know."

"Am I?"

You get the drill. After our first few months together, so did I.

And today she was the prettiest person in the restaurant. Why I needed to tell her that while my head was spinning with questions about Diane and what the hell to try next was beyond my comprehension.

"You look terrible," Sherry finally said, bringing me back to Earth.

"Thanks."

She shrugged, but extended her hand across the table and laid it on top of mine.

Lester's is an authentic 1950s-style diner with an aluminum rail-car look on the outside, and service at the counter on a swivel stool or at vinyl-cushioned booths running down the inside wall. Since the Broward Sheriff's Office was once housed in a nearby warehouse, the place became a favorite hangout for cops. Sherry liked it for nostalgia's sake. I liked the coffee.

One of the gray-haired, sixtyish-looking waitresses in a white, knee-length uniform with a yellow apron and a pencil stuck behind one ear came over to take our order. I succumbed to the ranch breakfast special while Sherry ordered only tea.

"Max, it's ten at night," Sherry observed after the waitress said, "Comin' up, hon," cracking her gum.

"Hey, a man's gotta eat," I said, not remembering when I had last done so.

I was now holding Sherry's hand in mine. We stared at each other in silence for a moment.

"Word at the office is that the feds are reviewing tapes of any traffic cameras that might have caught the Chrysler leaving the warehouse district and then using that as a point of reference in an expanding circle," she said. "When they get a second sighting, they can use that as direction and try to narrow the search."

I nodded.

"But it takes a lot of time and eyes-on," she continued. "Even with unlimited manpower, it could still take hours, maybe days."

I nodded again. She was preaching to the choir. She knew that I knew all of these tactics and the length of time a search could take.

"If they were smart, they wouldn't have had to run," I said, just voicing to Sherry what I'd been thinking since leaving Billy and asking her to meet me. Billy was not a brainstormer, but I was, especially with Sherry, who knew the lay of the land and had the experience to respond in kind.

"They could have stayed tight in a local safe house and waited. Hell, they were safe where they were. I was just lucky getting a tip that paid off.

"Maybe I flushed them," I said, putting it out there. "Maybe one of the informants let it loose, somehow."

Sherry reached across the table and took my hand away from my neck. Without realizing it, I'd left her hand lying there on the table. Mine had gone to the scar left by the bullet wound from Philly, my fingers rubbing the slick soft skin where the hole had been. It was an old habit, a tic brought on by stress and anxiety. I couldn't remember the last time I'd caught myself doing it.

"Max, they've got to know that the heat is never going to come off this," Sherry said. "Everyone will make this their top priority for as long as it takes." She took both of my hands and cupped them in hers, our elbows making a tepee over the table.

"You don't mess with a judge, a federal judge, in this country. Just like the state attorney said, we're scorching the earth on this."

"Don't know. Maybe it was taking longer than they'd thought," I said, still speculating on the kidnappers' reason for moving. "Maybe their plan was falling apart."

"If they've got a plan," Sherry said. "Far as I've heard, there's still no ransom demand."

"What else have you heard?"

When the waitress arrived, we sat back and cleared a space for my late-night breakfast. My appetite surprised me, and I went through the eggs and hash browns while Sherry went through a list.

The feds had sent everything they got from the warehouse to the FBI lab in Miami. They'd already found a fingerprint on the portable toilet left in the room where Billy had smelled Diane's perfume. If it was hers, good, I thought. If she was still cognizant enough to try leaving those kinds of bread crumbs, maybe they hadn't hurt her. The feds would run every hair follicle and sweat stain and tossed-away napkin from the Dumpster for saliva and try to make DNA matches. Sherry said they'd already tracked the pickup route for the company that serviced the trash and would start raking through the contents present and past.

"No blood samples," Sherry said.

I looked up from my last piece of toast with a quizzical look.

"They found sheets and towels and some discarded clothing in the Dumpster, none with blood stains."

I knew she was trying to give me good news—something to hold on to. And she was right. The lack of any kind of blood was always a good sign.

"You need to rest, Max," she finally said, and looked over her shoulder to alert the waitress. "You've got nothing to run on now. Let's go home."

I looked in her eyes and despite my anxiety, the days of no sleep, and the frustration, I went for selfishness and, yes, neediness. We paid the bill, tipping heavily, and went home.

Afterward, we lay in Sherry's bed with the overhead fan cooling the sweat on our bodies and the aqua light from her backyard pool seeping in through the window and painting the ceiling. Even though her skin was still hot from our lovemaking, she laid her head on my chest because she knew I liked it. I stroked her hair and stared up into the rippling blue light above us.

"Thank you," I said finally.

"For loving you?"

"For trying to relax me, take my head out of the game for a while."

"That's not why."

"Why then?"

"I was horny."

"Liar."

"Yes, but still—did it work?"

"It always works. But the sun still comes up tomorrow."

"And do we know what it might shine on when it does?"

"We are, as they say, waiting for a break in the case."

"Didn't you already create one break?"

"Yes, but the jury is still out on whether it helped or hurt."

"Juries get to judge after the fact."

"True."

We were silent again. Maybe we even dozed a bit, or slept.

My phone buzzed at 6:10 a.m. It was mine, not one of the burners. I rolled over and answered.

"Max, they picked up the Chrysler on a photograph from the tollbooth camera on Alligator Alley going west."

I am a light sleeper, even when I'm exhausted. It's an old cop thing. I deciphered the information coming from Billy with barely a blip in concentration.

Alligator Alley is the old name of what is now I-75, which takes you westbound across the state from Fort Lauderdale to just shy of Naples. It was built by a construction company in the late 1960s as a fast two-lane road from west to east coasts. When I-75, which goes all the way to Michigan from Florida, started using it as its main extension from Tampa to Miami, the name was officially changed. It was widened in recent times and the lanes separated because of increased traffic and the fact that when it was a narrow two-lane, head-on wrecks in the dead of night were of epic proportions.

There were two other things I knew about it. One, the far west toll plaza was dedicated to the memory of Edward J. Beck, a toll taker who was murdered on the job in 1974. Two, midway across are entrances to the Seminole's Big Cypress and the Miccosukee Indian Reservations. Together those Indian-held lands cover more than two hundred square miles of the Everglades.

"Did they catch it coming out at the Beck Plaza?" I asked Billy.

"No. No sign after that. But they could have gone north or south on State Road 29."

"Right," I said. Neither of us had to say it—Indians. Why the hell were Indians coming into all of this?

"You have some contacts out there, right, Max?"

"Yeah, in the Glades—one of the best. But inside the tribe is a lot tougher. You've got the big business casino boys pulling their 'privacy of a business entity' line and on the Indian side they stay behind their 'we're a nation of our very own' cloak. It'll be tough to crack in terms of search warrants or information coming out if tribal members are involved."

"I've got a legal connection," Billy said. "I helped with a case a few years ago when one of the tribe's big names got arrested for killing a Florida panther, a designated threatened species."

"They said it was a tribal custom," I said, remembering.

"They came to a mutual agreement," Billy said.

"Let's hope they're as cooperative this time."

"I'm also working another angle."

I waited.

"I'll get back to you, Max. I know you'll do what you do."

"Count on it," I said, and pressed the disconnect button.

CHAPTER 26

Braxton Hicks! Braxton Hicks! Oh God, please. Not real contractions. Braxton Hicks! I am not going into labor in the trunk of a damn car!

They were still driving, moving fast, but on a flat, straight trajectory that she figured had to be the interstate. But which one? I-95 north or south, or I-75 west?

And then came the contractions. No, no, no, she felt the squeeze in her uterus, muscles cinching up. She let go a gasp that only she could hear. She gritted her teeth as the pain increased and tried not to cry. A minute felt like ten; and then the muscles let go.

Diane tried to control her breathing, deep, regular breath, through the mouth, in and out, in and out. The air was terrible. The hood had been over her head for how long now? The smell of her own bad breath, the stink of moisture on the cloth pressed to her face. And she was in a damn trunk!

Breathe, Diane, in and out.

In her head, she tried to replay a scene from the childbirth classes she and Billy had taken at Healthy Mothers, Healthy Babies: Billy sitting so uncharacteristically on the floor of the classroom with her, still dressed in his Brioni suit, but sitting there nonetheless, encouraging the rhythmic breathing, reading the second-hand sweep of his watch with her, timing her. He was supposed to be counting out loud to her now. She was supposed to relax in between contractions. He was supposed to be holding her hand, letting her know she was not in this alone, that they were a couple, that this was miracle made for two.

Damn it, Billy, where are you now? Why hadn't someone come to rescue her? Why was she going through this by herself?

Diane knew her anger was misplaced, but there it was. Why her? What had she done to deserve this? And what if something happens to this baby? The marriage, the pregnancy, and the child she'd almost given up thinking she'd ever have before she met Billy?

Damn! There it came again, the squeeze starting at the top of her uterus and spreading down. She started breathing faster, faster, too fast.

Calm yourself, girl. Come on. Thirty seconds. Damn. Maybe a full minute—then the muscles relaxed.

Not drinking enough water can cause Braxton Hicks contractions; that's what the doctor had said. She reached again for the water bottle and drank. When she rolled herself as best she could to change position, Diane felt the fetus inside slide with her.

She was momentarily comfortable, or as comfortable as a pregnant woman could be in the trunk of a car, when she felt and heard the slowing, the deceleration, and finally the stop. They made a turn and then sped up again, but not as fast. A while longer and then another turn, and another, this time onto a rougher surface. They jounced along on a road that somehow felt soft, yet each lurch caused her body to move and push into the close space. When they finally came to a full stop, Diane heard the doors, four of them, open and close. Again, there were no voices. Not a word.

She sensed a change in the light despite her veiled eyes, and then the creak of metal hinges. A change in the air meant they'd opened the trunk. She felt coolness on her legs and arms. Someone reached in and scooped her up in his arms as if she were a child, and helped her, really helped her, get up and out, in distinct contrast to the way she'd been tossed in. She felt her bare feet touch something moist and stringy, which she recognized as some kind of grass. Two people again guided her with hands under her armpits, her belly hanging, unguarded.

She could feel a breeze and, despite the hood, she could smell something musty, like soil or plants. After several steps, she heard the slosh of water and then stepped into something wet. She recoiled at the feeling at first, but was prodded by her captors, who splashed their way forward. The ocean? No, there was no salt in the air. A lake?

She was calf-deep now, with soft muck between her toes. A hand grabbed her behind one knee and lifted her leg and planted her right foot onto something solid. She was urged to step up. When she put her weight on the object she could feel the stair or platform give a few inches—something unstable, something floating. With some uncomfortable pushing and twisting she felt herself finally placed into a hard seat.

When she leaned back carefully, she found herself in some kind of chair, and the hands holding her let go. There was clomping and bumping and again the feeling of instability as weight shifted, and whatever she was on rose and fell. All the sensations were causing her head to spin.

Then all of a sudden, she heard the grinding sound of a motor starting. When it finally caught, her ears were assaulted by perhaps the loudest eruption of noise she'd ever heard. In a panic, she reached up with her bound hands and began wrenching the hood from her head, but was immediately stopped by one of her guards, who grabbed her by the wrists and yanked her hands back down into her lap.

The noise continued to grow, burring with a physical force against her eardrums and vibrating through her body until she felt a rolling, wobbling movement. The engine noise increased and the movement continued forward. She could feel the wind increase with the sensation of speed; gathering her wits, she realized she was on an airboat. They were in the Everglades, she thought. Part of her deflated. She'd actually prosecuted two homicide cases in which bodies were dumped in the Everglades, one in which human remains had been found partially digested in the stomach of an alligator. Florida was full of conjecture that dozens of bodies of missing persons had been dumped in the Glades, where the chances of discovery were next to nil.

But as the boat increased its speed and the wind pressed the hood against her face and forced her to dip her chin so she could breathe, she had another thought: that her captors had made a big mistake coming to the Everglades, a place Max Freeman knew better than any investigator she'd ever been associated with.

She hadn't thought of Max during this entire ordeal. Billy would have called him, brought him on board immediately. Max was his man in the most dangerous cases Billy had gotten involved with, and Max was absolutely relentless when Billy put him onto something. She knew that Max had killed a man who was kidnapping children from the west Broward suburbs and letting them die in the Glades. She knew he'd worked a case for Billy that involved a serial killer in Fort Lauderdale that came to an end with the shooting of that man. She knew that he'd saved his girlfriend, Sherry, by taking on a gang of Glades fish camp looters and an oil company henchman.

You've screwed up, she thought of her captors, *stepping into Max Freeman's world. He will track you and find you and if history repeats itself, he will hurt you.*

CHAPTER 27

Rae was enthralled to the point of near-stupidity. What the hell are we doing? Where the hell are we going, in this wide-open and somehow gorgeous landscape with towering clouds like big sailing ships moving across the sky? It was fabulous. But if she could have somehow given the high sign to Danny, she thought the best plan would have been to jump out of the car and just run for it.

After what seemed like three hours on the freeway, they'd pulled off on some goddamn side exit. Geronimo had to get out and unlock a big swinging metal gate to drive through onto a thin macadam road. That, she thought now, would have been the spot to bail out on this fucked-up adventure.

Instead, they continued on, Danny driving the big car too fast on this back road with nothing on either side but this goddamn wheat field, which she could now see closer up was not wheat at all, but some kind of monster swamp grass. From down here instead of up on the elevated freeway, she could see the grass blades growing up out of standing water with only an occasional glob of some sort of tree mass that had sprouted up where they'd piled up the land to build the roadway. Sky and blade grass—that's all she could see for miles.

Where the hell are we going?

Finally, Geronimo, who kept checking his phone, which she figured must have a GPS app, told Danny to turn off. They followed a gravel trail down to a piece of land next to open water.

When they stopped and everyone got out, Rae was struck by the humidity that instantly wrapped around her like an invisible cloud. The AC in the Chrysler 300 must have been running full blast because the heat outside was choking.

There was nothing here, no structure, no person, just this weird-looking boatlike machine sitting halfway up on the shore and half-floating in the water. She watched as Geronimo went around to the back of the car and popped the trunk. He bent his huge back over and scooped the woman out, setting her carefully on her feet, and actually giving her time to get her balance.

Normally, Rae would have thought that the big asshole was being nice for once, but when he had bent to reach into the trunk, his shirttail had pulled up and Rae saw the ivory-colored handle of a knife sticking up out of his waistband.

Everyone had heard the stories of Geronimo's fucking monster bowie knife, the one some kids said they'd seen him throw and bury to the hilt in a fence post thirty feet away. The one they also said he used to carve up the bodies of missing persons from the casino before spreading them like droppings in the woods.

This was never supposed to be about knives! Goddamn Danny! This was never supposed to be about killing!

Rae turned her head and looked back up the road: Could she make a break for it? Could she run and make it back to the interstate? Get the hell out of this? Then she turned back to look for Danny. He'd already drifted over to the weird boat with the big-ass caged propeller on the back and was staring at it, fascinated by the mechanics. . . .

She'd be on her own if she ran now—be on her own like she'd been for so many years. Her mom used to say everybody's gotta have somebody whenever Rae had complained about the men who came and went from the house trailer. "Everybody needs somebody, Rae-Jay. That's the way it is."

And I got Danny, she thought, and started toward him as the Indian boys took the woman by the arms and led her to the water.

*   *   *

Now this was scary as shit. Yeah, she knew it was dangerous-fast, in fact much faster than she could have anticipated. It felt even faster because of the closeness of the water and the high grass. It was like nothing she'd ever experienced before and maybe that was the reason it was scary— but man, it was cool.

They'd loaded onto the airboat, Rae and the woman on a couple of hard plastic seats, the two braves on the row behind, and Danny and Geronimo higher up in the pilot seats. Rae had looked back at Danny when Geronimo sat in the seat next to the driver controls and said, "You're the wheelman, white boy. Get to it."

Danny said, "No problem," and started fidgeting with controls and working the stick lever for throttle and adjusting the foils in back to direct the air flow to make the damn thing move. Rae knew he'd never been on such a contraption in his life, but had probably told them he had. She also had enough confidence in Danny to know that if it had a motor, he could drive it. Still, when he fired up the airplane engine on the back and throttled it up, the noise surprised the hell out of her. Rae could only imagine what the hooded figure beside her was thinking; she had to be freaking. But the woman just bent forward, cradling her stomach with her still-flex-cuffed hands, and rode it out.

As Danny put the boat up on plane, Rae watched a tunnel of high saw grass start to fly by and felt the wind sweep over her face as well as the heat and humidity that went with it. She'd gone on many a speed-boat ride with friends and with Danny on Fife Lake, and the feeling was similar: the swing and the roll of the boat in water, the patter of the rippled waves slapping the hull. But when they broke through to open space here, on Geronimo's instruction, Danny pushed the thing out onto water sprouting sprigs and then even thickets of grass. She looked over her shoulder at him again.

Danny just throttled forward and plowed right across what appeared to be solid ground like he was behind the wheel of some kind of hovercraft. He had that damn look in his eye that she knew was adrenaline and thrill, the look he got when he'd boosted a car and they were flying down U.S. Route 72 back home "just to see what she's got." Or when they were on someone else's lakefront cottage deck, screwing like minks out under the stars, not knowing if someone would roll up into the driveway and catch them in the act.

She couldn't help it. His thrill infected her—the speed and the danger of it all.

But still, in her head she kept seeing that knife in Geronimo's waistband. Guns didn't bother her. Every boy she'd grown up with in northern Michigan had guns. Their fathers and grandfathers were all hunters: rabbit all winter, whitetail deer in November, spring turkey shoots. The boys grew up with guns in racks at the end of their beds or in cabinets in the living room. It was a way of life.

She'd even seen an early boyfriend and his father shoot rabbits with handguns. But Geronimo didn't have a gun. He had a big-bladed knife that wasn't for skinning game or filleting fish. He had it for trouble, and it was spinning around in her head that she and Danny could just as easily become the trouble as anyone else.

CHAPTER 28

Diane kept her head down, the wind pasting the hood to her forehead but leaving a ruffling, loose area around her mouth so that she could breathe. The airboat swerved at times and at other times slowed and lurched as if the pilot was finding his way on paths through the water. Intermittently, she felt the nausea creep up her throat, but kept it down. Though the noise of the engine was deafening, she occasionally picked up a barked order in a man's voice. They were quick guttural words, perhaps one telling the other what turns to take, which way to go. At times, she tensed her thigh muscles, found purchase of something solid with her left foot, and prepared to simply launch herself out off the boat and into the water. If they were planning to just dump her out there where no one would find her body, at least she'd be taking some control.

No, no, no, Diane, she chastised herself. *This is not just you anymore. You have another life you are responsible for. It's not just your choice. You will endure this, dammit. You will endure it until you are without choice.*

As the boat roared on, she lost all sense of time and direction. She tried to feel the sun, but had no idea whether it was morning or afternoon and what part of the sky the sun might be in. After a time, they slowed, first to a slog and then to a crawl. She heard the scuffle of feet, people moving about on board. The boat shifted and slurred and then clunked up against something solid. The engine was killed.

"Throw me that line," a man said. It was the first discernible sentence she'd heard since "Get her ready. We are going." But was it the same voice? Through the buzz still in her head from the engine noise, she thought, no, this was a younger voice, different somehow. And if he was asking for a line, coupled with whatever the boat had thunked into, she was praying for a dock.

Again, she was gripped by hands under her armpits and lifted up. As she scrambled with searching feet to find something solid, she was rewarded with some kind of platform instead of merely being tossed into the swamp in the middle of nowhere to die. Why were they keeping her alive? What the hell did they want? Were they bargaining her life for another?

She'd given up thinking this was about Escalante. Had she made such a dire enemy in the past that this was the result? Was her abduction some sort of statement about the federal court system as a whole? There were sure as hell plenty of radical antigovernment groups in Florida, but what would they be bargaining for? And why her? Antifeminism? God only knew the minds of human beings.

On the now-solid platform, they walked her several steps, their footsteps ringing on wood, her bare feet touching something solid and warm. She was beyond counting. Her stomach dangled; her legs felt rubbery and unable to support her. To the sound of a door being unlocked and opened, she was led into someplace without the touch of the sun. Another room? A room out in the Glades?

Diane's mind was muddled; she was exhausted. The stress had taken its toll. She was weak and tired and when they turned her and forced her to sit, she felt softness. A couch or a bed cushioned her. She curled her arms and her legs up into a protective wrap around her baby and lost consciousness.

She awoke to sensations: a voice in her ear, a touch on her shoulder, light invading her eyes, and the smell of food in her nostrils.

The perceived brightness actually hurt her eyes. She slowly realized that the cloth hood against her face was gone. She had to work against the stickiness of crusted eyelashes and her own reluctance to open her eyes. It had been so long. Did she want to see? Where was she, and what had become of her?

She gave it a minute, blinked, and then allowed some light in as she tried to focus and then to register the face in front of her.

"Come on. You've got to eat," a male voice said. "Rae says you've got to eat something, so please, wake up and eat."

Diane moved her legs, rolled her hips, felt the pull of her stomach weight, and instinctively reached for her pregnant belly before she realized that her hands were free.

She forced her eyes wider, and they drank in the swirl of color and texture that became a man's face. He was young.

Diane began to identify the odors: cooked eggs, warm butter, and coffee. She looked from the young man's face to the plate sitting on the seat of a chair pulled up beside her.

"Water," she finally said, barely recognizing her own voice.

The young man held out a plastic bottle of water, and she struggled to take it in her hand and tip it to her lips. She sipped slowly at first, moistening the dried membranes of her palate and throat, and then drew in more until she started coughing.

"Easy," the young man said.

"Thank you," Diane said instinctively, only later wondering where the politeness came from.

The young man stood from his chair and pulled it away. Diane worked to absorb his image: tall, but not as big as the beast that had appeared in her cell door and bashed her in the head. Her first impression of him had been young, and now she guessed late teens, early twenties, with haystack-blond hair and a wispy, half-grown beard on a solid jaw. He was dressed in jeans and a plain gray T-shirt.

"Please eat," he said again, and then turned and walked across the room.

Despite the jumble in her brain, Diane called out: "Wait. Wait. Who are you? Where am I?"

Instead of answering, the young man stepped out and Diane distinctly heard the metal-on-metal of a lock being set.

Slowly, she worked her way up onto one elbow. Then she swung her legs over the edge of the bed, and with her arms as a prop, hoisted herself to a sitting position. She tried to gather her wits and make sense of her surroundings. She knew first of all that she was not in a hospital. She was in a medium-size room, maybe fifteen by twenty feet. The bed she was on was big, a double with sheets and a comforter.

There was a small couch on the opposite wall and two comfortable-looking chairs in colorful fabrics. An armoire stood tall in one corner and folding doors, probably a closet, covered another wall. A second door, not the one the young man had left by, was opposite. The walls were made of some kind of natural wood, maybe pine, and the floor was also wooden, but covered by a large multicolored throw rug that looked handwoven.

To her right was a waist-high counter and what appeared to be a small kitchenette. On the wall to her left was a window through which light made its way into the room. When had the hood been removed? Obviously while she was out cold—but why? When they had been so careful in the previous place, not letting her see, not letting her hear their voices or see faces? The thought ushered in a heavier sense of dread; she'd overseen enough criminal cases to know that eyewitnesses were loose ends. Professionals knew better than to leave them alive.

Even though bits and pieces of her trip on the airboat were coming back, she could not resist the window and the view it offered of her new surroundings. She inched forward on the edge of the bed, planting her feet firmly on the floor, cupping her freed hands under her belly, and trying to stand. She lifted some of her weight using only her thigh muscles, but failed.

She sat back down and looked at the food sitting on the cushion of the chair next to her: scrambled eggs with some kind of yellow cheese melted into them; toast with a slick of melted butter; a large cup of coffee, still steaming; and perhaps more telling, silverware. The surroundings and the meal said hotel, or resort. But where? In the Glades? She knew there were such places, but would kidnappers check into a resort?

Determined, she ignored the food and with effort turned the chair next to her, slopping the coffee. Using the chair as a crutch, she cupped her stomach with one hand and pulled herself to her feet. The effort dizzied her, so she stood and closed her eyes, waiting for the vertigo to pass. Finally, she gathered her strength and walked in small steps to the window.

The scene outside was a mélange of honeyed saw grass, blue and unruffled water, and sprouts of green in the distance; that was it, all the way to the horizon. Her perspective showed no buildings, no signs, no obvious other life. She held on to the window casing and tried to peek to either side, but could discern nothing more. If she was in a room within a large building, she could not tell. If this was it—a fifteen-by-twenty-foot rectangle in the middle of nowhere—she still couldn't tell.

Carefully, she made her way back to the bed and sat and ate. It was the first solid food she'd had in, what? How many days had this nightmare lasted? And the eggs were still warm. They had to have come from someplace. The coffee was almost hot, but the idea of caffeine made her slightly ill.

While she ate, she kept looking up at the second door, as if some other danger lurked behind it. What had the young man said? He'd said that Ray wanted her to eat, that Ray said she needed to eat. Which one was Ray? Was he the huge backlit man? Was Ray in charge?

Had it been Ray or the young blond man who'd watched over her in the upstairs room before they threw her in the trunk and drove out into the Everglades? And either way, why were he and Ray being civilized to her now? The questions made her dizzy again, and she pushed them away but could not stop looking at the unopened door.

Finally, she used the chair back to raise herself, steadied her feet, and made her way across the room, this time to door number two.

She stood against the frame and listened to the silence. She tried the knob and it turned free. She opened the door slowly, exposing darkness, but the light from behind her began to leak in, and she made out a sink and a vanity. She spotted a light switch, which she flipped, and a ceiling fluorescent lit up a tiled bathroom with a commode and a glass-door shower. If she'd seen a golden fairy rise up out of the swamp, she would not have been more stunned. She went to the sink and turned one of the faucet knobs, the hot one, and left her fingers dangling in the stream until the water turned warm.

"My God," she said aloud.

Within minutes, she had thrown off her clothes and was standing in the shower, warm water coursing over her head and across her shoulders and flowing down over the skin of her bulging belly. She did not know that such a simple thing could be such ecstasy. There was even soap. She leaned against one side of the shower stall and slicked all the skin she could reach without bending. She luxuriated in the warm water stream, washing and rinsing and washing and rinsing, until the water started turning cold. Then she lowered her head and looked down and for the first time saw the pinkish swirl of the water that circled the drain. She was looking at a rivulet of her own blood running down the inside of her thigh.

Then she gasped.

CHAPTER 29

*T*hey were lying on their backs, looking up at a dome of stars that seemed so close you wanted to reach out and poke one. A thick comforter softened the hardwood deck beneath them. Danny was still breathing hard from his exertion and orgasm, but Rae had already recovered. She always wondered why he was the one doing the heavy breathing when she had been on top and doing all the work.

Not that she thought of it as work. She loved making love with him. But she also had her motive. She knew it was selfish, but what the hell, what did one of her high school teachers call her? A great multitasker? Yeah, that was it, two birds with one stone.

She did like the view out here. It kinda grew on you. When they'd started out in the airboat, it had been, yes, exhilarating, the speed and the wind in her face and all the stuff just whizzing by. At one point, Danny leaned down from his driver's seat and aimed out in front with his finger, and when she followed his line, she saw something just sitting on the surface of the water. Just before they came too close, she recognized it as the floating snout of an alligator. She watched with surprise as it whipsawed its tail and dove down just before they came close to clobbering it with the hull of the boat.

It reminded her of shining deer on the roads back home, the animal frozen in the headlights, staring at you with those weird luminous eyes, but most times breaking for the woods when you swerved. But a fucking alligator! Jesus. She'd only seen them on TV when those hick swamp assholes hooked them with baited steel and then head-shot them with shotguns.

It wasn't the only thing that amazed her on this damn trip. After about an hour of buzzing over the watery landscape, Geronimo had extended his long arm and pointed out something in the distance. As they approached, she'd made out a man-made structure low on the horizon. As they came closer, it became a floating collection of buildings and then a raised camp with four distinct cabins all squatting on a flat deck on pilings. It was a little wooden island in the middle of nowhere.

Danny had eased back the throttle, and then took them in slow and docked the airboat against a slanted ramp. When he killed the engine, the sudden lack of both noise and vibration felt like a cone had been pressed over Rae's ears; the sensation kind of stunned her. It was like when you stopped your snowmobile in the middle of the snow-covered woods at night and let the quiet envelop you.

Danny jumped onto the dock and called for one of the lines and tied up the boat. The braves were careful taking the woman off. She'd seemed to have lost her ability to stand on her own, weak and slouched. Geronimo pointed to one of the smaller cabins, and the braves half-dragged her across the big deck and took her inside.

Geronimo had gotten out and stepped up onto the deck and then just stood there, imposingly tall and straight, looking out at the sky and curve of the planet like he was some damn Indian elder in those old anti-littering ads on TV. But Rae knew this Indian wasn't going to have any tears running down his face. She looked at the spot on his back where she'd seen the knife handle and her mind was working, working, working: How the hell would they get out of this goddamn mess?

Rae had watched the big Indian survey the place. After her hearing had recovered, she picked up on the sound of a humming engine in the direction of the smallest cabin at the far end of the deck. Geronimo strode to the opposite end, to the biggest cabin, and without hesitating—like he knew it would be unlocked—opened the door and disappeared inside. Either someone was already here, or they'd set it all up for them. They weren't just pulling up on some abandoned place hoping for the best. Rae went over to Danny and, since they were alone, let him have it.

"Did you know about Geronimo's fucking knife?" she hissed as he bent over a cooler someone had loaded onto the boat. She heard the slosh of water and ice as he hefted it up onto the deck.

Danny looked into her face and said, "What? What knife?" and Rae knew he wasn't lying or covering. Although she knew she really didn't have the ability to see the future, she sure as hell knew when a man was lying to her, and Rae knew Danny's every twitch and tell. He was honestly surprised.

"In the small of his back—that big-ass bowie he carries," she said. "I saw it when he bent over to lift Ms. Prego out of the trunk."

She waited for some kind of reaction from Danny, who slid the cooler onto the deck.

"I never saw it when we were at the warehouse."

"Well, maybe things have changed since we left the warehouse," Rae said, recognizing the questioning tenseness in her own voice. Again, she awaited a reaction. Danny held to character, not jumping to answer. . . .

"Yeah, well, it ain't going according to plan, that's for sure. But I still want to get us paid, and then we'll get the hell out of here."

Rae was not so thoughtful in her reactions. Hers came from the gut.

"Uh, Danny, look around. Does it look like we control where we're gonna go to get the hell out of here?"

She was looking at Danny's cheeks and neck this time, but no coloring came to them. He simply nodded back toward the airboat.

"Geronimo could no more handle this thing than he could fly. Unless somebody else shows up, we've got control of the only way out of here."

She knew then that he, too, had been working on alternatives, had maybe become as wary as she was over this entire screwed-up operation, and had been formulating a plan of his own.

The braves came out of the cabin where they'd stashed the woman and headed across the deck to the big house, gawking at the surroundings. For the first time, Rae saw them whispering to each other. The code of silence might indeed be dead, but she and Danny ended their conversation and followed them.

Geronimo had gone weird and maybe Rae could see why. Inside the big cabin, the place was laid out like one of those huge private bungalows up at the Grand Traverse Resort and Spa. It was all done in some kind of polished pinewood: a kitchen with an island bar and stools on one side and then an open living area with big stuffed chairs and couches all done in muted green material. On end tables were what looked like hand-carved statuettes of Indians with waist-length coats and beaded necklaces and others standing up in narrow canoes with long poles in their hands. But the showcase was the western wall made of smoked, floor-to-ceiling glass with a view of the Everglades, its expanse reaching out to the end of the damn earth.

Geronimo was standing in the middle of the big room, silhouetted by the light from the huge window, staring at a large tapestry hanging over a stone fireplace on the eastern wall. The tapestry was made of some kind of woven cloth interspersed with strings of colored beads. The big Indian was stock-still, his thick hands clasped behind him, forearms encircling the spot Rae knew held the knife. If he was seeing something in the wall art that mesmerized him, it was beyond her. Yeah, it was pretty cool; the colors were bright and pure and interesting, but snap out of it, dude.

The braves wandered around, first opening the refrigerator and smiling at its contents. Rae noticed the light come on when they opened the door—electrical generator, she thought. That's what she heard coming from the smallest cabin. Mike Pierce's dad had one at his hunting cabin in the Upper Peninsula, where a bunch of kids from high school went after graduation just to party. Full electric, water heater, and everything—really roughing it.

The braves started going through the cupboards, probing like little kids in a candy store.

Finally, Geronimo seemed to snap out of his trance and turned to her and said, "Squaw, make us something to eat."

Rae looked at Danny and he looked back, awaiting her eruption at being ordered in such a way. He squared his feet in order to react, especially now that he knew Geronimo was armed. But Rae gave him a little nod. . . .

"No problem, Big Chief, what's your pleasure? A little alligator tail and some palm salad?"

Geronimo just gestured toward the kitchen.

"OK, Big Man, just let the little woman see what she can rustle up for you all."

Rae had been in enough restaurant kitchens to know her way around. She'd fended for herself since she was a child, cooking meals in her mom's little trailer. Not a big deal as long as you had the goods. As she rooted through the fridge, she found that the place was loaded: steaks, hamburger, peeled shrimp, pre-made salads, French bread, eggs, and butter. It conjured up a menu for anyone from anywhere. There was some mystery meat that might indeed have been alligator tail and some raw fish that she didn't recognize. But she stayed with what she knew and put together a dinner that the CEO of any Fortune 500 company would have loved. And while the Indians weren't looking, she spit in every dish she served them.

Those trips to the restaurant kitchens had taught her more than culinary arts.

Twice during the preparation and serving, Rae sent a plate of scrambled eggs with Danny out to the cabin where the woman was still locked up. Geronimo didn't question it. But Danny came back both times saying the woman was still out.

"I checked her breathing, Rae. She isn't dead, just sleeping."

"Did you try to give her water?"

"Yeah, I tried. It just dribbled off her lips, and she fussed a little but never opened her eyes."

"How do you know she didn't open her eyes?"

In a voice loud enough for everyone in the big cabin to hear, Danny said: "I took the damn hood off. It's fucking stupid to keep that thing on out here. What's she gonna see?"

Geronimo looked up from his steak for a second, but then continued eating without comment. Rae and Danny exchanged glances.

After the meal, which Rae had to admit was pretty damn good, all had withdrawn to their own corners of the wooden island as night settled in. Geronimo lorded over the big cabin, and the braves staked out the other cabin, a bunkhouse of sorts. Danny and Rae simply took some comforters and made up a nest on the dock where they dozed and made love in the cool open air and rehashed their situation in whispered voices.

"Should we just make a break for it?" Danny asked her. "I know I can get that boat started and get it moving. And in the dark, even Geronimo's not gonna throw a knife in our backs."

"And you know where the hell we are and how to get back to the road?" Rae said.

Danny hesitated. "Maybe."

Rae knew the difference between Danny knowing and maybe knowing.

"How much gas is in it? How long is it gonna run and how long if we get fucking lost in the dark?"

"We just get away and then shut it down and wait until daylight and figure from there."

"Ha," Rae barked sarcastically. "On the way out here, did you see any damn thing different from east to west to north to south?"

"No, but the sun rises in the east, Rae, so we go from there."

They were quiet for a while and then Rae rolled into him, wrapping one leg around his, and felt the warmth and knew he felt it, too.

"So we just run away with nothing?" she said. "Everything they asked us to do, we did. Don't you want to get what they promised us?"

"Ten thousand might not be worth all this."

"I'm thinking you're right. Hell, fifty each ain't enough for kidnapping a damn federal judge."

There. She'd spilled it, and now she had to wait for Danny's reaction, which wasn't nearly as slow in coming as it usually was.

"You're still thinking she's a judge?"

"She told me."

"And since when do you believe anybody, Rae? Maybe she just said that to make you scared."

"I checked," she said, going deeper into it now.

"What do you mean, you checked?"

"With Kelsey."

Danny's legs cinched up, squeezing hers, and then he rolled away. It was hard to check his eyes with only starlight to see by, but she knew anger would be there.

"Rae, Christ! You've got your damn cell phone? Geronimo will go fucking nuts if he finds out. You were supposed to leave all that shit back at the airport locker."

This time, she held on to her own response, letting the moment of her truth-telling pass.

"He hasn't found it yet and he isn't going to."

She'd told Danny of her hiding place before. He'd actually blanched and raised his eyebrow the way he did when he thought people were bullshitting him. But it was Danny who'd told her the stories of the prison work camp in Grayling where both the inmates and their women visitors hid packets of drugs and other contraband in their body cavities. He even told her of one woman who smuggled in a single-shot zip gun and ammunition that way. She hadn't believed him, but experimented and found out, yes, it was possible.

"So who the hell you been talking to, Rae, besides Kelsey—the fucking FBI?"

She let that go also. Danny knew she didn't like it when he was a smart-ass to her. She also knew he'd be contrite about it if she let him. After a few moments, she said: "I only texted her."

"Rae, they can track a text just as easy as a conversation."

"Yeah? Well, where the fuck is the FBI then, Danny? They didn't find us at the warehouse. They didn't find us on the road. What makes you think they're gonna find us out here in the damn middle of nowhere?"

They both stared up at the sky, quietly. Rae reached out in the starlight and found his hand.

"Look, all we have is each other, Danny. That's it," she said. "Something bad is going to happen out here and don't even tell me I'm wrong because I'm not. I can see what's coming and it ain't good."

Still Danny said nothing.

"That fucking knife is making me nervous," she repeated.

"No shit. You remember that story Randy Williams tells about seeing Geronimo pull that thing out of its sheath and flip the blade into his hand and throw the damn thing twenty feet into a fence post?"

"Yeah, I heard it was thirty feet."

"Whatever. If you've got your cell on you, get rid of it, Rae. We don't need to piss him off."

"What? Is he going to strip-search me?"

This time, Danny stiffened up.

"Not while I'm alive," he said, looking into her eyes with a seriousness that might have even made her neck color a bit. She reached into her shorts and came out with the phone, wiped it on the comforter, and gave it to him. He took it, got up, and walked toward the woman's cabin.

"I thought you were gonna toss it into the swamp," Rae said after him, before he got to the door, searching a little with the statement.

"Not anymore," Danny answered. "We might need it."

Rae watched Danny as he came back out of the prego's cabin and sat next to her with a look she'd never seen before. His eyes were diverted and his head turned away, but she took him by the chin and turned his face to her. There was an inward, unfocused dullness to his eyes, and even in the starlight, she could see the red glow of his neck pallor.

"What?" she said. But Danny kept his eyes off hers. "What the hell did she say?"

"Nothing," Danny lied. Rae always knew when he lied.

"Bullshit, Danny. I heard her voice," she lied right back to him. "What did she say?"

"Nothing, Rae," he repeated, but met her gaze. "She wants more to eat."

Rae kept her eyes on his. There was something going on in those damn mirrors of the soul, as her mom always called the eyes, that put Rae on edge. "Don't go getting all touchy-feely on her, Danny, now that you're having conversations and all," she said.

"Damn, Rae. It wasn't a conversation."

"But you took the hood off, Danny. You've seen her face, so now she's a person and not just a thing," Rae said, not going into the fact that he was now recognizable and everybody knows what that means for the damn eyewitness you don't leave behind.

"She was always a person, Rae. But maybe I should have thought of that before I got us into this."

"No, no, no way, Danny," Rae said, grabbing his shoulder and pulling him into her. "You didn't hold a gun to my head, baby. We're in this together. Don't take that away.

"Together," she repeated, holding on long enough to let him believe it.

CHAPTER 30

The bloody show: Why in God's name would they call it that? Diane stepped out of the shower and used a towel to dry herself and sop up the tinges of pink fluid that had streaked down her leg. She recalled the warnings that her obstetrician had given her: the bloody show was supposed to be just a small mucus discharge, blood vessels in the cervix rupturing. But it was hard to tell in the shower, mixed as it was with the water.

Now, she wiped herself again with one of the white washcloths, and again there was a pinkish stain.

Do not panic, Diane, she told herself. The periodic contractions—and she was now convinced that they were real contractions—would have naturally led to this. If her water had broken, it would continue to flow awhile. If it was the bloody show, it would stop. Either way, her baby was on its way; it was only a matter of how much time she had.

She wrapped a big towel around herself. *Do not panic. Be smart.* She took the bloodstained washcloth, folded it, and placed it carefully back in the stack of towels in the linen closet. She had already methodically pressed her fingertips in the corners of the mirrors and on any smooth surface that she thought a cleaner might miss. She was going to leave as much DNA as she could. She was determined to leave a sign that she'd been here.

Next she picked up her clothes from the floor. How many days had she been here? She'd lost count with the sleep and the darkness. She took her underwear to the sink and turned on the water and used a bar of soap to wash them as best she could and hung them on the shower door to dry. Then she filled the basin and began soaking her silk blouse, dipping the fabric into the soapy water and then rinsing it out: dipping and rinsing, rinsing and dipping . . .

While she washed, she looked into the mirror and saw the drawn, bleary-eyed face of a woman she hardly recognized. Tears were running down the woman's face.

"What am I doing?" she asked the face. "Am I nesting? Or getting ready to die? Preparing to be a mother, or a corpse?"

She turned the water on full cold and filled handfuls and splashed them into that woman's face, keeping her eyes closed, feeling the tingle, summoning the strength. Another contraction gripped her abdomen, and she put both hands on the vanity, steadying herself until the tightening eased.

By the time she'd made it back to the bed, darkness had filled the single window and she had her answer and lay down. She let the towel drop away off her belly and massaged the skin with the palms of her hands. She was going to give birth, by herself, in the middle of nowhere. So be it. She began running scenarios through her head, remembering the instructions about panting and being careful not to hyperventilate. She envisioned the position: she could use the extra pillows on the bed to prop up her back. She could get more towels from the bathroom for wiping the newborn's mouth and nose. She felt herself crying again, the tears running out of the corners of her eyes and down into her ears. She'd never felt so alone. And that's when she felt the baby kick.

"Oooh."

Not a hard one, but obvious. She'd been feeling movement for weeks but never considered the pushing and flexing going on inside her as painful. It had always made her smile before, the thought of her baby growing there, moving, and becoming more real in her head. But now she thought about the warnings she'd been given about the pain involved in natural childbirth.

She always thought of herself as having a high pain threshold. She'd been thrown from a horse when she was ten, but got back up, remounted the gelding, and rode back to the stable. They'd only discovered her broken collarbone after a doctor's visit the next day. She'd played lacrosse at Duke and had taken her share of cracks to the face and body and never flinched. Her parents called her too tough, but that didn't keep them from encouraging her to play polo at the Palm Beach Club, where her father the judge hobnobbed with the connected class and her mother frankly told her that more respectable suitors would be found there, even if Diane did take an occasional tumble.

Plus, she tried to convince herself, she was older and more mature than most new mothers. When she and Billy had gone to the birthing class, the other women seemed just girls, and she noted a few wincing at the instructor's description of contractions and what to expect. She overheard their jokes about demanding epidurals the minute they were wheeled through the ER door. She and Billy had not even discussed pain meds yet. Now, there wasn't going to be a choice. *But you can do this, Diane! You can do this!*

She pulled two pillows up behind her head and back and then raised her knees and looked down. Would she be able to see the baby's head crowning? Would she be able to reach down and ease its shoulder out? That's when she heard the lock turn in the outside door, and between her knees and in the light from the bathroom, she saw the young man who had given her food earlier step quickly inside.

"Oh, geez," the kid said when he looked at Diane peering at him through her raised knees from the other side of the kitchen counter, and then diverted his eyes as she lowered her legs.

"I'm sorry, I mean, excuse me. Sorry. I'm just . . ."

He glanced at the cupboards, the top of the refrigerator, not just avoiding her, but looking for something.

"It's OK," Diane said, "I just took a shower. I hope that was all right, I mean, taking a shower."

"Yeah, yeah, sure," the kid said. "I mean, of course."

He looked so young, she thought. Tall and athletic, but not exactly muscular, in a short-sleeved T-shirt that she noted had no logo or words on it. He was definitely not Hispanic. Her mind was still working, noting every detail as he moved about the kitchen opening and closing drawers and doors.

"Hey, can you at least tell me what you want? I mean, if Escalante wants deportation, maybe there is something I can do. Maybe if you let me talk to the Justice Department, we could come to an agreement."

She was trying to work the moment. This kid had been the only one to speak a word to her and maybe that was a crack to exploit. She was still not sure why they'd taken her, but maybe through this boy she could convince them that she was worth keeping alive and could help them get whatever it was they wanted by letting her speak to the outside world.

But the kid wasn't paying any attention and kept searching. Within seconds, he seemed to find what he wanted on an upper shelf. She heard a clunk of something on glass or china as he reached up into the cabinet and then withdrew his hand, closed the cupboard, and turned to leave.

"Uh, could I at least get something more to eat?" she called out to him. "Hey, is the water even safe to drink?" she added, but the outside door pulled shut and all she heard was the lock turn yet again.

Diane tried to analyze what she'd just seen. The kid seemed a bit embarrassed when he'd first walked in and caught her uncovered. But if he'd been watching over her for days in that other place he'd seen her squat on the toilet at least a few times, so big deal. And what was the searching all about? He didn't appear to take anything out of the cupboards; instead, he was leaving something. And he wasn't thinking about hiding it from her. Hell, he did it right in front of her.

Sure, he was anxious, and the sight of an old naked pregnant woman lying on the bed with her knees in the air might have thrown him off his game, but he had definitely left something behind to keep from someone else in his crew. Was it a sign of distrust? A little unraveling of the group? In her years as a prosecutor, she'd seen those grandiose schemes of so-called perfect crimes go south because humans will be humans and get greedy, scared, sometimes even have a moral conundrum, and botch up a good plan. Seasoned detectives always say the bad guys will eventually screw up. Maybe this was it.

She pulled a towel around her and rolled to the side of the bed. With resolve she wasn't sure she had, she got to her feet. She stood, steadied herself with the chair, and then walked to the kitchen island. She was finding strength from somewhere, maybe just survival instinct, mother-bear strength, instinctual strength to preserve her family.

With a hand on the counter, she made it around to the cupboards and went to the door of the room where the kid had been searching. He'd gone to the highest shelf, so she strained and stretched her side and arm to reach it. Her fingers fumbled at a stack of small china plates that clinked together, nothing odd or unfamiliar. She probed to the left and felt the shape of bowls or large coffee cups and pushed them aside. Maybe he put whatever it was to the back, behind the dishes where it couldn't be seen. She was on her toes now, stretching and feeling, but couldn't get to the back wall. The strain caused a sudden splint of pain in her side. As she came down off her toes with a gasp, a tall mug came out off the shelf with her hand, tumbling down onto the counter and spilling its contents—a cell phone.

Diane wasted a second staring at it just lying there on the counter. Then she ignored the pain in her side and scooped it up. It was an older model, but she found the power switch and clicked it on.

911? How would she describe her situation? Where was she? Should she even take the chance to call? Would someone outside hear her? The mug falling on the counter had made a hell of a noise. *Christ, Diane, hurry!* She thought for a moment more and then thumbed Billy's text number, the buttons making an eerily familiar clicking noise that she recalled from the room where they'd first taken her.

Carefully, she thumbed HELP MSMAC DNR and hit the SEND button. She thought of turning the thing off, but was afraid that if she did they wouldn't be able to track the location. So she took a chance, left it on, dropped it back in the ceramic mug, and then stretched beyond where she thought possible and put it back up on the top shelf. With that effort, she closed the cupboard, spun to the side, put her head down into the stainless steel sink, and puked.

CHAPTER 31

I had to reach Nate Brown on what I knew was a pay phone at a ramshackle bar just outside of Chokoloskee in the Ten Thousand Islands of southwestern Florida. Who has a pay phone these days anyway?

The pissed-off voice of a woman answered on the twenty-second ring. That was the beauty of the near-extinct pay phone—no switch to the message system. It rang until someone picked up.

"Loop Road Frontier Hotel, and you better have a reason for ringin' the damn phone off the wall," the woman's voice said.

"Hi, Patti," I said. I knew it was Patti, who could be the orneriest bartender on the planet and yet have the heart of an angel when the mood hit her. "It's Max Freeman. I'm trying to get ahold of Nate."

"Of course you are, honey. And it bein' five o'clock somewheres in the world, he's sittin' yonder in the corner drinkin' per usual."

There was a beat of silence.

"Well, can you get him to the phone please, Patti?"

"Well," she said, mocking my tone, "since I AM his private damn secretary I will endeavor to do so, MISTER FREEMAN."

She raised the level of her voice fourfold when she said my name, broadcasting it to the denizens of the bar as well as to Nate. I heard the receiver clunk against the wall, no doubt dangling on its metal-coiled cord. A few seconds later, a craggy voice picked up.

"That you, Max?"

"Yes, sir."

"Long time."

"Indeed."

"What's up? You gotta need to go fishin'?"

"In a sense," I said.

"Uh-oh."

Nate was never one for excessive use of words. I told him I was working on the disappearance of a judge from West Palm Beach who might have been taken to his area of the world, and I needed his help.

"That the one on the TV?"

"You have a TV, Nate?" A man who'd been born and raised in the Glades and had to be reached on a pay phone could surprise you.

"It's on right up there behind the bar this very second," he said.

"That's probably her then," I said. "Can you meet me at the rest stop at Route 29 and the Alley?"

"Name the time."

"Six in the morning?"

"I'll be there. But I'll tell you now, ain't nothin' in the air about that lady judge down here yet. And if they was trying to get her out by boat around here, the watermen would know."

I was disappointed, but not put off.

"I'll see you at six."

He hung up without saying good-bye.

Nate was a bit of a legend in the Ten Thousand Islands. Some say he just floated up in a canoe onto the shore of Florida Bay one day, a baby in swaddling cloth, so to speak. But Ben-Hur he was not. He was born sometime in the early 1900s of parents who'd been some of the first to try to live in the islands, subsisting on the fishing trade, shooting plume birds from the sky for the ladies' hat industry, or actually trying to raise crops on land mere inches above the waterline at the end of the Florida peninsula.

Nate was a crack-shot gunman, a fisherman who could smell the schools deep in the bay, a swamp hunter who could catch and de-tail a dozen gators in a day, and a distiller who could make moonshine in his secret still that would clean the rust off an antique railroad spike.

He'd lived and made his living on the salt water of the Gulf and its labyrinthine patchwork of shifting mangrove islands for so many years, his sense of direction and place was superior to any map or GPS system yet devised. In the early 1980s, in fact, this acute ability allowed Nate and those like him to thrive in the illegal business of off-loading bales of marijuana from big supply boats offshore in the Gulf of Mexico and bringing them to land using the water trails and routes that no law enforcement entity could ever find.

It is still a legend in Chokoloskee that when the DEA finally moved in, they arrested nearly every male resident of the island, Nate included. As a result, he'd spent several of his senior years in a federal lockup.

There was no one more knowledgeable or plugged in to the goings-on in the Glades. If Diane's captors had brought her there in an effort to hide her or move her to South America, there was a good chance Nate would have wind of it, or know how to find out.

That evening, I slept fitfully, if at all, on Sherry's couch. My tossing and turning was such that I'd abandoned her bed before midnight to keep the nightmarish demons to myself. Whenever I drifted off, I'd conjure some sight of dark and twisted mangrove tendrils twisting around legs and limbs and throats. They were always the body parts of clear-skinned women who had no business being in such an environment.

Startled awake, I tried to interpret the half-dreams and knew I was still beating myself up for taking Sherry out to the Glades and being responsible for the loss of her leg. If something similar or worse happened to Diane, I was once more somehow going to be responsible.

This time, I realized myself that again I'd found the bullet wound on my neck, once again worrying the small patch of smooth skin. Despite my flight from the streets of Philadelphia, my self-seclusion on the river, all attempts to rid my head of the past, it was for naught. No one forgets. Everything we've ever done is back in those memory cells.

There is no such thing as closure. You don't just get over it. All you can do is tuck it deep so it doesn't cripple you, but it will always be with you. I finally got up, dressed, and left for my rendezvous with Nate long before sunup.

From the tollbooth where the Chrysler 300 had last been photographed, I headed west with little traffic at 4:00 a.m. with sunrise chasing me. On the divided highway, I could see headlights coming at me from a mile away, but those behind me always went dim. I had the Fury up to 90 mph, and no one was holding with me. After an hour, the tops of the saw grass on either side began to glow with a red tinge, and within another twenty minutes, a crimson dawn created the effect of a thousand acres on fire.

"Red sky in the morning, sailor's warning." The phrase sat in my head for twenty stanzas before I shook it like an old song you repeat in your head for seemingly no reason. The Glades did indeed flame up on occasion, usually during long periods of drought when the saw grass and the muck it grows in became tinder-dry. Fires set by lightning strikes or cigarettes tossed by careless travelers or campers will spread like a flood, eating up acres in minutes, the switching winds on the open plain running it in such erratic directions that containment is nearly impossible.

And if it burns hot enough, long enough, the ground itself begins to smolder. The muck below is simply plant material that dies and falls, building layer upon layer. It is rich in nutrients and feeds a plethora of bioorganic species, but when it is dry and set afire, it can smolder several feet deep for months before the rains come again in amounts large enough to douse it.

Driving the arrow-straight expressway with nothing but horizon on either side can lull you. Before the Alley was modernized, there was nothing but two lanes, side by side. Now, between the separated lanes, there are grass medians and occasional turnoffs for rest stops and boat ramps spaced along the way.

Still, the first real stop is when Route 29 running north and south intersects. I finally turned into the gas station and food mart there and saw Nate's old pickup in the far corner of the parking lot. I pulled up beside it. You might guess the old Ford to be a 1970 or maybe even a late 1960s model. The paint is sun-bleached to a dust color. The bed walls and rails are scraped and scratched and dented by thousands of loadings and unloadings of crab traps and dinghies, bailing wire and lumber, gravel loads and yards of sand.

The man leaning against the tailgate looked the same: sun-faded in an oilskin jacket and jeans, a face creased deep with wrinkles and folds, a thin bony frame worn hard by manual labor and decades in harsh weather.

I got out and joined him at the back of his truck.

"Max Freeman," he said, his voice scratchy and low in timbre, his words drawn out to maximum length. He was a true Southerner in the most southern part of the country. He offered his hand and I took it, a dry and loose pouch of bones. The frailty took me aback at first, but his grip was still tight and his eyes, a nearly colorless pale from years of staring into reflected sun off the water, looked directly into mine. There was no telling the years. He could have been seventy, or ninety, or a hundred-plus.

"Nate," I said. "Long time."

He nodded and waited. I started in, foolishly recounting what I'd already told him on the phone, reiterating the possibilities we were both already aware of, and then leaving him to offer any others.

"You said Indians, but not Seminole nor Miccosukee?"

"Not from the description from a witness."

"So they ain't gonna look right if they headed north into Immo-kalee?"

"Not if they stop anywhere," I said, noting to myself that a tank of gas wouldn't get you much farther than Immokalee if you started from the warehouse in West Palm Beach and took the route across the Glades.

Billy and I—not to mention the feds—had no doubt already questioned the road taken by the kidnappers. If you were headed straight to the west coast of Florida, the shortest route would have been straight out 441 around the southern tip of Lake Okeechobee, onto State Route 80, and straight into Cape Coral. It was part of my gut feeling that their destination lay elsewhere.

"Lots of places to hide out here," Nate said, his drawl a slow but efficient monotone. "But ya'll better know somebody. Ain't a place for strangers."

The Glades have been a place apart for hundreds of years. They're a land away from civilization, and the people who live here like it that way. They don't like rules. They don't like intruders who don't have a history here. Toughened by the antihuman propensities of nature, they've paid their dues to live here. Others who have not paid those dues are looked at askance.

Gladesmen run by this credo: "We live off the land and the water like our forefathers and don't tell us we can't."

This has been the way through the days of the bird hunters who killed an untold number of fine feathered birds for the 1900s ladies' hat trade, the alligator hunters who trapped and killed gators for their skins and tail meat, the whiskey still operators and illegal rum runners who kept that trade alive over two centuries, and the fishing industry that continues today.

Since the nineteenth century, the Glades have been a destination at times for the lawless to hide, and a home for people who want no truck with civilization. They have adapted, made, trapped, shot, and peddled what they could, even when the regulators came in and brought laws that shortened or banned their hunting and fishing seasons or plain outlawed their old methods. For the old-timers like Nate, there is a pride in their heritage. And they are covetous of it.

"You could go north and ask," Nate said, nodding his head in that direction. "I've got names of people up the way, people who watch out. But since they got that bulletin thing out, I'd say you got that covered."

"Bulletin?" I said, meeting his eyes.

"Seen it on the TV this mornin'. Be on the lookout for a carload of people who are wanted for questioning in the disappearance of your woman judge."

Dumbass, I said to myself. I hadn't turned on the radio in my car. I hate listening to the radio.

"What else?" I asked, feeling stupid in front of Nate, a century-old man who was more technically informed than me, the so-called private detective.

"Said one of them was a giant Indian, like you said. At least two other men and a woman. Said they was in a silver Chrysler 300."

Jesus. The feds had actually taken me seriously. They took the descriptions I'd passed on, or they confirmed them with the crazy Jedi master in the warehouse when they caught up with him. Now, they'd put out a BOLO.

I was still looking down at the ground, maybe hiding my shame from Nate, when my cell phone rang. The number was Billy's. Probably calling to tell me the bastards had been arrested at some 7-Eleven on some citizen's tip. If so, and Diane was safe, wonderful, my ego be damned.

"Max, we've gotten the break we needed," Billy said.

"Yeah, I heard about the BOLO."

There was a slight hesitation.

"That may help, but I received a text—from Diane."

Relief, maybe even joy, locked my throat from breathing. Before I could react, Billy continued.

"Take down these coordinates," he said. "I have triangulated the cell phone signal, and it's out there in the Glades. Maybe you can get there."

I pulled a pen out of my pocket and a business card to write on, and fumbled to record the numbers.

"My satellite map puts it north of the Alley and west of 227, inside the Seminole Reservation around where the three counties meet up. There's an unnamed road. But maybe you can get there."

I was absorbing as much as I could of Billy's straight, unemotional recitation of information, but was admittedly stunned.

"Billy, what did she say? Is she OK?"

"The best I can tell, she is still under duress, Max. She only left me three words: *help msmac dnr.*"

Again, I was dumbfounded.

"It's an endearing term only I used when we were dating and she was still Ms. McIntyre. As I told the agents, she was obviously trying to distinguish the text from all of the false tips that have been flowing in."

"And the dnr?"

"Do Not Respond. It's an old text code we used when she was in a court session and couldn't talk. She didn't want me calling back to make the cell buzz or beep. I think she's surreptitiously using someone else's phone and doesn't want us alerting them."

"Smart woman," was all I could come up with. And then: "So are the feds on their way?"

"I have given them all that I have. They have responded with calls to the tribe since there are jurisdictional boundaries and so-called protocols about federal law enforcement entering the nation-state of an Indian reservation."

This time, I could hear the hints of anger and frustration in Billy's voice. He was dealing with the red tape of government. I was not.

"I'll get back to you when I get there, Billy."

I got off the phone and turned to Nate, who was staring out toward the horizon—his way of giving me privacy while I talked with Billy.

"I need to find out where this is and how to get there," I said to the old Gladesman, and held out the card with longitude and latitude figures on it.

"Is it out here?"

"It's where they're holding the judge."

Nate looked at the numbers, nodded his head, and motioned me with a gnarled finger. I followed him into the convenience food store without question.

The place was no different than a million other stop-and-shops or food marts: rows of snack foods, a wall of glass refrigerator doors behind which every soda, flavored water, and beer known to man was stacked. The only things that may have set this place apart were a rack of cheap fishing lures, a prominent display of BullFrog Mosquito Coast insect repellent, and a stack of ball caps with jumping bass emblems on them.

When Nate walked in, the clerk behind the counter recognized the wizened old man and nearly genuflected to him on the spot.

"Mr. Brown, sir. Well, I'll be. Mr. Brown," said the guy, who might have been in his thirties. He fumbled to speak as he walked behind the counter in step with Nate toward the back of the store.

"Man, my daddy and my granddaddy know you. It's an honor, sir."

Nate nodded and asked simply, in a way that somehow didn't sound like he was ignoring or just waving the guy off: "Rowdy in?"

"Yes, sir, he is. He'd be right there in the back office, sir. Y'all just go on back."

Nate never broke stride, as if he intended to do just that

whether Rowdy was actually in or not. But the old man did rap on the door marked OFFICE. EMPLOYEES ONLY. before entering without waiting for a reply.

A large man with a bald pate, a florid, fleshy face, and an enormous belly bulging out in front of him was already standing up from behind his desk by the time I inched my way in behind Nate. The office was tight with filing cabinets, the desk overloaded with stacks of paper and catalogues, and a wall of bookcases sagged with the same.

As we shuffled our way in, Nate offered his hand and asked his question at the same time: "Rowdy, you got some of them topographic maps of the Glades y'all use for findin' fishin' sites and such?"

Again, Nate's presence seemed to cause mere mortals to discover marbles in their mouths and stars in their eyes.

"Uh, yes, I do, Mr. Brown. I do," the man called Rowdy said, as he first glanced about his own office and then turned to start rooting through corners and beside cabinets.

"It's a pleasure, sir, uh, Mr. Brown," he stumbled. "Any particular area, sir?"

"Three-county corner," Nate answered.

"Uh, yes, yes," Rowdy continued, as at last he found a tepee of long cardboard tubes standing in a short metal wastebasket. He finally decided on one and then turned and with a few sweeps of a big-pawed hand cleared a space on his desk, seeming to ignore the piles of paperwork that spilled onto the floor.

He slid a rolled map out of the tube and unfurled it on his desk.

"Now, this here is the three corners," Rowdy was saying when I reached over and offered the business card with the coordinates.

"Max Freeman," I said to Rowdy as introduction. "This is specifically where we're trying to get to."

"This here is a friend of mine," Nate stated.

The big man looked up, met my eyes, and reached out a hand before going back to anchoring the corners of the map with paperweights, a stapler, and a heavy logbook from his desk.

"Any friend of Mr. Brown, sir," he said, and did not have to finish as he took the business card and set to plotting the numbers. It took less than a minute.

"Right here, Mr. Brown," he said triumphantly when he'd lined up the intersects.

Nate bent over the desk and studied what was useless to my untrained eye.

"Hell, Rowdy, that ain't but a couple miles from the north park boundary."

"Yes, sir," Rowdy agreed, both of them looking closely.

"On the rez."

"Yes, sir. The reservation boundary is right here," Rowdy said, moving his finger on the map.

"I believe I used to gig some four hunnert frogs a night outta that piece a few years back," Nate said.

"Could be, sir."

"Then the Seminoles built themselves some kinda camp all fancy and such right about there. Brought in the pilings and pounded them down and put up a big ole place."

"I believe you're right, sir."

"Scared all the damn frogs away."

"Word is the top Seminoles take their big-time visitors from the casinos out there now, sir. You know, to show 'em the real Everglades," Rowdy said, staring down at the map and starting to move his finger. "But if you're lookin' for a place to gig frogs, Mr. Brown, I do have another spot you might consider."

A sudden change in the air set the room to silence as the big man realized his mistake. Nate had looked up into his face.

"Rowdy. Do you think I need a young boy like you to tell me

where to find giggin' frogs?" Nate said, again in a way that showed no anger or disrespect. But the big man could not meet his eyes, and an obvious red glow of embarrassment colored his heavy cheeks.

"No, sir, I do not."

"We ain't huntin' frogs, Rowdy, and I thank you much for the use of your maps," he said in a tone that indicated that we were done there.

Back outside at the tailgate of Nate's truck, I awaited instruction I knew was coming. This was his world. His knowledge of it would be my ally and maybe Diane's savior.

"I know a man out that way," Nate said after nearly a minute of full silence. "Name of Mason Jumper. He ain't a tribal member 'cause he's a half-breed. Momma was a Seminole and daddy a Cuban immigrant. He runs a huntin' an' fishin' outfitter out on Snake Road 'bout as close as you're gonna get to that spot on the map."

"Tell me how to get there, Nate. I appreciate your help."

"Naw. I'll lead ya. Jumper ain't a fella you can just walk up on without introduction."

With that, Nate climbed into his truck. I had to skip back to get to the Fury in time to keep up with the old man before he left me in the dust.

We got back on Alligator Alley and headed east in the direction I'd come from. Despite the age of Nate's pickup, the old man rolled it up to 75 mph and never faltered for the next fifteen miles. The sun was now sitting at thirty degrees above the horizon and was full in my eyes. I kept glancing out to the north, where I knew we were ultimately headed, and the sight of pure, flat Glades grass now honey-brown in the full sun told me once again that this was an unforgiving land. The thought of Diane out there, captive, under duress, as Billy had put it, started to conjure nothing but poor scenarios in my head.

I'd heard of airboat men who had broken down only a couple of miles from a main road out in those grasses and thought they could walk out, but ended up dying of heat stroke and dehydration.

I'd been in Florida for only a few months when a DC-9 airliner leaving Miami International lost power after takeoff, went into a dive, and speared itself and the 110 passengers and crew aboard directly into the deep Everglades muck. When rescuers got on-site, the entire plane had seemingly disappeared. All that was left were scraps of baggage and assorted pieces of metal. So deep and consuming was the River of Grass that the bodies of those who perished were impossible to recover. Only a marker stands over what became their last resting place.

Foolishly, I hadn't brought a thing to help me if I had to travel into that milieu. I was still wearing my canvas boat shoes, my black cotton cargo pants, and a stupid button-down long-sleeved oxford shirt. Other than the P226 Navy, I didn't even have a knife or a pair of binoculars to help me. I had my phone and two throwaway cells that hadn't rung in days. And I still had several thousand dollars in cash in the trunk. I hoped Nate's friend the outfitter would be well supplied and a willing businessman.

I was still in my head when my eyes recognized the brake lights on Nate's truck come ablaze in the straight-shot monotony of the interstate. At first, I thought his truck had broken down from the sustained speed, until I picked up an unmarked turnoff in the distance. We slowed and I followed him across the median onto a graveled lane, jumped the westbound lanes, and drove onto a thin asphalt lane that led north. Nate stopped at a chain-link gate entrance that stood ajar and I pulled up beside him. He got out of the truck but stood at his open door with one foot still in the cab, so I did the same.

"This here gate is usually locked up," he said, looking up the road. There was a sign on the gate that read OFFICIAL USE ONLY. DO NOT ENTER.

I knew that such signs were but a minor nuisance to a man who had hunted, fished, and poached this land for generations. Nate was simply stating that someone else had passed this way, an observation he knew might be of interest to me. And he was right. If the so-called big Indian and his troop with Diane in tow had brought the Chrysler 300 through here, we were now on their scent. The knowledge sent a tweak of adrenaline into my blood.

"Let's get to it," I said.

Nate climbed back into his truck, moved forward, and without regard for the resulting scratches on his front bumper, pushed open the gate as he passed through. I followed.

Snake Road had nothing to do with S-curves or rolling, undulating contours. It was a straight shot, albeit in a ditchlike furrow through the saw grass. The sky was visible above the walls of stalks, blue with clumps of passing clouds that seemed as substantial as landmasses themselves. And down here, close to sea level, you could see the ubiquitous water off to either side of the roadway. A skid off the apron and you were in the drink.

As I followed, I had to keep asking myself, *Why? Why out here?* As the old Gladesman had said, you don't come out here if you don't know someone. Who the hell would a kidnapping group of non-Seminole Indians know out here on what to them would be a foreign reservation? I hadn't heard a word from my street-level drug contacts. Not a word from the sleazy attorney who was as plugged in as anyone to the next level of the world of narcotics. And Billy's work with the upper echelon of Colombian insiders had brought nothing. The connection with Escalante was fading.

So who were these people, and what motive did they have to kidnap a sitting federal judge working an extradition trial? Billy had made a fleeting mention of another judge. He hadn't explained, which was like him. Billy didn't speculate. He dug to the bottom of things. He checked out his theories before making sloppy, unprofessional statements of semi-truth. He could never be a politician or a pundit. I admired his stance, even though as his best friend I sometimes resented his close-to-the-vest processes. It was Diane in whom he confided.

But was I so different? Sherry was my sounding board. Everybody needs somebody.

Again, Nate's glowing brake lights alerted me. He slowed, and I saw him drift into the western lane and then take a left onto a dry two-track path that seemed to lead into nothing but saw grass. But within a hundred yards, the track opened up, and a two-story clapboard building with a couple of sheds fronting a marl beach appeared out of what was distinctly nowhere.

Nate pulled up just short of two airboats sitting on the bank of a small lagoon of open water. I parked beside him. When I got out, the heat and humidity seemed to rise out of the ground. Though my river shack was on the edge of the Everglades, a canopy of ancient cypress trees kept my place in constant shade and helped make it tolerable. Out here, everything was at the mercy of the naked sun.

As the two of us walked toward the big building, a man stepped out of one of the sheds and started toward us. He was thin and mocha-skinned and had the distinctive straight black hair of an Indian native. He walked with the square-shouldered, confident gait of a man meeting important clients. But as the gap between us closed, I could see a wide smile grow on his face.

"Mr. Nate Brown, as I live and breathe," he said before reaching us and extending his hand in greeting.

"Mason Jumper, you grow younger by the year," Nate said, in what I considered a more intimate response than I have ever seen him give any man.

I stood back and let the friends have their moment. They clasped hands for a long time, smiling into each other's faces. I almost expected an embrace, but it didn't go that far.

Jumper, who appeared to be in his forties, was by this time looking beyond Nate, first to me and then to the cars we had parked.

"Still with the old pickup, eh, Mr. Brown?" he said, though his black eyes were moving from me to the cars to Nate's face.

Nate stood back.

"This is my friend, Max Freeman," he said. "He only drives a police car. He's not a cop."

The designation as Nate Brown's friend brought a change in the man's attitude that was like the flip of a light switch.

"Then welcome," Jumper said, immediately smiling and stepping closer to extend a hand. His skin was dry to the touch, yet stained in its pores and creases with dark lines of oil or machinery grease.

Nate did not waste words. He explained to Jumper that I was tracking a cell phone signal and gave him the coordinates.

"Just plain old Glades out there," Jumper said. "A mile or two from the Big Cypress National Preserve."

"I tol' Max that it looks close to that new fish camp the tribe built a couple of years back," Nate said.

Jumper was nodding before Nate finished.

"They don't use it much. It just sits out there like some kind of showpiece," he said, looking off to the southwest. "About three miles out. I know the man who takes supplies out there when they're bringing visitors. They call him and tell him when guests are arriving and he takes out food and bait and starts the generator.

"I know because Charlie usually gets the bait from me," he said, turning back to his own buildings. "I could get them anything that they need, but it's a tribal thing. Charlie says it's mostly casino people. High rollers and gaming executives who want to see the real Glades or the real Indians."

The timbre of Jumper's voice changed when he mentioned the casino people and put a sarcastic note on the "real Indians."

"I'd like to get as close to the place as I can," I said, speaking for the first time. Jumper turned and held my eyes, an unusual trait for a Seminole.

"You know it is forbidden to enter reservation land without an invitation?"

I nodded.

"It's the safety of a woman friend I'm concerned with."

Jumper looked to Nate, who gave his assent by saying nothing.

"I can put you in an airboat. But I suspect you might want a quieter approach?"

I pulled a stack of bills from my pocket. Jumper looked from the money to my eyes.

"You said there was a woman in trouble?"

"Yes."

Jumper turned away without another glance at the cash.

"I will get you whatever you need and I can take you as close as you want," he said, walking away toward his shed.

It took less than an hour to put together what I thought I might need from Jumper's well-stocked outfitter store: a kayak that he often rented to fishermen and frog giggers who liked to be close to the action—not your usual tourist orange or yellow, but a camouflage green and brown; bottles of fresh drinking water; some beef jerky; and a high-intensity flashlight. Since I didn't know how long I'd be, he threw in a portable GPS for those who might get lost in the tall saw grass. Then he added sunscreen and a dark, wide-brimmed camo fishing hat to ward off the direct sunlight.

I loaded all the loose items into a backpack I carried in the trunk of the car. While I was there, I took out the P226 Navy and put it in my cargo pants pocket.

Nate was out at Jumper's airboat, knee-deep in water, lashing the kayak down when I joined him. He'd been my guide on a couple of forays into the Glades when I was chasing some very bad men. But he knew my rules; I liked to work alone.

"I got my old British Enfield .303 in the truck," he said without turning to me. "Use it for takin' bear at a distance. Could be of help."

"Thanks, Nate, but I tend toward close work," I said.

"So I heard."

Jumper came striding down from his store, ready to pilot the airboat.

"I called Charlie," he said. "He got a call two days ago to supply the camp. Said they asked for enough for six people for a couple of days. No bait. Said he didn't have to ferry the visitors out there, they'd do it themselves."

"Helpful information," I said. "Thanks."

Jumper held his cell phone in his hand.

"Modernization," he said. "The tribe put up a cell tower up on Josie Billie Road a couple of years ago. They're businessmen now. Have to keep in touch."

I heard Nate hack up a bit of phlegm in his throat and spit in the water. Jumper and I shared a look and a grin, and we got up into the seats of the airboat. Nate might eschew the new ways, but that cell phone connection might be what we needed to save Diane's life.

CHAPTER 32

Airboats are not nimble or comfortable or even a particularly fast mode of transportation. They are top-heavy. They are wobbly. They are noisy as hell and I've never been a fan. But they do go places that no other vehicle can go, and when it comes to the Everglades, they are often the only option.

Mason Jumper drove with an abandon perhaps fueled by the idea that there was a woman in peril, or maybe he always drove this way. Once we left his tiny beach and looped around some large mangrove outcroppings, he pretty much made a beeline for our destination somewhere out there on the horizon. I kept checking the GPS he'd given me, but he was guided by native memory and experience. For him, this section of the Glades was his neighborhood. If you go back home, you don't need street signs and intersections to find your way.

When the water opened up, he pushed the throttle full forward, creating his own massive windstorm. If short-grass marshes got in the path, he slid right over them. If a thick, three-foot wall of saw grass blocked us, he slowed but then plowed right through. The flat-bottom boat will simply skid right over dry land given enough power. After thirty minutes of bullet-line travel, Jumper cut back the engines and handed me a large pair of binoculars and pointed west.

"There about a mile out, you can see the ripple in the air above the marsh line. That is the exhaust, the pollution. They have the generator running for their electricity."

In any other situation, I would have thought the man was kidding, but I took the glasses and focused on the farthest line where sky met earth. It took me a while, but finally I saw the waver in the light. It was like seeing heat waves rippling off a summer highway.

"If we get much closer, they will hear our engine and be warned," Jumper said. I nodded and got down out of the seat beside him to begin unstrapping the kayak and settling it into the water.

"Should I wait for you? Can you give me a sign if you need help?"

I slid into the tiny boat and got my balance.

"I think you're going to know when it's safe to come in," I said. "The federal government is on its way, and they don't do things subtly."

Jumper nodded as if he knew, and maybe he did.

"I will stay within reach just in case."

"Thank you," I said, and shoved off.

"Good hunting."

Within ten minutes, I was sweating through the camouflage T-shirt that Jumper had given me. The early sun was out full now, climbing the sky and warming the air. But even when you're above water out here, you're still in moisture. I could guess at the humidity level at eighteen inches above the waterline: 90 percent was my low-ball estimate.

It is essentially the way the Everglades and South Florida work. The one hundred thousand acres of the Glades lie out on the unshaded open plain in the center of the southern half of the state. Its water crawls constantly and ever so slowly southward, like the laziest of rivers. The daytime sun causes evaporation and moisture floats up. Clouds form and move their bulk with the prevailing winds to the coast toward the coolness of the Atlantic Ocean, where especially in summer the meeting of those two systems produces rain.

Now, I was at the bottom of that chain of events: on the skillet of the rising steam. I kept paddling, an even, steady stroke toward my destination. Compared to the roar of the airboat engine, the kayak was uncannily quiet. The occasional sound of a birdcall, the rustle of grass in an errant wind current, accompanied the rhythmic *plunk* and *swish*, *plunk* and *swish* of my paddle.

The water was flat and clear, and I could see the stalks of saw grass reaching down into the mucky bottom some two feet below. As is my habit when I take nightly canoe trips on the river where I live, I found myself counting strokes. After every five hundred, I stopped and floated, got out the binoculars, and searched the horizon for a sign of the fish camp I knew was out there. I was being careful.

I wanted to get close enough for an assessment but didn't want to run right up on the place and be spotted. Jumper had said there was a tall saw grass marsh just to the east of the camp, and I planned to use it as cover. Each time I stopped, I drank from my water bottle, knowing that dehydration was the big danger out here. The overblown myths of alligators and monster pythons are nothing compared to the deadly effects of heat stroke and dehydration.

I thought of Diane: Would her captors know this? Did they have any idea how the South Florida sun and heat could drain a person, especially a person in her condition? Jumper said the custom-built camp was luxurious by any standard. And we had seen the sign that the generator was operating, but would the people who had her be smart enough or care enough about their captive to watch over her?

I kept moving, another five hundred strokes, and another.

After my fourth set of paddling, my check of the skyline found the rippled air of exhaust vapor Jumper and I had seen from a distance. Now, I slowed and sought out the marsh edges and stayed away from open water where I might be seen. I stopped after a hundred slow strokes, checked the glasses, and picked out the plume again. Another hundred and I found a roofline. I started making my way to the east toward the cover Jumper had told me about. On my final stop, I could see partial walls above the waterline in the field glasses and knew I'd have to move deeper into the grasses to stay unseen for the rest of the way.

Silence was all around me: no distant voices, still no sound of the mechanical generator. As I stayed still and quiet in the grass, a sudden shearing of wings ripped the air and from the corner of my eye I picked up the swoop of a bird. Closer, I saw the dark body of a snail kite soar by.

All around me were tall stalks of saw grass, but in my singular focus I'd missed the rows of tiny olive-brown apple snails lining the thicker strands. I was in the middle of a feeding ground for this South Florida hawk, and it was no doubt pissed at my intrusion. I stayed still, and soon I swear I felt the beat of wings on my ears as the kite hovered and clutched onto a saw grass stalk an arm's length away, then deftly ripped a snail off the blade with its scissor-sharp beak and jumped away into the sky. Silence followed the quick strike of violence.

I stayed completely still. A living thing kills a living thing to survive—the way of nature in this place. But why was I bringing my human violence into it? I didn't have an answer, and it wouldn't help me if I did. I had one goal: to help Diane, whatever it took.

I eased forward, now using my paddle like a pole, finding purchase in the muck below and pushing my kayak forward, trying my best not to create unnatural movement in the top of the grass that an eye might pick up.

It took another half hour of slow, meticulous movement for me to come even with the camp; I finally could hear the hum of the generator. Ten yards deep into the grass, I unstrapped my fanny pack, stowed it, abandoned the kayak, and eased myself into the water. My feet touched the soft muck below. It was like walking in oatmeal, but there was enough purchase to push myself forward. The water was warm as it soaked through my clothing, but I knew that it was momentary. It wasn't 98.6 degrees. If you spent enough time in it, hypothermia would still set in.

But the immediate problem was pushing aside the saw grass

stalks, so named because their blades' edges are saw-toothed and sharp. Rubbed against the grain, they will cut you like a hacksaw. You have to move with them, not against. And still they caught at my long-sleeved T-shirt and tore at my trousers.

When I got to the outside edge of the grass, I went low, my chin touching water, with only my camouflaged hat and face floating above.

There were thirty yards of open water between me and the raised platform. From here, I could see the sides of three buildings and the roofline of a fourth rising above and beyond the others. The generator noise appeared to be coming from the closest, smallest cabin. There were windows in the other two. From Jumper's description, I knew the dockage was on the far south side. I was approaching from the east as planned.

I still saw no movement, heard no voices. If there were lookouts, I couldn't spot them from here—which made me nervous. Would the kidnappers all stay inside in the middle of the day? Were they arrogant enough to think no one could find them? Which cabin would Diane be in? Could she be tied up in the generator shack? Or be kept close in the biggest structure? It was information I didn't know, but I couldn't just sit here. I needed a better angle, a cleaner vantage point.

I kept moving along the grass line in my floating camouflaged hat, with sunglasses peering up from the brim. Water skimmers skittered on the surface in front of me, and sparks of sunlight danced in their tiny wakes as I made my way south. On the other side of the generator shack, I could finally see the outline of an airboat tied up next to the edge of the deck. Just beyond it, I finally picked up movement: the figures of two men came into focus at the farthest point west, next to the largest cabin. They appeared to be dancing near the edge of the raised platform, moving to the edge and then springing back.

Neither was big enough to be the huge Indian my Yoda witness had described, but they could be Indians. I was too far to tell, but not too far now to pick up yelps and guttural whoops coming from their direction. I tucked myself back into the tall grasses and watched. I let minutes go by. What the hell were they doing? Their movements were erratic, but they seemed focused on something. No one else appeared.

Without visual confirmation, I didn't even know if Diane was here, or long gone since her mysterious text message. The others could have manned another airboat and been off to Tampa by now. And where the hell were the feds? Would they drop in on helicopters? Come by airboat or some damn black ops inflatable? Or would they come at all?

One part of me said wait for backup, let the big boys do their thing. The other part urged me forward to gather intel—to *do* something. I'd left my cell phone in the kayak. I knew it would be ruined by the water anyway. I'd learned a terrible lesson when I'd taken Sherry out to a Glades camp and a playful rollover in our canoe resulted in the destruction of our only contact with the outside world, with a hurricane bearing down on us.

But now I felt more than helpless. Water that initially felt warm had now sapped enough body heat so that my teeth were beginning to chatter. With no one else in sight but the dancing goof-offs on the far side of the camp, I abandoned my conservative side and moved out to cross the yards of open water hoping, perhaps beyond hope, that my hat would look ever so much like a sunning turtle shell or a useless clump of floating sedge grass.

I tried to move as slowly as possible—leave no wake, attract no attention. My ears were full of water, my eyes kept low. The dancing men could be standing there waiting for me by the time I reached the pilings on which the deck was built. But they weren't. I slipped into the shadows, grateful, but with an uneasy feeling about the slipshod ways of this crew. They had to know that every law enforcement group in the country would be on alert for the kidnappers of a federal judge. Yet they'd left no lookouts on guard? Were they arrogant or stupid? I was hoping for the latter.

Under the raised deck, I had better footing. Whoever built this place must have drilled into the limestone below the water and muck before pounding in the pilings. The excavated stone formed a kind of anthill around the base of each piling and spread outward to provide a sounder bottom on which to make my way. When I stood, I was in waist-high water, and the underside of the deck was barely above my shoulders, so I had to duck down to move under it.

There was enough light to see three distinct plastic catch tanks strapped underneath three of the cabins. I approached the first: waste tanks, installed to catch sewage. The Seminoles were being environmental while still giving their special guests flush toilets—how grand. There were also pipes leading to the three cabins from the generator shed that were drawing Glades water and probably running it through a filter before sending it up to faucets: a true AAA tourist destination.

I moved around all of this and made my way west and south around the pilings to where I knew the airboat was docked, thinking of sabotage and a closer look at the men on the deck. If I could disable the airboat, they'd have no escape. If I could get a better assessment of the kidnappers, I could get back to my kayak and report in to whoever might, and I mean might, be coming. I could stay here till dark, but I'd have to get out of the water. My body temperature was still dropping, and I could feel a slight numbness in my fingertips.

As I got closer to the western edge, the sounds of the voices above echoed down—that, and the occasional noise of splashing water. I crept to the sunlit edge near the airboat dock and peered carefully through wood planks toward the spot where I'd seen the men. Thirty feet away, I saw the plunk of something tossed into the water only a few feet from the dock, and then the roiling gush of water and the flash of an alligator's snout.

They were feeding the goddamn gators! They were actually tossing food into the water and then yelping at the sight of the alligators snapping it up. After each explosion of the water surface, I could hear the footfalls of the two men skittering back on the plank deck and guffawing over their game.

Jesus, maybe they were just idiots. But as I stood on the limestone marl next to a piling, I felt the distinct bump of something moving against my leg. When I looked down, I saw the disappearing slither of a gator tail. It was a small one, probably a three- to four-footer. The activity ten yards away was drawing members of the neighborhood, but as in all such encounters, the big boys were muscling out the little ones, leaving them the possible scraps. I ignored them. I didn't look like prey. I didn't look like leftovers. Even the bigger ones would have little interest in me.

Instead, I turned my focus to the airboat. I could try to cut a fuel line, but the engine on such a craft was well above water and would be in full view of the men. I could try to gouge some holes in the hull to swamp it, but cutting through a metal bottom with a knife would be difficult and noisy as hell.

I was still thinking of alternatives when a scream, a woman's scream, seared through the planks of the deck and lit a firestorm of adrenaline in my brain.

It wasn't a scream of "help me."

It wasn't a scream of frustration.

It was a scream of pain like I'd never heard before.

CHAPTER 33

G*eronimo wants to see us," Danny said. Rae knew from the inflection in his voice that he was scared, and Danny was never scared.*

"Fuck him," she'd said, but got up from the comforter she'd been sitting on, watching the sun continue its climb into the eastern sky. Danny said nothing.

"What, the scrambled eggs were runny? He wants a fresh pot of coffee?"

Rae had risen before dawn and without being asked had gone into the big cabin and started making breakfast for everyone. During the night, she'd sent Danny into the lady's cabin five or six times to check her breathing. He'd said the woman seemed out of it, but was alive.

At sunup before Rae had dished out Danny's breakfast, she'd told him to take a plate and some coffee to the woman. She didn't want to do it herself, not with the lady's hood off. Rae was still holding out hope that she and Danny might get out of this fucking thing with money and anonymity. This summons to the big house might answer that hope or dash it altogether.

When they walked in, the two bucks were at the kitchen counter, playing with food from the refrigerator. Geronimo had taken up his now-familiar position standing with his back to them, staring out of the big windows at the vast Everglades. He had changed his clothes, had found a colorful jacket in the patterns similar to those on the wall tapes-

try. He had also braided his long hair into two black ropes and pinned them to either side of his head.

Rae's nose wrinkled at the odor of some kind of incense or burning seed that scented the air. Geronimo left them standing in silence, posturing on purpose, Rae thought, before raising one hand, a signal for the other two, who gathered up a bowl of raw chicken parts and hurried out the door.

Danny waited until the door was closed and then stepped forward, a move that Rae had seen before in other situations, which meant he was done taking the backseat and was ready to drive or move on.

"You wanted to see us?" Danny said.

Geronimo turned and made himself big in front of the sunlit window, but still said nothing.

"What's the plan, Alvin?"

Danny was using Geronimo's given name, another clue to Rae that he was done with the bullshit. It was a joke among the kids who knew Geronimo that he was a Chippewa and that Alvin was the name of one of the chipmunks of cartoon fame. It was usually used behind his back.

"Ah, Danny boy," the big Indian said. "You are now the brave one, eh? No more letting your squaw be the mouth?"

Danny let it go.

"This isn't what we signed on for, Alvin. I was the driver. A couple of days safely hiding out and then we were supposed to get our money and split. That was the deal, not taking some mystery trip out into the middle of God's country and hanging on to some pregnant federal judge for who knows how long."

The words federal judge even made Rae twitch. She'd only found out from texting Kelsey. But again Geronimo didn't flinch.

"You obviously have some people with money backing this whole gig," Danny said, raising his hands palms up to indicate the camp. "So how about I drive us back to civilization, you get on your fancy cell phone and talk to whoever it is you talk to, we get our money, and we'll be on our way."

This time, Geronimo stepped forward.

"So, driver, you are now the white man who's going to take over and tell the Indian what to do and when to do it, and then send him back to the rez? Is that what you think?"

Rae could feel the tension in the room rising by the sentence, and even if she couldn't really tell the future, when Geronimo moved both of his hands behind his back as if taking an at-ease position, the recollection of the bowie knife stuck in the back of his waistband made her reach out and touch Danny's elbow.

"Look, guys, let's just ease back, OK?" she jumped in. "Chief, we're just a little uptight with all of this change-in-plan stuff and want to know what's up, you know? You're the man. You're the one deciding. We just want to be let in on what's happening, all right?"

The big Indian seemed to look beyond them instead of at them, and then said: "You will get your money."

"When?" Danny said, not taking the edge off his voice.

"Tomorrow. In the morning, we go to Tampa and you get your money," the Indian said, and then began turning back to his window. Rae had started to exhale when Danny asked his next question:

"And what do we do with the woman?"

When Geronimo turned back, he was wearing a grin, the first time such an expression had ever creased his face, Rae was sure.

"Ah, great white warrior. I think I will leave that decision to you," the Indian said, making his face an even more obscene mask by raising one eyebrow.

In the silence that followed, Geronimo turned back to the window again and spoke to the glass.

"You decided to break the rules. And now you live with that decision. It is your face that she has now seen. You are the only one she can identify. Everyone else, including your squaw, can walk away. Been to Florida lately? No, I've never been to Florida, Officer. Well, we have an eyewitness who says otherwise.

"So you decide, get-away driver. If it was my decision, I would let nature decide," Geronimo said, raising his hands to the vision of the Glades before him. "Five miles from this place, she can be set off the boat in the middle of this ancient wilderness and let nature take its course, as it always does."

Again, silence. Rae knew Danny was doing his thinking, not jumping in with a reaction without first rolling it over in his mind. The catch had not surprised her. She'd thought of the conundrum the first time he'd told her he'd taken the woman's hood off. But she had let it sit. Cross that bridge when it came. Well, here's the trestle. She looked at Danny, who was blank-eyed, looking inward.

"OK. Look . . ." he started. But his words were cut off by a searing sound coming from outside, a wailing that penetrated not just the door of the cabin, but the soul of a young woman who had heard such a rending scream of pain before.

CHAPTER 34

The contractions—and there was no doubt about them now—were longer and coming only a few minutes apart. And yes, despite all of Diane's bucking up and self-convincing, they hurt like hell. This wasn't a high ankle sprain in one of her lacrosse games, or a collarbone break, or a fall off a damn horse. She'd been gritting her teeth and had even begun sticking a wad of sheet into her mouth at the peak of the contractions to keep from crying out.

She didn't want them to know outside: not the boy or the rest of them.

Endure, Diane, she kept telling herself. *Pant and endure. Pant and endure. You know Billy's on his way. He got the message. They tracked the phone. Help is coming. Endure.*

She closed her eyes. In the classes, they'd emphasized trying to relax in between contractions. Save your strength. Breathe deeply and regular, but don't hyperventilate. Roll from side to side to keep this damn backache from destroying you. Think pleasant thoughts and scenarios: your favorite spot on the beach, the sound of surf, and the feel of warm sun.

Yeah, right. I'm having a baby alone. Outside the door are kidnappers who may end up killing me anyway, even if they do get whatever the hell they want. My first child is going to be born in a strange room in the middle of nowhere, and there won't be a single person to care for it.

Another contraction hit. Was that three minutes since the last one, or even two? She'd only been guessing about the time. She'd been trying to count seconds between the contractions since they began, but after the boy had left and she'd found the cell phone, she'd lost all focus. Now, she was just trying to stay conscious.

Please, Billy, get here. Please get here.

She rolled onto her back and raised her knees and then the tightening came again. She squeezed her eyes tight and *OH MY GOD, THAT HURTS LIKE HELL . . . ARRRRRGH!*

It was dark and she heard a wolf cry. Not a call into a lonely night, but a howl of intense pain, a ragged, screeching response to a leg caught in a snapping iron trap, a cry of some sixty, maybe ninety seconds that felt way longer. Diane opened her eyes, blinked back to consciousness, and saw light and then a ceiling, and then her raised knees. When she tried to swallow, she felt the rawness in her throat—and knew that she was the howling animal.

CHAPTER 35

The cries of a woman's pain tore a hole in my heart.

I spit out a curse and then took a quick look up at the men who had instantly stopped their idiot game at the sound of the howl. I tried to contain both my fury and the urge to charge up the boat ramp and just start firing. Then I heard a door fling open and the sound of footsteps on the wooden planks above, one set light but quick, and the other heavier, but following the first. Their direction was toward the third cabin in pursuit of the painful wails.

Yet again, I held. How many times had I jumped too quickly? How many times had I not waited for backup when I was a cop in Philly, including the night I ran into the robbery on Fifteenth Street and caught a bullet in the neck for my impatience? Despite the blood now pounding in my ears, I dared to wait, and the howling stopped.

Was it Diane? Was she being tortured? Jesus, why torture her now? For what reason? Kidnap victims weren't tortured; kept in isolation, yes, abused through living conditions, yes. Their lives were bargained for politics or money. But torture didn't make sense.

I dared another glance up at the men, who were now shrugging their shoulders and looking toward the door of the big cabin. Two minutes? Less? And the wail began again and to hell with backup!

I was up and out of the water, striding up the boat ramp and pulling the P226 Navy from my pants pocket at the same time. The two men instantly swung their heads to me and the look in their eyes would not have been different if one of those gators had roared up onto the deck after them.

"Down!" I yelled, motioning with the barrel of the P226 Navy. "Get the fuck down, hands behind your head."

Again, they looked at each other, but followed the order, onto their knees and then bellies to the wood. It was six long strides with the painful screeching in my ears, but I kept repeating in my head, *Protocol, Max. Disarm. Secure who you have. Do not screw up. You're no good to her if you screw up.*

I jabbed the nose of the P226 Navy into the back of each man's head as I slapped his pockets, checking for firearms. Nothing. Unarmed guards—what the hell was I into?

"If a face comes up, I will shoot it," I growled. "Got it?"

Heads bobbed, noses stayed down. Now, with that pain shrill in my ears, I turned to the middle cabin, but heard another door open behind me. I spun to the big house to see a figure of enormous size fill the frame.

The big Indian took two steps into the sunlight, glanced at the others lying on the deck and then at me. Stoic—he had to be the man that rooftop Yoda had described. But under the present circumstances, he also had to be the calmest human being I'd ever seen. He was dressed in a colorful Seminole jacket, but he was no Seminole. His black hair was oddly braided. He went easily six foot six and near three hundred pounds.

There wasn't a single discernible emotion in his eyes: no fear, anger, or surprise. His hands were at his side. My gun was pointed at his chest. I worked the scene in my head: two on the ground, two more who had run to the third cabin, one big fucker in front of me staring like it was a soft summer day, and the wrenching cries of my best friend's pregnant wife over all of it. The big Indian made up my mind for me. His right hand went for something behind his back.

"Don't do it, Chief!" I yelled. "You're a dead man if you move!"

"Then so be it," the deep voice said with no more emotion than was in his face. His arm moved with incredible speed. I picked up on the flash of steel in the sunlight, and from fifteen feet away I fired the P226 Navy four times. All four of the water-sealed rounds worked as manufactured, finding a grouping within an eight-inch circle on the big man's chest. The first bullet hit a piece of sternum bone, which sent it tumbling and tearing through the superior vena cava of the man's heart, and then bouncing off a rib and spinning through the viscera in the middle lobe of his lung.

Two others passed through his body just below the sternum and bored expanding holes through upper liver tissue and exited through his back. One path was never determined by the medical examiner. The big man went down, first onto one knee, then onto a tripod of palms and knee, and finally over onto one side on the deck. There was no Tarantino spraying of blood or ridiculous propulsion of body through the doorway behind. Bullets pierce and rip and tumble and internally destroy. Trained cops go for center mass with intent to kill, never just to wound. It is not a circus; it's real death.

I looked over at the others. They were still nose-down on the planks, though they'd cut their eyes to the big man when the shooting started. I stepped across the deck to the big man's body, and there was no doubt that it was a body. Death is not hard to recognize: total, and I mean total, lack of movement—nerve, muscle, or respiratory. Lying next to him was a huge-bladed knife with a carved-bone handle. I put my foot next to the weapon and kicked it across the deck into the water where the young men had been feeding the gators. They wouldn't be going in after it.

With my gunshots still echoing across the open Glades, I went for the door from which the sound of agony was still roiling. I hesitated for only a second at the frame, but when I heard the distinct but ragged voice of Diane Manchester say, "Please, Billy, please," I went hard, shoulder-first, splintering wood and wrenching open metal-lock hardware. I came into a single room crouched low with the barrel of the P226 Navy sweeping chest-high at anything that moved.

*   *   *

A white kid about the same age as the two outside, but definitely not of the same family, turned when I bashed in the door. When he saw the P226 Navy swinging toward him, he raised his palms and said: "Whoa, whoa, whoa."

I swung my sights from wall to wall and then stepped to my right. Behind the kid was a strawberry blonde girl, face turned away, who did not look up. On the bed lay Diane, her back propped up by a mound of pillows, her face a ghastly pale, her mouth providing the only noise left in the room—that of a raspy panting and blowing.

I took two more steps forward, let my eyes move down her body, and said: "Oh, geez."

"No kiddin', right?" the kid with his hands up said.

"Shut the hell up and help already, Danny," the girl said, and finally turned and looked first at the gun in my hand and then into my face.

"And if you're gonna keep shooting that thing, then get to it, mister," the girl said. "'Cause we're having a baby here, and it isn't waitin' on you."

I was still mesmerized by the girl's audacity when I heard the rasping voice say my name.

"You're done shooting, right, Max?" Diane said, and the words caused me to lower the P226 Navy and move to her side.

"Diane? Jesus, Diane."

"No, it's not Jesus, Max. It's a baby," she said. If she was trying to make a joke, it was an awfully brave thing to be doing at that moment. Then she shifted her eyes to a spot behind me. "Where's Billy?"

Even if I knew, which I didn't, I had no time to answer as Diane's face suddenly turned into a mask of grimacing pain. A throbbing blue vein rose on her left temple as she tucked her chin to her chest. "ARRRRRRGH" came out of her mouth like an unholy eruption.

"OK, OK, push, push, push," said the girl at the end of the bed. Every living muscle in the room tightened for the next ninety seconds.

CHAPTER 36

God, that wail!

The cry of pain that speared through the door of the big cabin went straight to Rae's heart, and she had no check on her reaction the way Danny always did. She'd bolted, just turned and ran out the door and went straight for the woman's cabin as if the throat-burning howl had physically reached across the deck and dragged her to the room.

"Mommy?" she thought she heard, in a tiny girl's voice that she hadn't heard outside her own dreams for many years. And there it was, the nightmare appearing behind her open eyes as if the thing had happened yesterday, or this morning, or right this moment.

That day, years ago, she'd walked home alone to their trailer from the bus stop like she had dozens of times when her mother was too sick to meet her there. "Sorry, Rae-Jay, but Mommy's a little sick today, you know? But I do have your Oreos up there on the counter, baby."

And indeed the package of Double Stufs was there, right next to the near-empty bottle of Allen's brandy, which Rae had always thought was named after her mysterious uncle whom her mom talked about having to go see, as in, "Got to go visit old Uncle Allen tonight," as she walked out after doing her makeup and hair and whispering, "Girl, you still got it," into the bathroom mirror.

But that day, her mother was not on the couch with the iced washcloth on her forehead when Rae walked in. At the tender age of seven, Rae had simply gone to the couch herself and found the remote for the TV and pushed the ON button. It responded with a howl that seemed to vibrate the thin walls of the trailer. At first, she was confused, as if the volume had been left up at maximum, and the noise caused her to start fumbling with the remote—before she realized the horrific sound was not coming from the television, but from down the hallway.

She got up from the couch and started toward her mother's bedroom and the ugly sound. At the time, she didn't know why tears were running down her face. When she got to the doorframe's edge and peeked around into the room, she saw the man on the bed first. He was in an unfamiliar pose above her mother, straddling not her hips this time, but her chest and shoulders. The fingers of his left hand gripped a fistful of her mother's beautiful hair, and in his right hand he held a knife with a flashing blade against her mother's cheek as he said: "Isn't gonna be so pretty no more for them other fellas now are you, Glory?"

In between Rae's mother's cries of pain as the knife edge cut deep into her perfect unblemished skin, she somehow sensed Rae's presence and looked over at her daughter with those penetrating green eyes and called out: "Run, Rae-Jay. Run, baby, just run."

Rae had run. But it was the last time. She had not run from anything in her life since and never would: not from the funeral that followed. Not from the men who would later try to lure her and mistreat her and disrespect her, who ended up with a fist to their own faces or a gouge from a sharp key on the paint job of their fancy Town Cars. Not from the life she swore would not belong to anyone but her. Now, she was running toward the sound of a woman's cries of pain and not away, never away again.

"Shit, shit, shit," Rae said as she entered the cabin and saw the woman lying on the bed, her back propped up, her knees in the air, her feet planted at the bottom edge of the mattress. What, are you just gonna pop it out onto the damn floor? she thought as she moved around the kitchen *island and without so much as a plan grabbed a chair, positioned it at the end of the bed, and then sat between the V of those quivering thighs.*

"OK, lady," Rae said. "You're OK now. This is all gonna be OK."

The cries had subsided. The woman had gone quiet but was breathing as if she was gulping air in short supply. Rae knew, and didn't know how she knew, that this was not a good thing, as she'd once seen a stupid girl get all hyper at a party in the woods back home and fall into one of these air-sucking binges to the point where she passed the hell out. Rae knew instinctively that a pregnant woman having a baby should not be passing out.

"Easy now, ma'am. Try to calm down, OK? Slow down that breathing, OK?"

Damned if the woman didn't just obey her. The lady calmed. Her breaths became shallow. She opened her eyes and focused on Rae's face and the tendons in her neck loosed. The throbbing blue vein plumped up on her left temple eased back into her pale skin.

"Oh God, thank you. Are you a nurse? Who else is here? Are you with a rescue team?" The woman started babbling, looking past Rae as if a damn ambulance crew was going to come through the door. But Rae knew the only one behind her was Danny, and she could see the flicker of disappointment in the woman's eyes.

It was the first time that Rae had actually seen the lady's face: her large green eyes all moist from the effort and pain of the contractions, her skin pale and perfectly unblemished just like Rae's mother's, and her auburn hair damp from sweat still beaded up on her forehead. She was a pretty woman, Rae thought, and then immediately wondered how a woman could still be pretty after all the shit she'd been through over the last few days.

"Get some more towels from the bathroom, Danny," Rae said, ignoring the woman's questions. "And some water for her to drink."

She did not turn around while giving the orders and instead actually reached out and gently pushed at the insides of the lady's knees, widening the view and recognizing the urgency. "Jesus, Rae," Danny said from behind her. "You know how to do this?"

"The woman's having a baby, Danny, it ain't rocket science. You been down to Morgan's farm during calving season, right? Well, it's the same thing. You just help a little if you need to and let nature do the work."

It was that last statement that made her look up again into the woman's face and say, "Sorry, ma'am," with the realization of who exactly was doing all the work here. The lady's eyes were focused now. Even if she'd missed the distinctive sound of gunfire outside, she seemed rational and remarkably in the moment. Even Rae had flinched at the pop, pop, pop, pop sound and had told Danny to lock the door behind them. She was thinking of Geronimo and the sight of that damn knife in his belt. But the woman was thinking other thoughts.

Rae took a bottle of water that Danny brought over and offered it to the woman. She drank a little while looking directly at them. Then the lady asked the loaded question: "So, Danny and Rae, are you a couple, or just a couple of kidnappers?"

Rae's first reaction was to say something bitter, something about being the only two people here that could help her now, when the woman's contractions began yet again. But the pretty face twisted up. Now, all the woman could say in between her cries was, "Please, Billy, please."

Then hell itself seemed to rush into the room when the door to the cabin exploded open with the sound of splintering wood and wrenching metal.

Danny started saying "Whoa, whoa, whoa," but Rae kept her attention on the crowning head of the coming infant and did not look back.

CHAPTER 37

When Diane came out of the contraction, she opened her eyes and felt relief—the tingling, burning sensation that her obstetrician had aptly warned of as a "ring of fire" had subsided. Then she felt hope as she began to recognize that a young woman was at the end of the bed, poised as if to help her. This was followed by confusion as names and utterances and connections began to make less and less sense.

"Oh, thank you," she said when she realized that this young woman, not much more than a girl, was sitting there, looking oddly but attentively into Diane's eyes.

"Who are you?" Diane asked, and then looked past her. "Who else is here?" She was thinking rescue team, paramedics, cops, Billy.

But the young woman did not answer. Instead, she turned to the guy standing next to her, whom Diane recognized as the young man who had given her breakfast and been embarrassed when he'd walked in to find her nude on the bed after her shower. He was the one who'd hidden the cell phone she'd used to send Billy her plea for help, what, hours, a day ago?

The contractions had started in earnest after that trip across the room to reach the phone, and her sense of time had warped as she tried to keep track of how many seconds each one lasted and how much recovery time she had between the absolutely agonizing periods of pain and overwhelming urges to push.

When the girl ordered the guy to get more towels out of the bathroom and called him "Danny," Diane had tucked the name away. Then the girl reached out and carefully pushed Diane's knees apart, and Diane wondered if the baby was crowning. It had to be crowning now with the sensations she felt, but she couldn't see from this angle.

Then she'd heard the boy say, "Jesus, Ray. You know how to do this?" and Diane was hoping the girl would say, yes, she'd been a midwife for years and knew exactly what she was doing, but instead she made some crude barnyard analogy. So Diane had focused instead on "Ray."

It wasn't a man's name the boy had uttered before; it was a girl, this girl.

But before either could answer yet another contraction began, and all Diane could do was close her eyes and push, push, push. Intellectually, she knew these late contractions were supposed to last a minute, maybe a minute and a half, but damn, they felt like an eternity. Even if she couldn't see, the baby had to be crowning, its head showing, but AAAAAAAGH. *Damn it, child, enough already!*

This time, when the pain subsided and Diane opened her eyes, the surprise wasn't a slick new baby, but the face of Max Freeman peering over the young woman's shoulder. Diane took a deep breath and felt such relief that when she heard the girl say something to Max about shooting someone, she asked where Billy was.

"He's coming, Diane. He's coming," Max said. The seriousness of his face, his familiar face, and the realization that they'd found her, found her alive, and that finally this nightmare was going to end gave her both a sensation of relief and one of purpose.

"I'm having a baby, Max," she said stupidly, and felt a smile come to her face, an actual smile she had not felt in forever.

"Yeah, I see," Max said. "But it doesn't look like you're in any shape to wait, Diane. So maybe we need to get to it. Aren't you supposed to be breathing or something? Getting ready for one final push?"

"Yeah, yeah," Diane said. "I need to do this. We need to do this." She looked from him to the girl between her knees and made eye contact with this young woman she did not know. Diane still had no idea what role the girl had played in the nightmare.

"Hold my hand, Max," she said aloud. Max stepped over and took her hand and then for reasons she might never understand, she looked at the Danny kid and motioned with her other hand for him to come and take it. The kid moved to her side and Diane squeezed both of their hands as the ring of fire lit anew.

You didn't have to be a seer to know this was it, Rae thought to herself. The new guy in the room, this soaking wet guy with a gun, who obviously knew the woman and was here to rescue her, seemed to put the lady into an upbeat, let's-get-it-done headspace.

The woman, whom the new guy called Diane, asked for his hand and the guy gave it to her, which was good, Rae figured. But then she blew Rae away when she actually asked Danny to come over and hold her other hand and Danny didn't even hesitate, which maybe was good also.

The head of the baby was already starting to show and when this Diane person looked Rae in the eye, Rae saw her mother, heard her mother tell her to run. But goddamnit, Rae wasn't running again. Instead, she started telling the woman to push, push, and push.

The head got bigger, impossibly bigger, thought Rae, and then it seemed to slide past some final fraction of an inch and Rae could see an ear and a tiny chin and then what must have been a shoulder. With her finger, Rae reached and slipped the shoulder through, and God, the whole baby came sliding out onto the towels Danny had put down.

Holy crap—there it was, lying there. Instinctively, Rae picked up one of the clean washcloths and wiped the tiny face and it just opened up its little mouth and started in with high-pitched crying. There was no hanging her upside down. No slap on the butt. The kid just did it all on her own. This damn beautiful noise came out and filled the room.

I felt the very air in the room change, no more profoundly than if you walked from dark into light, cold into warm, storm into calm. The girl was urging Diane to push and I copied the mantra, like some stupefied fan in the crowd. Diane had asked for my hand and I gave it. Then she asked the kid for his and he stepped up like a trooper.

When Diane dipped her chin and started growling from the throat like a hair-raising lioness, her grip tightened to the point that my already-cold fingertips turned purple. It was as foreign an experience as I had ever had and I couldn't turn my eyes away, watching as the girl probed and caressed something down there as a nearly inhuman sound came from someone I felt somehow responsible for.

Then I saw the slick, wet form of the baby's head slip out into the girl's hands and Diane let out an "aaahhh" of relief that seemed to blur my vision. When I looked up at the kid across from me and saw tears running down his cheeks, I realized I was crying, too.

Then the baby started to cry and that pure sound, that announcement of life, infused the entire room with relief and wonder, and yes, a word I'm not sure I have ever actually used—joy.

"Oh, man," the kid across from me said. "Oh, man, Rae, you did it! You delivered a baby! How the hell did you do that?"

The kid may have been confused as to who did all the work here, but the girl paid him no mind and wrapped the infant in a towel and placed the bundle up onto Diane's chest. The new mother seemed to fall into a rapture all her own.

"Your new baby girl," the young woman said, and then sat down and leaned back in her chair.

Diane pressed her lips to the newborn's and said: "Victoria."

Before long, a minute, two, maybe five, the newborn's crying and Diane's hushing tones were competing with and then overwhelmed by a mechanical sound coming from outside the room. Then the growing noise was joined by an amplified voice yelling: "This is the FBI. Come out with your hands over your heads. Come out now. This is the FBI."

The two kids finally made sense of the cacophony and looked at me. Diane closed her eyes.

"Any weapons in here?" I asked them.

The kids looked at my waistband where I'd tucked the P226 Navy and shook their heads.

"OK. Then let's be cool. They've got to have paramedics with them. You two just follow me out with your hands on your heads and do what I do."

When I came through the busted-open door of the cabin into the sunlight, I picked up on at least half a dozen men dressed in dripping wet SWAT gear moving up on all sides of the deck with weapons raised in firing position. Two entered the big cabin. Two more moved on top of the Indians still lying on the deck, preparing to flex-cuff them. Two more were already checking the body of the big man. I took three steps forward with my hands on the top of my head and all the guns swung to me.

"OK, OK, OK," I said, and went down on my knees into a position of submission so that no nervous trigger finger would make a disastrous mistake. "Two more coming out behind me," I said, hoping the kids were doing what I'd asked them to.

The men over the big Indian's body came first to me with the gun sights of their automatic rifles on my chest, dead center, as trained.

"Handgun in my waistband," I said, as calmly as I could. "I'm not touching it. You take it, Officers."

While one covered me, the other stepped forward and yanked the P226 Navy away. The sound of yet another outboard engine whirred as reinforcements arrived on black inflatables.

The words *clear, clear, clear* were coming from the cabins. Only then did someone with the look of authority come out of the growing pha-lanx in dark clothing and a baseball cap. I recognized him immediately as Agent Howard, from the street where Diane had been abducted.

"Well, well—Private Dick Freeman," he said, his eyes hidden again by sunglasses. "I see you've found your friends."

He nodded at a place behind me and I turned to see the two kids on their knees while other agents bent to zip-tie their hands behind their backs.

"No, Agent, my real friend is the judge who has just given birth to her baby in that room and is in need of immediate medical assistance."

Howard glanced behind the kids at another agent who was half inside the doorway and nodding at my statement.

Howard went for his radio and called for an immediate landing of the medical evacuation chopper to the south side of the platform.

I put two and two together and asked the obvious.

"You've been waiting?"

Agent Howard did not answer.

"You've had a medevac team hovering above us? For how long?"

"Until we could get eyes on the ground, Freeman—real eyes, professional eyes. Team eyes."

I wasn't one of them and didn't want to be. When I'd gotten here, I wasn't so sure how long I was going to be waiting in the shadows. My first plan had been simply to gain intel, swim back to my kayak, and phone it back. Hearing Diane's wails of childbirth pain and mis-judging them as the sound of her possible abuse had moved me to action. No one had yet tried to cuff me as I talked to Howard, so I rose to my feet. I don't like being looked down on. I admit I enjoy the height advantage I have over most people. Howard did not object.

"So what made you finally move, Agent?" I asked.

He turned his sunglass lenses to me. "ShotSpotter," he said.

I knew the lingo. ShotSpotter was a new technology law enforce-ment was using in the city that detected the noise of a weapon firing and supposedly put a pinpoint location on the distinctive sound. How accurate it might be out here, I had no idea.

Howard turned away from me and indicated the body of the big Indian, now being ignored by the federal team as they moved about the secured camp.

"I'll assume that is some of your close work, Freeman?"

Even though it was technically a question, I stayed silent.

"When the ShotSpotter picked up four firings of a weapon, we moved in the interest of potential harm to the hostage."

"So how long have you been waiting out there out of sight for an indication of potential harm, Agent?" I said, copycatting his vernacular. "An hour? Three hours? You knew I was here. You were using me."

Howard almost cracked a grin, a smarmy little twitch at the corner of his lip.

"We've known exactly where you've been since the day you showed up at the federal building, Freeman. Your old-school cop car is parked about three miles in that direction," he said, nodding to the northeast. "Your cell phone is much closer, probably a stone's throw away. I was a bit surprised you hadn't used it yet."

"Yeah, well, I was busy," I said, and then felt some urgency to explain myself. "The dead guy was apparently the leader of this little tribe. I shot him in self-defense. His knife is about four feet off the dock over there in the water. His prints will be all over it."

While Howard and I went back and forth, a helicopter outfitted with pontoons came sweeping down out of the southern sky with a whooshing of wind and landed just off the dock. The rotors slowed to a stop. Lines were tossed, and the machine was pulled dockside.

First out was a medical team that disembarked with their gear and strode past us into the cabin where Diane still lay with her baby. Billy was out the door of the chopper right behind. He was dressed in a white oxford shirt and odd-looking rubber boots and stopped only for a second to take my hand and say, "Thank you, Max," before moving on to see his wife and newborn.

"You're going to have to be debriefed, Mr. Freeman," Howard said, still looking off away from my face. "So don't go swimming off, OK?"

He walked away, giving out orders as he went, and left me standing there. I was a suspect in a deadly shooting; the cause and veracity of my self-defense claim had yet to be determined. I had probably broken more than a few laws inserting myself into a federal investigation. What tribal laws I may have broken, I didn't give a shit.

The two cuffed kids had been moved out of the way and were sitting cross-legged with an armed agent standing guard. In all the hustle, they had not yet been separated and were whispering together; getting their stories straight, I figured.

I walked over, assuming that since Howard had been talking with me but had not cuffed me, the guard would allow it. I went down on my haunches.

"Whoever you two are, whatever your involvement in the kidnapping of that woman in there is, you helped her give birth to her baby," I said. "Use that, for yourselves and for whatever comes after. Otherwise don't say a word to anyone until you have a lawyer."

Then I stood and moved away to the north side of the second cabin, looking as if I were tending to one of the inflatables tied there. When I looked back, the two kids were being separated as protocol demanded. They sat the girl next to the door of the big cabin, and the boy over by the airboat. But they could not keep the two from making eye contact, and for some reason I rued the fact that this might be the closest they would be for the rest of their days. Then I surreptitiously lowered myself into the water from the opposite deck side and quietly swam away.

CHAPTER 38

Twenty-four hours later, I was in the visitors' area of the maternity ward at Broward Health Medical Center, being briefed by my lawyer, friend, and new father, Billy Manchester.

After slipping unseen into the water of the fish camp—or perhaps not unseen at all and simply let go—I made it back to the kayak and called Mason Jumper on the cell I'd left there. He hadn't moved from our rendezvous point, even after he got a call that agents had come to his store asking for him, even after he saw the air support sweep in over the skies above the fish camp.

"How is the woman?" was all he asked before starting the engine of his airboat.

When we'd arrived back at his place, I was surprised to see that my Fury was still parked, untouched. I was not surprised to see that Nate Brown's truck was gone. If Nate dislikes anyone more than the game warden, the park rangers, or the state alcoholic beverages agents, it would be the feds. He would help me whenever I called, but he wasn't one to hang around and provide witness statements.

It was after midnight when I made it back to Sherry's place. I was exhausted, sunburned, hungry, thirsty, and not a little bewildered by the events of the past several days. My best friend's wife and newborn child were safe. The plot to kidnap a federal judge was still a mystery. The fate of two young people who had shown their

243

humanity in the end was just as unknown to me. I had killed a man, and witnessed the birth of a precious and innocent life, in the span of a few minutes.

When Sherry arrived home, she rustled around in the kitchen for a few minutes before bringing a bucket of iced beer to the pool-side lounge chair. Then she slid in next to me and didn't say a word. She knew I'd be there. She knew I'd get to it in time. We drank, went to bed, then slept and perhaps dreamed.

In the morning, I explained it all to her. She told me that Diane was listed in stable condition. The baby was still considered guarded. I had arrived at the hospital ward, showered and shaved, as Billy was emerging from Diane's room, where he said both she and the baby were asleep.

"Sh-she is three weeks pr-premature, b-but extraordinarily healthy, c-considering," Billy said to my first question.

"She is exhausted, d-dehydrated, euphoric, and grateful," he said to my second.

"I'm r-relieved, euphoric, and grateful," he said to my third. And though euphoria was not something Billy did well, I believed him.

My fourth question was not answered so succinctly.

"Billy, what the hell was this all about?"

"D-diane is r-resting. Victoria is asleep. C-come, M-max. T-take a r-ride w-with m-me."

We took the Fury, heading north, back to the federal courthouse where Diane's office now sat empty, the feds gone, and her case with Escalante on hold. While I drove within the acceptable speed range for I-95, Billy stoically explained.

"D-do you remember Judge Krome?"

"Stubby guy who does card tricks? Yeah."

"He c-continued t-to regularly inquire on th-the st-status of the FBI s-search," Billy said. "Wh-why s-so n-nosy? He b-barely knew m-me or D-diane. T-too interested. S-so I d-dug d-deeper."

"No stone unturned" should have been Billy's motto, not the government's.

As we passed exits and traffic, Billy stared out ahead, spelling out the case as if in a grand jury hearing. Krome, he explained, was overseeing a disputed legal judgment involving private investment interests and Indian casinos. It was a boring white-collar feud, but with a huge amount of money at stake. A ruling, or lack thereof, would have implications across the Indian gaming industry countrywide. It probably would have been the highlight of courthouse coverage if Diane hadn't been adjudicating Escalante.

I stayed silent.

"Indian gaming is a s-seven-b-billion-d-dollar industry in th-this c-country, M-max."

Money talks, I was thinking—nothing new there.

Billy went on to explain that the case hung on a single contract, which was due to go into effect last week. For one side to win, Krome didn't even have to actually make a ruling: he just had to keep granting extensions for the casino's lawyers until the contract went into effect. Past that date, the money had to be paid. Some people were going to be very rich. But granting such extensions is carefully watched.

"If anyone is w-watching," Billy said, and now I was picking up a grit in my friend's speech, a hint of heat he rarely, if ever, let slip through.

"Distraction," I said, finally getting it. "All this for distraction?"

"A m-magician's indispensable pl-ploy," Billy said. "All eyes go t-to th-the abduction of a f-federal judge wh-who is d-deciding th-the f-fate of a c-cartel l-leader. All eyes are off th-the b-boring m-money c-case n-next d-door."

"Provable?" I asked.

Billy sat quiet for a few seconds.

"If I have anything t-to s-say about it, yes."

When we finally pulled up to the federal building in West Palm, I parked in the visitors' lot. Billy said we wouldn't be long.

As we walked the corridors of the courthouse, Billy was his pleasant but no-nonsense self. Several people who knew him approached to offer congratulations or simply to express their relief. He took their hands lightly, whispered "thank you," and moved on. I let him lead us directly to Judge Krome's office. The judge's assistant recognized Billy as we walked in and rose from behind her desk.

"Mr. Manchester, we are all so relieved," she said.

"Th-thank you, D-donna. Is th-the judge in?" he replied, pointing to the private chambers' door.

"Why, yes, let me tell him you're here," the woman said, and began to reach for the intercom button on her phone.

"N-no!" Billy snapped. The woman's hand jerked away from the phone with the same surprised motion I adopted when the emphatic word came from my friend's mouth uncharacteristically.

I watched as Billy strode to the door, banged the handle lever down, and pushed the panel open. He stepped inside and hesitated. I waited a beat, and then followed.

"Why, Mr. Manchester, what a surprise," the judge said as he rose from behind his ornate desk and stepped around.

Whether Billy's hesitation at the doorway was intended to bring the man out from behind the desk, I did not know. But I closed the door behind us.

Krome stepped around his desk and began to offer his hand, but Billy was already reaching into his briefcase and bringing out a sheaf of documents.

When Billy spoke, he had lost his stutter, the intensity of his anger in the presence of Krome completely overwhelming it: "This is a certification of ownership of the warehouse where my wife was held hostage for days," he barked. I had never heard my friend bark. "Your ownership."

Billy tossed the papers onto the corner of the desk and continued: "Here is an extensive list of the gambling debt that you owe to the Seminole Hard Rock Casino."

I thought of the Seminole attorney Billy said owed him a favor. "Here is a police identification report linking the kidnappers to an Indian casino in Michigan whose owners are one of the primary beneficiaries of your latest nonruling on a joint appeals case."

How Billy got that so soon, I had no idea. "And here is my petition to the court to demand a grand jury investigation of your personal participation in the kidnapping and abuse of Judge Diane Manchester and her child, Victoria Manchester."

I don't use the word *befuddled* much, but the twitches in Krome's face, the spasms in his throat as he tried to speak, and the flash of fear in his eyes brought it to mind. "Why, I, uh, I have no idea what . . ." the judge uttered, trying to gather himself. But explanations were not what Billy had come for. My friend, my mild-mannered, never-get-your-hands-dirty friend, set his feet, the left slightly in front for balance and power, and delivered a straight right-hand punch that caught his judgeship square between the eyes. Krome stumbled back against a wall of legal tomes and slid down until his opulent butt was on the floor, eyes dazed, decorum finished. I might have been as stunned as he was.

Billy simply turned, opened the door, and walked out of the room. As I followed, we passed the judge's aide, who looked into the chambers as we filed out and took in the sight of her boss on the floor. When I turned to close her outer door, she looked into my eyes and gave me a big thumbs-up with her right hand.

As we marched down the courthouse hallways toward the exit, I said: "Bribery?"

"Undoubtedly," Billy said.

"Provable?"

"D-depends on w-witnesses."

As we continued out and across the parking lot, Billy hooked his thumb back toward the building.

"Wh-what d-do you th-think? Assault and b-battery?"

"Depends on the witness," I said, smiling.

As we walked, I asked Billy if he'd really obtained an updated police report.

"Th-the FBI was tr-tracking IDs on th-the d-dead m-man and th-the t-two other Indians, b-but had already verified th-they w-were m-members of a Ch-chippewa tr-tribe in n-northern M-michigan," he said.

The two living men were already "spilling" to federal interviewers that they were only hired and had no idea who Diane was, or why they were paid to take her off the street.

When I asked about the two kids, Billy's details were even sketchier. Using the girl's cell phone, they'd traced her to Traverse City, Michigan, where she apparently lived alone. But investigators had already elicited the help of a Michigan State Police homicide investigator by the name of Annette Cook, known for her skill in interviewing young female suspects, who was sent to the location tracked by text messages sent on the girl's phone.

"A friend of your young midwife, one Kelsey Preece, was quite helpful in filling in names and relationships when assured it was the only way she was going to help her friend," Billy said.

"The Preece girl verified that the young woman, Rae McCombs, whom she called Radar, was in Florida with her boyfriend, Danny Peters, and that she thought they'd gotten in some kind of trouble."

"Radar," I looked quizzically at Billy, but then kept my mouth shut.

"They were apparently a couple. How they got involved and what their role was is still uncertain."

We both went silent. The Florida sun was heating the pavement, the glaze of humidity rising, the day, even in the wake of what I considered an extraordinary event, simply moving along. As we walked, I noticed Billy shaking his right hand, as if trying to loosen something from his fingertips. When we reached my shaded car, he stopped before opening his door and grasped his hand, massaging the knuckles.

"D-does it always hurt th-this b-bad, M-max?"

"Yeah, sometimes," I said, suppressing a grin.

He opened the door, but again hesitated before getting in.

"D-does it always f-feel th-this g-good?"

"Yeah," I said, giving up the smile. "Sometimes."

EPILOGUE

Don't ever call me on this line again."

"Relax, it's done now."

"Done? It's in the shit."

"The contract is good."

"Christ, there's a man dead. People are in jail. Your people."

"I don't have the slightest idea what you're talking about."

"Right."

"Like I said, the contract is good, Your Honor. They can appeal until hell freezes over. Your money is coming."

"Great. I may need a good lawyer."

ACKNOWLEDGMENTS

To those who made this work possible. I'd like to thank Jessica for her insights on a young woman's perspective, Kathy and Twist for their early reads and advice, Rob for his guidance on weaponry, and the late Totch Brown for introducing me to and schooling me on the ways of the Everglades. Continuing thanks go to my agent, Philip Spitzer, who has been there from the start.

ABOUT THE AUTHOR

Jonathon King is an Edgar Award–winning mystery novelist and the creator of the bestselling Max Freeman crime series. Born in Lansing, Michigan, in the 1950s, King worked as a crime reporter in Philadelphia and Fort Lauderdale for twenty-four years before becoming a full-time novelist. Along with the seven books of the Max Freeman series, King has authored the thriller *Eye of Vengeance* (2007) and the historical novel *The Styx* (2009).

THE MAX FREEMAN MYSTERIES

FROM OPEN ROAD MEDIA

Available wherever ebooks are sold

OPEN ROAD
INTEGRATED MEDIA

OPEN ROAD

INTEGRATED MEDIA

Open Road Integrated Media is a digital publisher and multimedia content company. Open Road creates connections between authors and their audiences by marketing its ebooks through a new proprietary online platform, which uses premium video content and social media.

Videos, Archival Documents, and New Releases

Sign up for the Open Road Media newsletter and get news delivered straight to your inbox.

Sign up now at
www.openroadmedia.com/newsletters

FIND OUT MORE AT
WWW.OPENROADMEDIA.COM

FOLLOW US:
@openroadmedia and
Facebook.com/OpenRoadMedia

CPSIA information can be obtained at www.ICGtesting.com
Printed in the USA
BVOW08s0019060815

412055BV00001B/1/P

9 781504 001656